COCO DU CIEL

ELISE NOBLE

Published by Undercover Publishing Limited

v3

ISBN: 978-1-912888-42-9

Edited by Nikki Mentges, NAM Editorial

Cover design by Elise Noble

www.undercover-publishing.com

www.elise-noble.com

Do not be too timid and squeamish about your actions. All life is an experiment. The more experiments you make the better. What if they are a little coarse and you may get your coat soiled or torn? What if you do fail, and get fairly rolled in the dirt once or twice? Up again, you shall never be so afraid of a tumble.

— RALPH WALDO EMERSON

CHAPTER I

RHYS

Rhys Evans groaned out loud as he tried to get comfortable in the old armchair. No matter which way he shifted, he ended up sitting on a lump, and what was more, the TV kept changing channels all by itself. Kind of creepy when you were stuck in the middle of nowhere. Rhys gave a nervous laugh as repeats of *Come Dine with Me*, *The Great British Bake Off*, and *EastEnders* cycled through in rapid succession. When Uncle Albert had asked him to house-sit while he went on a two-week botany expedition to the Himalayas, it had seemed like a good idea. Now? Not so much.

"My usual girl's gone on a sponsored bike ride from Stuttgart to Paris," Albert had said on the phone last month. "I'm in a bit of a bind."

Woodside Lodge, with its backdrop of rolling hills and evergreen forests, was only four hours away in North Wales, but it might as well have been in another world. Rhys had never even visited before. On the rare occasions he'd crossed paths with his uncle, Albert had come to England to catch up with his late sister—Rhys's mother—and the last time had been years ago. Albert had turned up wearing a tweed jacket and Wellington boots, if memory served correctly, and then troughed down all the food in the house. He seemed harmless enough, though, and family was family, so Rhys's mum had always said.

"I'm not sure. I've never looked after a house before."

"I'll pay you thirty pounds a day," Albert offered. "All you have to do is fetch the post in and keep the plants watered."

In the end, it wasn't the money that had swayed Rhys, more the opportunity to escape his shared house for a couple of weeks. There were too many bad memories in that place, not to mention the fact that he could do with some peace and quiet to work.

It was only once he'd spent fifty quid on petrol, forked out another tenner on a dried-out jacket potato at Telford Services, and unpacked his holdall into the cavernous wardrobe in one of his uncle's spare bedrooms that he realised he'd made a grave mistake.

"I'll just explain about the plants," Albert said, passing him a lever arch file full of papers. "I've written a few notes in case you forget anything."

A few notes? Rhys goggled at the novel he was holding. Exactly how many plants did his uncle have?

The answer? Most of them.

"This is the hothouse," the old man explained as he led Rhys through the first of six giant greenhouses. "It's kept at thirty degrees in the daytime and cools to twenty overnight."

The place was a bloody jungle. Trees and vines and exotic blooms filled every inch of available space, and the humidity left sweat running down Rhys's back. He half feared wild animals would start popping out of the under-growth when the sun dropped.

"What was that sound?"

"Oh, just a fox. They like to wander around at dusk."

"In here?"

Albert chuckled. "No, outside. You're not much of a country lad, are you?"

No. No, he wasn't. Who wanted to live all the way out in the sticks? It was two miles to the nearest shop, and Rhys's only experience with gardening was watering a mate's house-plants while the lucky bastard went to Marbella for a fort-night. It was only after he'd caught a "Say No to Drugs" ad on the TV that he realised precisely what type of plant they were, but luckily, the police hadn't arrested him for possession.

At least Uncle Albert wasn't a stoner. And he'd carefully stuck colour-coded labels on everything and provided Rhys with a handy index in the back of the file.

"You'll find the watering and feeding instructions on pages one through a hundred and thirty. And see here, I've left the number of my plumber in case of any hiccups with the water supply. The temperature shouldn't be a problem since it's June, but just in case it chills off and there's a problem with the heating, the local electrician's on call."

How on earth had the Amazon rainforest survived for thousands of years without human intervention? It was a mystery.

"Yeah, I'll memorise the numbers and study the book in the evenings."

"Good, good." His uncle missed the sarcasm. And Albert's last words before he walked out the door? "Look after my babies."

Babies? Did he think they were...human?

Since Albert's departure, Rhys had received thirty-nine text messages, each asking whether things were okay and reminding him to dim the lights at seven thirty sharp, and there were still eight days to go.

Was it any wonder his uncle had never married?

Mind you, Rhys was hardly one to pass judgement. While he was sitting in a draughty living room, watching snippets of some depressing reality show about one man's search for true love, Stacey—his ex-girlfriend and the woman he'd once thought was his future—was back in Uxbridge shagging his housemate.

Rhys's mind drifted to the last day of the semester, to that nightmare of a Friday when his life had fallen apart. First came the horror of realising his web architecture exam was in the morning and not the afternoon as he'd initially thought. He'd kept his head and winged it, only to arrive home and find the love of his life naked on the sofa with Gary, a wannabe DJ with too many earrings and a tattoo of a mermaid on his pasty arse.

He'd never forget the look of shock on Stacey's face. The way she'd tried to cover herself up. Her stammered words.

"We… I… I wasn't expecting you home yet."

Maybe *she* wasn't, but Gary definitely had been. Rhys had bumped into him outside the exam hall first thing that morning and mentioned he'd be back for lunch. Which meant the needle-dicked asshole had not only stolen Stacey, but also planned the big reveal with careful precision.

Why had he done it? Because he was still bitter about the drums? Rhys had accidentally backed his car over Gary's drum kit on the day they both moved into the house on Cardon Street, and although he'd paid for the damage, Gary had been decidedly cool towards him ever since. And petty. But missing shower gel and loud music late at night were one thing; with Stacey, he'd taken the animosity to a whole new level. And although Gary spent most of his time at her place now, when he did set foot back in the shared house, the atmosphere made an igloo seem cosy.

And even when he was at Stacey's, he still managed to stick in the knife. She lived right opposite, and one night when they "forgot" to switch the light off, Rhys had been treated to another faceful of Gary's arse, this time as he pounded Stacey against the wall. The way her expression had changed from ecstasy to horror when she opened her eyes and realised he was watching from the living room window... How had he misjudged her so badly? She'd said she was sorry, even cried, but that didn't stop her from flaunting her new relationship all over campus.

And why couldn't he forget her? He tried his damnedest to block her from his mind, from his dreams, but she was always there, and at night it was worse. Close his eyes, and he'd see her baby blues. Turn over in bed, and he'd feel her hair tickling against his chest. Despite every-thing, a part of him still missed her company. Why didn't he simply move out, you ask? Because he was tied into the lease until the end of August, and a tight budget meant he couldn't afford to throw away two months' worth of rent. Not when he could just lock himself in his bedroom and work.

A sudden blast of sound sent Rhys shooting from the armchair, his heart pounding until his brain caught up and reminded him it was only the stereo. Four o'clock sharp, and the intro to "Feed Me" from *Little Shop of Horrors* began playing—Uncle Albert's idea of a joke. The old man's sense of humour took some getting used to. Rhys stretched, trying to relieve the chair-induced backache. At this rate, he'd be spending half of his thirty-pound-a-day stipend on chiropractor fees when he got back to Uxbridge.

Once he'd put his shoes on, he snagged the manual off the coffee table and trudged out to the greenhouses. Time to feed the plants. His record so far was two hours and twenty-five minutes from start to finish, but today, he managed it in two hours and ten. Not bad.

Ah, dammit. He'd forgotten about the two fancy trees.

"The coco du ciel palm," Albert had told him, eyes sparkling. "*Lodoicea oriella*. They're the jewels in my collection, so make sure you look after them."

"Really?" Tesco sold prettier plants in the veg section. "What about all the orchids?"

The coco du ciels were just plain old palm trees—big, yes, but there was nothing remotely ornate about them. Lumpy trunks branched in odd directions, and some sort of chunky fruit lurked among spiky green fronds. Or was it a nut? Rhys leaned to the side to get a better look. The thing was curved like Stacey's arse. Dammit, he had to stop thinking about her.

"The orchids aren't a patch on that pair." Albert followed his gaze. "What you're looking at up there is something special. The fruit's almost ripe, and it's priceless."

Priceless? Really? To Rhys, it looked like an oversized coconut. "What makes it so special? I mean, I can see it's big, but size isn't everything, right?"

At least, that's what Stacey had always assured him.

"*Lodoicea oriella* is the rarest tree on earth. There are only twenty-seven mature specimens outside Brazil, and this is the only pair."

"How did you get them?"

Albert tapped his nose. "That's a long story, lad."

Rhys flipped to the page his uncle had marked with a pink tab, a yellow stripe, and three black dots. Yep, that matched the label on the coco du ciel trees. Even though he'd followed the same instructions for days, he still liked to check.

Each Sunday, Tuesday, and Friday, mix one scoop of powder from the red pot on the bottom shelf with one large can of water and sprinkle it over the roots. No more, no less.

Where was the red pot? He rummaged around in the gloom. The lid looked more pink than red, but since he couldn't see anything else close, he'd been using it the whole time and the trees were still alive. Yeuch, the stuff stank, a weird metallic smell that turned his stomach. Rhys held his breath as he scooped out the right amount, mixed it in a watering can, and slopped it over the ground at the bottom of the trees. One more day done, thirty quid in his pocket, and he could finally crawl into a cold, lonely, lumpy bed.

What was that noise?

After two hours of sleep and six hours of tossing and turning, Rhys's brain still wasn't functioning properly, and it took a moment to recognise Mariah Carey warbling the lyrics to "Thirsty." Okay, okay, he got the hint.

Since he was alone, he gave his T-shirt and jogging bottoms the sniff test, deemed them good for another day, and traipsed out to the Welsh rainforest. With a week to go, he swore he'd never buy a houseplant, not even a cactus. If only there were some way he could foist a future plant-sitting mission onto Gary as payback... Nothing would ever compensate for him stealing Stacey, but exiling the prick to the wilds of Gwynedd for a month in winter would certainly make Rhys feel better.

Did Uncle Albert have any other trips planned?

Rhys hummed to himself as he unwound the hosepipe, a tuneless rendition of Dev's "In the Dark," which played every evening as a reminder to flip the master light switch before he turned in for the night. He'd quite liked the song at first, but now it was stuck in his head as an earworm and he never wanted to hear it again. The watering should take an hour or two, and what was the next task? He drew the line at weeding, not that he'd be able to tell the difference between a weed and a plant anyway.

A chirp overhead made him look up. Was that a sparrow? Should he open the doors? Hmm, not the best idea—that would let Albert's precious heat out. The feathered fiend alighted in one of the coco du ciel trees and started squawking.

"Sorry, mate. I haven't got any birdseed."

But maybe there was a spare slice of bread in the kitchen, or... Wait.

Hadn't there been a giant nut up there yesterday?

CHAPTER 2

RHYS

Ah, shit. Rhys shifted to get a better angle and gaped up through the foliage. The nut had been a huge thing, at least three feet wide. Where had it gone?

Apart from a small circle of bare earth around the trunk of each tree, the ground was a tangle of foliage, but he had to find the thing. Then if he could get hold of a ladder, maybe he could...hmm, stick it back up there?

"Ow, you bastard."

He cursed as a thorn poked into his thigh, then stubbed his toe tripping over a rock. This "job" should come with hazardous-duty pay. And probably a flak jacket too, because there was his uncle's precious nut-fruit, smashed to smithereens on a carpet of blue flowers, which meant Rhys had roughly one week left to live. *Fuck.* For a second, he considered superglue, then smacked his own head. The damn thing had exploded. Jagged shards of seed case and creamy flesh lay scattered among the undergrowth. There was no fixing that mess.

Uncle Albert was going to do his nut, which was a

terrible pun under the circumstances, but "furious" didn't even begin to cover it. Would he believe the truth? That Rhys had played no part in the damage? That it was all just an accident?

A flash of something pale darting through the foliage caught his peripheral vision. Another bird? No, it was too big for a bird. The fox, perhaps? If that mangy creature was responsible for this disaster...

Rhys turned off the tap and listened. A rustle came from the far end of the greenhouse as whatever it was moved again. Should he run? Hide? What if it was a burglar? Or a plant rustler? Did such a thing exist? When he didn't hear anything else, curiosity got the better of him and he tiptoed in that direction, brandishing a handy shovel as his heart thumped against his ribcage.

There...a glimpse of white among the green.

What *was* that?

He found her crouching behind a *Fatsia japonica*. Or was it a *Gunnera manicata*? Which one had the bigger leaves? Why the hell was he even thinking about leaves? *There was a naked freaking woman in front of him.*

Who was she?

Why was she in the greenhouse?

And why did she look so scared?

So many questions, and absolutely no answers.

As Rhys looked her up and down, she shrank back farther, cowering against the base of whatever damn plant it was as she attempted to cover herself with her hands. He reached out and bent one of the leaves in front of her, and her knuckles turned white as she snatched it and gripped the edge.

"Uh..." he started. What on earth was he supposed to say? "Are you...all right?"

Time ticked by, and the bird swooped past, squawking. That startled her too.

Finally, she gave her head a quick shake. No, she wasn't all right. Hardly surprising, given the situation.

"So, this may be a silly question, but what are you doing here?"

She hugged the leaf against herself and gazed at him with eyes the colour of molten chocolate.

"I don't know," she whispered, so softly he could barely hear.

"How did you get here?"

She shook her head again, damp brown curls cascading over her shoulders. "I don't know."

"Did you walk? Come by car?"

"I think I fell."

"You fell? From where?"

Was naked skydiving a thing?

"I woke up in the dirt under that tree." She started to point at the closest coco du ciel tree, but the fatsia-slash-gunnera leaf pinged away and she had to grab it back to save her dignity.

Wait a second… A broken nut, priceless according to his uncle. A mysterious trespasser. Had she climbed up to steal Albert's pride and joy and then slipped? It seemed like a definite possibility. Should he call the police? How else was he meant to deal with a naked burglar?

A naked freaking burglar.

"Did you touch that thing?" Rhys pointed at the foliage.

The girl followed his gaze. "What thing?"

"Well, obviously it's not there anymore. But it was a giant nut, and it's broken right where you claim to have landed."

"I… I don't know. I don't think so."

"You'd better tell me the truth, otherwise I'm the one that's gonna get it in the neck when my uncle gets home."

"I swear, I don't remember touching it." She glanced around, brow creased. "Do you know me?"

"Lady, do I look as if I know you?"

"Where am I?"

She didn't know? Maybe she needed an ambulance as well as the cops? And possibly a straitjacket too. Where had she come from? Her accent was bland, difficult to pin down, and Rhys was ninety-nine percent sure he hadn't seen her on his trek to the village shop. A pretty girl like that? He'd definitely remember.

"You're in Llanefion."

Her blank expression said that didn't help.

"It's a village in Gwynedd." Nothing. "Wales?"

"Wales?"

"The country? You know, sheep. Mount Snowdon. Daffodils, dragons, rugby."

"In Europe?"

"Yes." Finally, they were getting somewhere. "Are you here on holiday? Vacation?"

"I don't know."

They'd hit an impasse. Rhys's phone was in the house, and now the girl was shivering despite the fancy heating system. Probably he should act chivalrous and at least get her a blanket before he asked any more questions.

"Don't go anywhere, okay? I'll be back in a minute."

"Okay."

Rhys backed away. At least if she bolted, someone would notice. Even in deepest, darkest Wales, a naked woman skipping through the countryside would raise eyebrows.

As he jogged into the house, Rhys paused to pinch

himself. Was he still asleep? Was this his subconscious getting Wales and Stacey and that brunette from last night's TV game show all mixed up? Ouch. Apparently not. He ran through a mental checklist—no, he hadn't been drinking, or smoking anything funny, or getting adventurous with any pharmaceuticals. But he'd eaten mushrooms on his pizza last night. Could some joker at the supermarket have swapped them for the magic variety?

When Rhys got back to the greenhouse with an old grey woollen blanket—the best he could find—he half expected the girl to have vanished. Or perhaps that was just wishful thinking? It would undoubtedly have made his life easier if she'd taken off. But no, there she was, exactly where he'd left her.

"Here." He held out the blanket. "Sorry it smells a bit fusty."

She didn't make eye contact until she'd wrapped it around her shoulders like a cloak. When she straightened, she only came up to his chin in bare feet, and at five feet ten, Rhys had never considered himself particularly tall. She licked her lips the way Stacey sometimes did, but it was a nervous gesture as opposed to Stacey's usual confident teasing.

"What now?" she whispered, glancing towards the door.

Words stuck in Rhys's throat. What was the proper etiquette for dealing with an admittedly pretty, very naked stranger who didn't know who she was or where she'd come from?

"You'd better come inside, I guess. I mean, you can't stay out here in the greenhouse."

He offered a hand, but when the girl just stared, he

slowly retracted it. Gee, this wasn't awkward in the slightest.

"Uh, follow me."

She stopped a foot inside the kitchen door, hesitant to go any farther. Rhys couldn't blame her—he was a stranger too, after all. And truth be told, he didn't particularly want her in the house.

"So, er, do you want a cup of tea?" A good cuppa was the British answer to everything.

She gave the tiniest of nods.

Uncle Albert still had an old gas kettle rather than an electric one, and Rhys set it to boil on the stove. Mugs lived in the cupboard beside the fridge, and he picked out the two with the fewest chips. Every item of crockery was decorated with flowers, and worryingly, Rhys could actually identify some of the blooms now.

"Do you take sugar?"

"I don't know. I don't know anything."

Her eyes began to glisten, and Rhys took a step back. Bloody hell. He could cope with nudity and amnesia and even the prospect of his uncle's anger, but tears were beyond him.

"Hey, it's okay." Rhys patted her stiffly on the shoulder, then plucked a leaf from her hair. "We'll get this sorted out. Somehow," he added under his breath.

"I'm s-s-so sorry. For being in your greenhouse, for interrupting your morning, for whatever I might have done to that plant."

Was it possible that she'd escaped from somewhere? A hospital?

"Here, have a tissue."

Okay, it was a paper towel, but it would have to do.

Rhys helped her onto a stool at the breakfast bar just as the kettle started to whistle.

"Thanks." Her hand trembled as she wiped her eyes. "I can't imagine I've ever been this scared before."

She wasn't the only one shaking. He slopped boiling water across the counter as he tried to pour it into the mugs. Plenty of milk, two sugars for the strange stranger.

"You really don't remember? Nothing's coming back?"

Tick, tick, tick... The old-fashioned grandfather clock in the hallway was the loudest thing in the house, and its steady countdown only served to remind Rhys how fast his heart was beating.

"I know your accent is English and this is a kitchen and the sky is blue. But specifics? Anything about me?" She shrugged. "There's nothing."

"Sounds like amnesia," Rhys said. "We should try the hospital."

And with any luck, they'd take her off his hands.

"But I'm not injured. I feel fine."

Rhys's ringing phone interrupted the conversation. In an ideal world, he'd have ignored it, but he recognised his uncle's ringtone, and when he'd accidentally missed a call from Albert last week, a flurry of panicked text messages had quickly followed.

"Uh, excuse me, I have to take this." He stepped into the hallway. "How are the Himalayas?"

"Bloody freezing, lad. You've got the better end of the deal, that's for sure."

When he thought of the waif sitting in the kitchen and the mess in the greenhouse, Rhys knew that was a lie.

"We'll have to agree to differ on that."

Uncle Albert laughed heartily. "Just so long as you're not slacking. Those plants won't look after themselves."

"I've been following your instructions to the letter."

"Everything going okay?"

Rhys should have fessed up about the incident with the coco du ciel tree, he knew he should have, but he didn't want to ruin Albert's holiday. At least, that's what he convinced himself. There was also the small issue of facing his uncle's inevitable fury, and why do today what you could put off until tomorrow?

"Absolutely fine. Couldn't be better."

"I should get going, then. *Saussurea gossypiphora* is calling me."

"Sassy-what?"

"It's a herb. A rare herb. Tell my babies I said hello."

The line went dead, and Rhys let out a long, shaky breath. Okay, he'd bought himself a few days. If he timed it to perfection, perhaps he could leave a "Sorry I screwed up" note and be halfway back to London before Albert started yelling? A definite possibility.

But he'd worry about that tomorrow. Today, he had the mysterious girl to deal with...

CHAPTER 3
RHYS

Rhys lingered in the hallway for a moment before he headed back into the kitchen, hoping once again that the girl would have disappeared as suddenly as she arrived, taking his problems with her. Well, not *all* of his problems—that would be impossible—but certainly the ones that had the potential to keep him away from work today. He designed apps for a living, and one advantage of staying in the countryside was the peace and quiet.

But Lady Luck wasn't smiling down this morning.

The brunette gazed up from her seat at the breakfast bar, those doe eyes wide and watery. What should he say? Even before Stacey had knocked the stuffing out of him, he'd never been the most confident around pretty girls, let alone pretty girls who'd dropped in from another dimension.

"Tea all right?"

"I don't think I take sugar."

"I'll try to remember that." She seemed quite sweet enough without it, just really, really odd. "Are you hungry? Do you remember when you last ate?"

"Yes, and no."

"I'll make you some breakfast. Toast okay?"

It had better be—the Rice Krispies had gone soft.

"Toast's good."

Her eyes tracked him around the kitchen as he fetched bread, butter, and plates. As an afterthought, he turned on the local news, just in case there was any mention of an escaped psychiatric patient, or a failed mind-control experiment at a nearby swimming pool, or an alien spaceship crash. You know, the usual.

"What happened to your clothes? Did you take them off?"

"When I woke up, I wasn't wearing any."

Ordinarily, a man would dream of hearing those words, but this was more of a nightmare.

"I'll find you something to borrow. You can't sit there in a blanket all day."

Was that a blush?

"Thanks."

Rhys hadn't brought many clothes with him, and he certainly hadn't envisaged a situation where a rather shapely female might need to borrow them. For a moment, he toyed with the idea of checking his uncle's wardrobe, but he wouldn't wish a pair of unfashionable corduroy trousers on anyone. The girl would have to make do with tracksuit bottoms and a sweatshirt. When he got back to the kitchen, he found her trying to hold up the blanket with one hand and scrape the burnt bits off the toast with the other.

"Sorry, I forgot to say the toaster's dodgy." He should have mentioned it, but funnily enough, he'd been slightly distracted. "Half the time, it doesn't pop up when it should."

"I'm sure I've eaten worse, and right now, I'm so hungry I could eat charcoal." She glanced at the blackened bread. "Which is just as well, I guess."

"Want me to toast you another slice?"

"No, this is fine." She took a bite and made a face. "Really."

"You don't eat butter?"

"Butter? Right, butter."

The girl grabbed the knife again, but with the wrong hand, and the blanket slithered to the floor. Rhys moved to pick it up, and they cracked heads.

"Sorry."

"Sorry."

It might have been funny if it wasn't so weird. This chick was seriously spaced out. Was she on something? Prescription drugs? Regular drugs? Didn't some plants have psychedelic properties? What if she'd snuck into the greenhouse intent on pilfering, got high on leaves, and this was the result? That seemed the most plausible scenario so far. But where were her clothes? Still in the greenhouse? Rhys needed to check.

"Here, let me do the butter. And I brought you spare clothes to wear."

"Thank you."

Ah, damn, that smile was dangerous. Just a tiny quirk of her lips, but it was enough to make Rhys twitch in places he shouldn't. Why were the pretty ones always trouble?

She ate like a starved dog, hunched over, barely chewing one mouthful before she took the next. Cannabis munchies? Rhys's ex-housemate Dave—now sadly in jail—had eaten eighteen Greggs sausage rolls and six steak bakes after he got high one night, and then he'd fallen asleep, dead to the world. Unfortunately, he hadn't woken until the bakery manager arrived for work the next morning and found him curled up in a pile of broken glass.

"Still hungry?" Rhys asked as she swallowed the last crust.

"I should go change. Like you said, I can't sit here in a blanket all day."

He showed her to the downstairs bathroom and left her to it. Part of him questioned the wisdom of having a suspected thief in the house, but Uncle Albert kept his valuables in the greenhouses. No self-respecting twenty-something would nick a china ornament or a dusty encyclopaedia.

Besides, what other option did Rhys have? He could hardly kick her out naked.

While she changed, he ran out to the greenhouses to search for any evidence of clothing. A discarded sweater, a pair of trousers, underwear... But there was nothing. And the only footprints he found were in the hothouse around the coco du ciel trees, all bare, directionless, a patchwork of panic in the damp earth. Sunlight sliced through the spiky leaves, shimmering onto the lesser plants below while Albert's prized specimens stood majestic. Kings lording it over their peons.

Odder and odder.

Rhys had made it back into the kitchen when the girl reappeared, and he got his first good look at her without feeling like a pervert. She was slender but not to the point of malnourishment, and she had the palest skin. White, almost translucent, as if she'd spent her entire life indoors. Her dark hair provided a sharp contrast, untidy but not greasy. She must have washed it recently. And her eyes... They were the window to the soul, or so the saying went, and the girl's puzzled him. A rich brown with flecks of gold, they spoke of secrets and past regrets that her mind didn't register.

"So," he said, more to himself than her. "What should we do now?"

A shrug.

"You still haven't remembered anything?"

"This place, the plants, you... I have no idea what I'm doing here."

"What about further back? Your parents? Your childhood?"

Tears rolled down her cheeks. Ah, shit.

"Okay, okay. We should speak to the police. Someone must know who you are, and maybe they filed a missing persons report. Probably you should get checked out by a doctor too."

"I guess."

"The hospital here isn't too bad. When Uncle Albert put a garden fork through his foot, they fixed him up. Besides, the sooner you get your memory back, the sooner you can go home."

"Will you come with me? To the hospital?"

Who could resist that pleading note in her voice? Not Rhys, unfortunately.

"As long as I'm back in time to water everything this evening."

Rhys had never embraced the student lifestyle to its fullest extent. While his housemates partied and spent their student loans on two-for-one happy hour in the Students' Union bar, he'd kept nights out to a minimum and lived frugally, tucking his spare money away for the future. But he'd splurged on a car. Okay, not splurged, exactly, but after the old chap who lived next door to his previous home had a near miss with a dustbin lorry, his daughter had banned him from driving, and Rhys picked up his fifteen-year-old Ford Fiesta for a song. It was only a matter of time until it made its way to the great scrap heap in the sky, but by some miracle, it had got all the way from West London to Wales without any vital parts falling off along the way. Gary took the piss out of him for driving a banger, but since Gary's only goal in life was to do as little as possible, Rhys discounted his opinion. He wanted to finish the travels he'd started before his mum died. See the sands of the Sahara and the desolate beauty of the Andes before he settled down. And that would take cash.

Still, as he swept an empty crisp packet and a stray glove off the passenger seat, he wished he'd at least given the car a tidy. The girl didn't seem bothered, though.

"Seat belt," Rhys reminded her.

"Huh?"

"You need to put your seat belt on."

"Oh. Right."

When she made no move towards doing so, he reached across her and clipped it into place. The last thing he needed was a fine, although if the Old Bill pulled them over, it might save him a trip to the police station. He could just hand the girl over.

Where was the police station, anyway? Six miles from Llanefion, according to Google, and the hospital was three miles farther.

"Police first?" Rhys suggested.

He took her shrug as a "yes."

In hindsight, they should have gone to the pub next door to the station instead. Not only did Rhys need hard liquor by the time they'd finished speaking with the duty sergeant, but the landlord would probably have been more helpful.

For twenty minutes, they sat on hard plastic chairs in a room where the stink of week-old vomit had battled disinfectant and won. The lady beside them picked at her fingernails while a guy in a suit berated the woman behind the desk over an impounded car. Park in a tow-away zone, get a ticket—what was so difficult to understand?

"Are you waiting?" Rhys asked the lady.

"Been waiting for hours. The sergeant went to check the database or something. Probably gone for lunch."

Great. As if hanging out with a complete stranger in Uncle Albert's kitchen hadn't been bad enough, now Rhys had to endure the scrutiny of every cop who walked past, plus a cleaner. The girl sat on her hands and gave him the silent treatment.

"Who's next?" the desk lady asked as Suit Guy slammed the door hard enough to make the hinges rattle.

"We are."

"Yes?"

"We need to report a missing person."

"I'll need a name and description."

"I don't know the name, but this is her." Rhys gestured at the brunette, and she tried a tentative smile.

"How is she missing? She's right here."

"Okay, so she's not missing exactly, more found. But she must be missing from somewhere."

"Is this a joke? Because wasting police time's a criminal offence."

"No, I swear! She's got amnesia. I found her wandering around my uncle's garden this morning."

Desk Lady clicked away with her mouse, but when Rhys glanced at the framed *Don't Drink and Drive* poster on the wall behind her, he saw the reflection of a game of solitaire in the glass. Good to see his taxes were hard at work.

"This morning? So she hasn't been missing for more than twenty-four hours?"

"No. At least, I don't think so. I suppose she might have been, but she can't remember."

"We can't do anything until she's been missing for more than twenty-four hours."

"But she has amnesia. In twenty-four hours, she probably still won't know who she is."

"Well, come back tomorrow and file a report."

Rhys had never been a violent man, but he stuffed his hands into his pockets just in case the urge to wipe the superior smile off the woman's face became too strong.

"That's—"

The brunette interrupted. "I understand you're busy, but I can't remember who I am or where I came from. So unless you want me sleeping in your lobby, I'm going to need your help to find my family."

"You can't stay here." Desk Lady pointed at a handwritten *No Loitering* sign. "We've got rules."

"Do the rules mention playing solitaire during working hours?" Rhys asked.

Busted. His turn to smile.

"Fine." If looks could kill... "Fine, I'll call the duty sergeant, but I don't suppose he'll be able to do much."

What happened to serving the community?

CHAPTER 4

RHYS

Another half hour passed before the sergeant turned up, and then he spent ten more minutes explaining to the woman with ragged fingernails why he couldn't arrest her neighbour for having a bonfire too close to her washing line. She slammed the door on her way out too.

"Right. I hear you're looking for a missing person?"

"No, I've found a missing person."

"You'll have to explain."

So Rhys did, and now he understood why vigilante justice was a thing. Was a written report too much to ask for?

"So, love, you say you can't remember your name?" the sergeant asked the girl.

"No."

"Or when you came to the country? Your accent doesn't sound Welsh."

"I don't know."

"I'll have a look at the missing persons database, but if no crime's been committed, I can't do much else."

The clock on the wall was ten minutes slow—even inanimate objects couldn't be bothered to work properly around there—and the room was a soulless space, probably designed that way on purpose so people gave up waiting and went home. No magazines, no pamphlets, not even a vending machine. They were missing a trick there. In all the excitement, Rhys had skipped breakfast, and by the time the sergeant strolled back in, he was craving a packet of crisps.

"Did you find anything?"

The sergeant shook his head.

"Nobody fitting your description's gone missing locally for months," he told the girl. "You might want to try the university. It's what, five miles away? They take a few foreign students. Maybe someone there'll recognise you." His no-nonsense expression softened infinitesimally. "Good luck."

Good luck.

Rhys didn't need luck, he needed help. Over beers in the pub, finding a naked girl in the garden might sound like a comic-book fantasy, but as Rhys was finding out, the reality was very different.

"Are we going to the university now?" the girl asked as they walked to the car.

"Let's try the hospital first."

Assuming it had a psychiatric department, there was a better chance she'd come from there than the uni anyway. The girl climbed back into the car, obedient. Submissive, almost, and Rhys found that unsettling. If Stacey had been in this situation, she'd have been freaking out by now. This girl, she just put on her seat belt, folded her hands in her lap, and waited. Waited for the next paragraph of her story to be written. For the page to turn.

The problem? Neither of them had a clue about the plot.

At the hospital, they found a parking space right beside the entrance to A&E, which seemed like a blessing until Rhys reached the ticket machine.

"Four quid an hour to park," he grumbled as he stuck the ticket to the windscreen. "That's taking the piss. Do they think everyone's made of money? Bet we'll be waiting for ages too."

"Sorry."

The wobble in the girl's voice took the edge off his annoyance. "It's not your fault."

She didn't answer, but as the automatic doors parted, she suddenly pressed one hand to her forehead. Her face screwed up in pain as she clutched at Rhys's arm, and his heart raced. What was wrong? Was she having a stroke? Some sort of panic attack?

The receptionist took one look at her and beckoned them both past the other people waiting. A kid with a Lego brick stuck to his arm glared, and Rhys glared back. Whatever was wrong with the girl certainly trumped stupidity with superglue.

"Are you okay, love?"

Would they have come to A&E if she were?

"I-I-I tripped and f-f-fell," the girl said.

What? No, she didn't.

"You hit your head?"

The girl nodded and winced. "It hurts."

"Did you black out?"

"I don't know. Maybe? I don't remember. I don't remember anything."

The receptionist turned to Rhys. "Can you tell me what happened?"

"I'm not sure. I just found her outside my house like this." At least that part was true.

"Is she a friend of yours?"

"I never met her before this morning."

The receptionist sucked in a breath and gave a single nod. "Right. Right, I'll get you booked in, love. What's your name?"

"I don't know."

"You don't know?"

Rhys's turn to speak. "When she said she didn't remember anything, she meant she doesn't remember *anything*."

"But…"

"Not one single thing," the girl said.

"What about ID?" the receptionist asked. "Do you have a wallet? A phone?"

"She was naked when I found her."

The woman's eyes widened, and Rhys noticed that everyone else in the queue was listening too. Perhaps he should have been peeved, but right now, the more people who knew the story, the better. The local gossip mill might be able to shed some light on the girl's identity.

"Naked?" the receptionist repeated, as if she might have misheard.

"No clothes in sight."

"Well, you did the right thing by bringing her here. Take a seat, love, and I'll get the doctor to see you right away."

They sat, and the chairs in the hospital weren't any more comfortable than the ones in the police station. But hopefully they'd be sitting on them for less time.

"Why didn't you tell me your head hurt?" Rhys whispered. "I could have given you paracetamol."

"Given me what?"

"Paracetamol."

"I don't even know what that is."

Huh? "Then what do you normally take when you have a headache?"

"Acetaminophen." And Rhys had no idea what that was. "Hey, I remembered something. That's good, right?"

"Right."

"And I don't have a headache. I just said that so we wouldn't have to wait in line again."

"Uh, nice one." Although now Rhys felt guilty for glaring at the kid with the Lego. "Well, I believed you. Maybe you used to be an actress?"

"Do you think?"

"I'd give you an Oscar."

And it also gave them a potential lead—if the hospital and the university were dead ends, Rhys could try local theatre groups.

Five hours later, the girl had been thoroughly examined, not only by the doctor but by half a dozen medical students too. Because why not use this horror show as a teaching experience? They'd taken blood and urine samples, checked her blood pressure, and run an ECG. Then they'd given her a pregnancy test, and when that came back negative, they ran a CT scan. When that showed nothing, they tried an MRI scan as well. Apart from the results of a few blood tests that were yet to come back, the investigations yielded a big fat zero.

"So far, everything's clear," the doctor declared. "To all intents and purposes, you're a healthy girl in your mid-twenties."

"Then why can't I remember anything?"

"I'm afraid I can't answer that. There's no evidence of head trauma. It's possible that you may have dissociative amnesia, which is caused by emotional shock, but the good news is that the condition is usually temporary."

"Emotional shock?" The girl clutched at Rhys's arm again, and he wasn't so sure she was acting this time. "What do you mean, emotional shock?"

"Some sort of stress, an event that you witnessed or were involved in."

"Such as what?"

The doctor shifted from foot to foot. "Possibly physical or sexual abuse, the death of a loved one, something like that."

Rhys focused on two words in that sentence. *Sexual abuse.* He'd found her naked, for crying out loud. The girl had gone even paler, if that was possible, and what the hell was he meant to say?

"Did you, uh... The sexual abuse... Did you check?"

The doctor nodded. "There are no obvious signs."

Thank goodness. But that didn't mean she hadn't seen something terrible, and what would be bad enough to make a girl lose her entire memory? Rhys didn't even want to think about it.

But he could hardly walk away, could he?

"What happens now?" the girl asked. "Where do I go?"

"I'm afraid we can't keep you here. We just don't have the beds. But I can refer you to a counselling service, and if you need the number of a local hotel, Janet at the reception desk will be able to help."

"But I don't have any money. Not a penny."

"The council has a program to help the homeless. I think we have leaflets somewhere—I'll ask Janet."

"Okay."

One word, so tiny and quiet. The doctor mustered up a kindly smile.

"I know a reporter for the local paper. They might be able to run a picture, see if anybody recognises you. Do you want me to find his details?"

A nod.

"I'll be back in a jiffy. Just wait out the front."

In the waiting area, the girl sniffled quietly as she perched on one of the hard plastic seats. Rhys hated to see her upset, and at the same time, he was surprised she'd managed to hold it together for so long. It couldn't be easy having your whole life disappear into a black hole. She had courage, and he had to admire that.

"I'm staying at my uncle's house for another week. There's a spare bedroom if you want it?"

"Really? He wouldn't mind?"

Probably not, and Rhys didn't even intend to tell him. Call it payback for Albert's claim that the broadband was super-fast when it was barely a megabyte above dial-up.

"Nah, it's fine. Perhaps in a day or two, you'll remember something?"

And what else was Rhys meant to do? Find her a cardboard box for the night?

CHAPTER 5

RHYS

When they got back to the house, the stereo was pumping out Mariah again. The girl looked at Rhys, confused.

"Someone else is here?"

"No, and this isn't my music, I swear. It's my uncle's way of reminding me to water the plants."

"Maybe I could help?"

"Don't you need to rest?"

"I'm not tired, and I think... I think that I should just try to act normal?"

"Well, if you're sure you don't mind... There's a tap by each door."

The process went much faster with two pairs of hands. They split the six greenhouses between them, and Rhys explained which plants needed a lot of water and which hardly needed any. Honestly, these plants couldn't have been more pampered if they spent the weekend at a health spa. *Six more days to go...*

With the watering finished, Rhys turned off the squeaky tap in the final greenhouse and rolled up the hose. Uncle

Albert might have had green fingers, but Rhys certainly hadn't inherited them. Gardening made returning to his student dive and putting up with Gary and Stacey seem like an attractive option. Where was the girl? Yelling "Hey you" seemed rude, so he traipsed through the other greenhouses until he found her standing under the coco du ciel palms, staring up at the huge spiky leaves.

"I wish they could talk," she said. "They'd be able to tell me where I came from."

"If these plants started talking, we'd have an even bigger problem."

"I guess."

"Keep your chin up—we'll solve the mystery. Maybe that copper was on to something when he suggested trying the university? Students do crazy things when they're drunk."

"How crazy? Do they run around with no clothes on?"

Rhys thought back to some of the wilder parties he'd attended. He might not have socialised often by choice, but he wasn't a complete hermit, and Stacey had dragged him out most weeks. He recalled the bikini vodka fight on the roof, skinny-dipping in a local duck pond, that time one of Gary's mates had got himself arrested for public indecency...

"Uh, yeah. Sometimes they lose their clothes."

The girl looked him up and down with fresh eyes, and Rhys felt a sudden pang of regret when he recalled the gym membership he'd taken out during freshers' week and rarely used. Not that it mattered what she thought of him. Give it a day or two, and she'd be gone. Hopefully.

"We'll carry on asking around in the morning," he promised in an attempt to move the conversation along. "But in the meantime, what should I call you?"

A shrug. *Please don't cry.*

"Perhaps a nickname?"

"The doctors called me Patient A."

"Sounds a bit James Bond, doesn't it? You know, having a letter instead of a name? I could call you A."

The girl didn't smile. Did she even know who James Bond was?

"Wouldn't that confuse people?"

Probably. Rhys glanced around, seeking divine inspiration, and what do you know? It came.

"How about Coco? Like the trees?"

"Coco? Isn't that kind of...girly?"

"Well, you *are* a girl."

Rhys realised his gaze had dropped to her chest. *What a bloody arsehole.* His cheeks burned as he focused on her face again. Had she noticed his faux pas? Yes, it seemed—her lips had flattened into a thin line, but then she caught herself too and forced a smile.

"Fine. Call me Coco."

Dinner was an interesting affair. Eating fish and chips in silence felt awkward, but what did two people discuss when one had no memory of any events before the previous day?

"So... The weather's meant to be nice tomorrow."

"Sunny?"

"Apparently so."

"I think... I think I like the sun. Where are we again? You said the name of the village, but I forgot it."

"We're in Llanefion, North Wales, and the nearest city is Bangor. Ring any bells?"

Coco shook her head. "Have you lived here for long? You sound different from the other people we spoke to. Your accent, I mean."

"No, I live near London. I'm only here for a couple of weeks, house-sitting."

"And you're a student? I saw a bunch of textbooks in the living room."

"I've just finished a computer science degree."

In some ways, it was like speaking with a child. Almost every sentence that came out of Coco's mouth was a question.

"How long does a degree take? Four years?"

"Three years. But I started late. My..." Rhys paused to take a breath. This was the part that hurt. "My mum died when I was nineteen. Sudden—a drunk driver knocked her off her bike while she cycled home from work. So things got...delayed."

He'd been backpacking at the time, working on a farm in Australia. The call had come in the early hours. One day, he'd been picking fruit and flirting clumsily with girls in the local bars, and the next, organising a funeral. The driver had been uninsured. Money had been tight. Rhys had deferred his uni place for another two years while he saved up enough to live on, and then finally moved to Uxbridge.

Coco squeezed his hand. "I'm so sorry about your mom."

Rhys jolted at her unexpected touch, but as quickly as she'd reached out, she snatched her hand away.

"It happened almost five years ago. I've learned to live with it."

A bland answer, and one that glossed over the pain that still burned in his gut. He'd found that was the best way to deal with the past. To pretend it didn't exist.

"What about your dad?"

"Not in the picture."

"I'm sorry for that too."

"Don't be—he was an arsehole." Rhys barely remembered the man, only the yelling. He'd been glad when his father left. His mum had been happier as well, but now Uncle Albert was the only family he had left. "I don't suppose you remember your parents?"

Coco gave a helpless shrug. "Sorry."

The questions carried on... What year was it? Was it winter? No, summer, although it didn't seem like it. Did it rain every day in Wales? Where was Uncle Albert? Why did he have so many plants? After dinner, Rhys turned the TV on, and although Coco vaguely understood football, she only recalled the American game which was more like rugby with a bunch of standing around.

But underneath the confusion, she was whip smart, maybe even *too* smart at times. Tell her something, and she analysed and challenged. Coco might have been forgetful, but she definitely wasn't stupid. And Rhys enjoyed the evening with her more than he'd ever thought he would.

The grandfather clock had chimed midnight when he finally showed her to the nicer of the two empty guest bedrooms. Woodside Lodge was far too big for one man, but at the same time, Rhys couldn't imagine Uncle Albert living anywhere else. An eccentric old house for an eccentric old man and his menagerie of plants. Albert would go stir crazy in a retirement flat.

The bedroom smelled musty, but apart from a thin layer of dust, it was clean. Not as nice as a hotel, but definitely better than a cardboard box.

"Make yourself at home, I guess."

He started to close the door behind him, but she stopped him with a quiet whisper.

"Rhys?"

"Yeah?"

"Thanks. For, you know, everything."

"No problem."

What sort of man would he be if he'd left her to fend for herself?

The next morning, they started the hunt for Coco's true identity in earnest.

"Smile," Rhys said as he snapped photos with his phone.

"What is there to smile about?"

He crossed his eyes, and she giggled.

"Better. I'll make up a bunch of flyers with your picture. Somebody must know who you are."

It took him twenty minutes to mock up a poster in PowerPoint and another thirty to convince Albert's printer to talk to his laptop. The thing had to be five years old, practically an antique in tech terms, but at least his uncle hoarded ink cartridges the same way he hoarded canned goods.

"Have you seen this woman?" Coco read. "I sound like a lost dog."

"Do you have a better idea?"

"I guess not."

"I just hope people don't think this is a bloody joke."

After all, full-on amnesia was rare, something that happened in movies more often than in real life—Rhys had researched the details on the internet last night after Coco went to bed. And the fact that there had been no sign of outward injury worried him more than he let on. If the doctor was right and Coco's memory loss had been caused by emotional trauma, then living in ignorant bliss might actually be preferable to remembering what happened.

First, they called the doctor's contact at the local paper, who agreed to run a small article, and then they tried the university. The lady in the student liaison office insisted they had no missing students, but she made sympathetic noises in the right places and offered to put up some posters.

Rhys and Coco spent the afternoon traipsing around Llanefion village and the neighbouring town, taping flyers to trees and lamp posts and bus shelters. By the end of the day, the only thing they had to show for their efforts was aching feet. Coco was wearing Rhys's spare trainers with three pairs of socks, but they were still too big for her.

She groaned out loud as she sank onto somebody's garden wall for a rest.

"You okay?" Rhys asked.

"Just tired. Why hasn't anyone called?"

"We haven't finished putting up the posters yet."

"Don't remind me. Why do I get the feeling this is all a big waste of time?"

"Have faith."

"All I want to do is go home, and I don't even know where that is."

"Somebody'll recognise you." Eventually. "We can get you better shoes tomorrow."

"How? I don't have any money, remember?"

"I'll lend you the cash. Let's go back to Woodside Lodge, okay? Get some rest."

A teenager shuffled past in a leopard-print onesie, and Coco turned to stare. "What *is* that boy wearing?"

"That, my dear, is fashion."

"Oh. Wow. Then I'm quite glad I'm unfashionable." Her eyes widened as she realised whose clothes she was wearing. "Sorry! I didn't mean…"

"Chill, I get it. We'll buy you some clothes tomorrow too. Any idea what style you like?"

"None whatsoever. But not…" She took one last glance at the wannabe leopard. "Not that."

Rhys made a mental note to chuck his tiger-print onesie in the bin. Not that he wore it often, honest. He'd only bought it for a fancy-dress party. Then he caught himself— why did it matter? The onesie was in Uxbridge. It wasn't as if Coco would ever see it.

CHAPTER 6
RHYS

Back at the house, Rhys stood in front of the pantry, surveying the contents with Coco beside him. Was Uncle Albert a prepper in his spare time? There were so many cans. And packets, and jars, and boxes...

"What can you make out of chickpeas, olive oil, and dried pasta?" Coco asked. "I'd say my mind's a blank, but we both already know that."

"There's an app with the answer to that very question. You know what an app is?" Rhys didn't want to make any assumptions.

"Like a program for your phone?"

"Exactly."

"And it tells you how to cook spaghetti?"

"Yup. It's called Pan Friday."

Rhys should know—he'd written it. Pan Friday hadn't made him rich, but by living frugally, he'd managed to graduate debt-free and also save up enough cash to finish the trip he'd started five years ago. Plus he'd learned twenty new things to do with baked beans. Eating them on toast was so last century.

Returning to Australia would be bittersweet, but his mum had always encouraged him to follow his dreams. He hoped that his new project—a subscription app called Fit4Life he was writing in collaboration with a fitness coach who'd found fame on YouTube—would allow him to travel for an extra year at least. And with any luck, it might help him to get in shape too.

"Yeah, you just enter the ingredients you have, and it tells you what you can make."

Rhys didn't write the recipes himself—a good thing too, because he was shit at cooking—but instead, he used a database he'd built up over the years to direct users to an appropriate recipe on the internet. He got income from the app purchases, and the food writers got additional traffic to content already on their websites—a win-win situation.

"So what can we make?"

"How about pasta with chickpea-and-tomato sauce?"

"I guess that's okay. I mean, I have no idea what I like to eat, so..."

"Then we'll just have to try a different type of food each night until you remember."

Her face fell. "How long do you think I'm going to be here?"

"I meant until you go home. Maybe a day or two? We can pick up groceries tomorrow, anything you want."

"Sure."

Unlike last night, Coco barely spoke as they ate, just picked at admittedly overcooked pasta in between staring blankly out of the window. What was going through her mind? Worry? Confusion? Nothing at all?

Two days into the search, Rhys was even more baffled than he had been when Coco emerged from the foliage in her birthday suit. Why hadn't anyone reported her missing? Perhaps he was being judgemental, but she didn't seem the type of girl to fly under the radar. Coco was beautiful. He hadn't missed the heads that turned as the two of them taped up posters, and he also knew what those people were thinking—what was a girl like her doing with a man like him? Not that Rhys was hideous or anything; he was just average. Average in every way. Coco was in a whole other league, and not only in terms of looks. She was clever, funny, and kind too. A lethal combination, at least when it came to a man's heart.

Good thing she wouldn't be around for long.

"I guess we can cross moussaka off the list?" he said when she put her fork down.

"Huh?"

"You didn't like dinner?"

"Oh, I... It was good. I appreciate you cooking."

"Really?"

Whenever he'd suggested cooking in Uxbridge, Stacey had immediately reached for a takeout menu.

"I just... I think I might not like eggplants. All those fleshy little lumps." She hesitated a second, then clapped both hands to her cheeks. "Flesh? Do you think I saw a murder?"

"Do *you* think you saw a murder?"

"I don't know, but the doctor said trauma, and... Okay, I'm clutching at straws."

Probably, but Rhys was going to follow every possible lead. "I'll check the internet in case any deaths have been reported locally. And after I've watered the plants, we can watch the news too."

"Do you need a hand again?"

"I wouldn't say no."

In retrospect, that decision turned out to be a mistake.

The humidity in the greenhouses meant that Coco stripped down to her T-shirt, which left Rhys kicking himself for not taking her somewhere to buy a bra. *Put your filthy mind away, you utter dick. Think of something else. Computer code, cars, anything.* The poor girl had been through quite enough without a virtual stranger lusting after her.

And the news was a problem too. There wasn't a single item of interest on *Wales Today*, but then the international segment came on and it turned out that a cruise ship had capsized off the coast of Spain. At least thirty-seven people were known to have drowned, and Coco took the news worse than half of the people on the ground. She tried to blink away her tears, then gave up and used a sleeve to wipe them.

"All those poor people. The water…"

"Rescue teams are there now. They'll help."

"But what if there are still survivors trapped inside?"

"They'll get them out. Look, there's a diver."

Coco bit her lip, and Rhys passed her a tissue. Mental note: find a comedy to watch tomorrow. Assuming Coco hadn't gone home, obviously. She might have been sweeter than Stacey, but she was a hell of a lot more complicated to be around.

The following day, Rhys bankrupted himself buying more ink cartridges, and they postered the nearest town in the other direction as well as stopping at a department store to get clothes for Coco. And underwear, but he let her find that while he checked out the electronics section. Shopping for undies with a girl he shouldn't have liked but kind of did would be only marginally less embarrassing than finding her naked in the greenhouse.

"Lunch?" he asked once she had what she needed. "Fancy going to Greggs?"

"I don't have a clue what that is, but sure."

What? How could she not know what Greggs was? Despite the amnesia, Coco had been perfectly familiar with McDonald's, although she couldn't recall whether she preferred Big Macs or Quarter Pounders.

"Greggs—you know, the bakery chain?"

Coco shrugged, both hands out.

"Where else would you buy your sausage rolls from?"

"My sausage whats?"

This was getting weirder and weirder. "Sausages wrapped in puff pastry?"

"I don't think I've ever had one of those."

"How can you not have?"

Surely she wasn't a vegetarian? Once she finally settled on a Big Mac yesterday, she'd wolfed it down. Plus Greggs did vegan sausage rolls now. No, that couldn't be the issue.

"Maybe they don't have a Greggs wherever I'm from?" she suggested.

Impossible if she came from the UK. There was no escaping them. Going to Greggs was a rite of passage for every student, office worker, and hung-over twenty-something in the country. That was the biggest hint yet that Coco wasn't from around there.

Another hint came when they got into Greggs. Coco sniffed the air and smiled, studied the cabinet, then asked the assistant for a sausage roll and chips.

"We don't sell chips, love. You'll have to go to KFC for those."

"So what are those packages?"

The woman followed Coco's gaze. "You mean crisps?"

"Ah, yes, crisps." Then almost to herself, she added, "That's what British people call chips, isn't it?"

So that meant Coco...*wasn't* British? Her accent had been difficult to pin down. When they first met, Rhys thought he'd detected the faintest hint of American, but that had faded as they spoke. And today, she'd adopted a definite Welsh lilt. Where had she been born? The USA? Had she moved to Wales recently? Or was she just great at imitating people?

Rhys's thoughts were interrupted by his phone ringing, and when he saw an unknown number on the screen, his heart jolted.

"Hello?"

A pause. "I thought this number was for the girl on the poster?"

"Yes, it is. I'm a friend of hers."

"Can you give me *her* number?"

"Do you know her?"

"No, but I'd like to *get* to know her."

Ugh. Rhys hung up, then realised Coco was watching him, a hopeful smile on her face.

"Sorry, just a crank."

The smile faded. "I ordered you a sausage roll."

"Thanks, babe." Dammit. "Uh, Coco."

Shit. Rhys definitely needed to get her back to wherever the hell she'd come from, and fast.

The next call came at twenty past four as they walked back to the car, carrying half a dozen bags of groceries and clothes between them. And at first, the lead sounded hopeful.

"So you reckon you saw her? The girl on the poster?"

Coco leaned in to listen, and Rhys wished he'd stepped away. The brush of her breast against his arm did nothing to aid his concentration.

"Oh, aye. For sure. Last week, mebbe? Or the week before?"

Was he asking Rhys or telling him?

"Where?"

"So I was at this party…"

"And the girl, she was at the party too?"

"Naw, man. I saw her afterwards."

"On your way home?"

"Naw, on the ship."

"Ship? What ship?"

"The spaceship. Those little bastards have been abducting me for years. Years! And she's one of them. One of those freaks! The bald ones, they drill holes in my head, but she sucks my—"

Rhys hit the "end" button and muttered, "Sorry."

What a waste of time. Two days of searching, and only two calls. Nothing from the police. Nothing from the hospital. Who the hell was this girl?

CHAPTER 7

RHYS

Now what? All week, the clock had been counting down to this moment. Tomorrow, Rhys was due to drive back home, and Coco? She still had nowhere to go.

The handful of calls they'd received had yielded a big fat zero—several people wanted to know if there was a reward, one guy said she reminded him of a girl he'd seen at his cousin's wedding, and a woman threatened to report them for littering after they stuck a poster to her fence. The wedding lead had sounded promising until they tracked down the cousin. The mystery girl turned out to be his sister-in-law, and the guy who called must have been wearing beer goggles because she looked nothing like Coco.

"Did you water the orchids?" Coco asked.

"Not yet."

"I'll do them."

She hadn't smiled once today, which was a crying shame because when she did let down her guard, she lit up the world. If scientists could find a way to harness that energy, mankind's dependency on fossil fuels would reduce overnight.

"Do you want to order Chinese afterwards?"

Pizza had been her favourite so far. No pineapple, though. Over the past week, they'd gleaned a few other snippets of information about her past, tiny clues that helped to build up a picture of the girl she'd once been. She liked animals. When a neighbour's mutt strayed into the garden at Woodside Lodge, Coco had played fetch with a stick until the owner showed up. Pop music was her favourite, the cheesier the better, and she'd dance around the greenhouses when she thought Rhys wasn't looking. And she could draw. Give her a pen and she'd doodle, and those doodles would turn into detailed sketches. She drew a lot of buildings. After the first, Rhys thought she might be drawing a memory of her home, but no, it just seemed to be a favourite theme of hers. Ornate mansions, quirky apartment buildings, modern townhouses... She produced them all.

"We still have groceries left. Can't we use that magic app?"

She still didn't know he'd designed the app, so her comment was unexpectedly flattering.

"Chickening out of using chopsticks again?"

"No." Her sulky tone told him he'd hit the nail on the head. "I should probably learn more about cooking."

"Sure, we can cook."

They needed to discuss the future too. He'd offered to lend her cash to stay in a bed and breakfast or rent a flat, but she'd been hesitant to accept. Rhys knew why—guilt. She had no idea how she'd pay the money back, and quite frankly, neither did he. How could she get a job with no identity? Sure, some dodgy places would pay cash in hand for waitressing or crop-picking, but Rhys didn't want her to be stuck in that life. He already cared about her more than he should.

Fuck.

It was his turn to pick at his food, and her turn to act concerned.

"What's wrong?"

"Just pondering what to do tomorrow. I'm worried about leaving you here alone."

"I think... I think I'll have to borrow the money you offered. I don't like doing it, but..."

"There might be another option."

"Really?"

What was he doing?

"I've got the room in Uxbridge until the end of August. If you want to share it, then you're welcome to." Had he lost his mind as well? "I mean, not the bed because that would be awkward, but we could get a futon or something."

Yes, it was official; he'd gone crazy. Why else would he have asked the loveliest woman he'd ever met to move in with him, albeit temporarily? His heart hammered in his chest. If she turned him down, it would hurt like hell.

"I realise it's not a brilliant offer." Great, now he was babbling. "And you might have a better chance of connecting with your past if you stay here, but—"

"Are you sure?"

"Am I sure?" No. "Uh, yeah? I mean, definitely."

She treated him to one of those dazzling smiles. "Then I'd like to come with you."

Thank goodness.

And holy shit.

The relief that flooded through him should have been a warning, but in that moment, he was too happy to heed it.

"So I guess we need to pack."

"What about that pod thing? Should we clear it up before we go?"

The question had weighed heavy on Rhys's mind all week. To sweep up the sorry remains of his uncle's coco du ciel nut might be construed as an admission of guilt, and Rhys had done nothing wrong.

"Let's leave it. Maybe Uncle Albert will think it fell down right before he got back?"

"Maybe." Her tone said she didn't believe that. "You're not going to stay and speak to him?"

Rhys knew he *should*—Albert was his only living relative, after all—but if his uncle was annoyed, putting a few hundred miles between them seemed like a good idea. Not only that, Rhys didn't want to answer questions about Coco either. If Albert found out she'd been in the greenhouse that night, then *she* might get the blame. Now that Rhys had gotten to know her, he couldn't imagine her committing an act of vandalism, but his uncle might not be so willing to give her the benefit of the doubt.

"I'll phone him later."

As they set off for Uxbridge, Rhys said a silent prayer that his ancient Fiesta would make it the whole way back. He hadn't bothered to get it serviced seeing as he planned to scrap the vehicle before he left the country, and now he was regretting that oversight. An extended stay at Watford Gap services would hardly be the best start to Coco's new life.

She was fidgety too, of course she was. Once again, she

was heading into the unknown. And the house in Uxbridge... Okay, so Rhys might have glossed over some of the details because the masochist in him didn't want her to run screaming into the distance. Let's just say it would be about as far away from the peaceful solitude they'd shared in Wales as it was possible to get.

Black smoke was pouring from the back end of the Fiesta by the time they pulled onto Cardon Street. The dingy Victorian terrace he shared with three others sat halfway along on the right-hand side, a thorn among roses. As he drew to a halt at the kerb, Rhys kept his fingers crossed that he'd put his dirty underwear into the laundry hamper and remembered to bin the remains of the noodles that had been his last meal before he left for Wales.

"This is it?" Coco asked, looking up at the grubby facade.

Once upon a time, the building had been white, but over the years, the paint had faded to a dirty grey that blended in with the smoggy sky above it. Paint peeled from the door and window frames, and the tiny front yard had as many weeds as Uncle Albert had flowers.

"Home sweet home." Rhys opened the front door, and Jorge—the least offensive of his three housemates—wandered past scratching his unmentionables. "Well, sort of."

Things didn't get much better when they walked into the lounge. Hashim was sprawled on the sofa, surrounded by a sea of empty pizza boxes. Brilliant.

"Didn't you lot clear up at all while I was away?"

Hashim shrugged. "Nope. Football was on." Then he noticed Coco behind Rhys and grinned. "Hey, you upgraded Stacey!"

"Who's Stacey?" Coco asked.

Hashim choked on a laugh. "Whoops."

Rhys steered Coco out of the room. "Let's talk in the kitchen. I'll make us some tea."

Or coffee, as it turned out, because they'd run out of teabags. Black, because there was no milk either. Coco sat opposite him at the scarred kitchen table and raised an eyebrow.

"Stacey?"

He closed his eyes, which did nothing whatsoever to help. Fuck, this was embarrassing.

"We dated for a year and a half, but then she decided she preferred one of my housemates."

Coco glanced back towards the living room, nose wrinkling. "What, one of...?"

"No, not them. Gary. I caught them at it on the sofa."

Rhys hadn't sat on it since, and not just because it was permanently covered in crumbs.

"He still lives here?"

"Unfortunately."

"Has he no shame?"

"He doesn't know the meaning of the word," Rhys said on a sigh. "I just try to keep out of the way. My lease is up soon, and I mostly stay in my room, working."

"Is there anything I can do to help? Poke Stacey's eyes out, kick Gary in the balls, that sort of thing?"

Rhys managed a lopsided smile. He was tempted to take Coco up on the second option, but that would only create more tension.

"To be honest, just having you here's done wonders for my street cred."

"What do you mean?"

"You must know you're pretty. Did you see Hashim's and Jorge's faces when you walked in?"

"Am I pretty? I guess I never really thought about it."

Coco's answer was genuine. She wasn't fishing for compliments.

"Not just pretty. Beautiful."

The words left Rhys's mouth before he thought to apply a filter, and he cursed himself. *Shut up, you fool.* Coco, ever the sensitive one, noticed his discomfort and lowered her gaze to the table for a moment.

"So I guess I'll just...hang out?"

"Sorry this place is such a dump."

"Hey, it's better than being homeless."

Dammit, that note of sadness had crept back into her voice.

"You'll never be homeless, I promise."

Think before you speak, asshole. Don't make promises you can't keep.

"I won't be here forever. As soon as I can find out..."

"I know." This was getting too heavy for a Wednesday afternoon. "So I guess I should show you my room. Our room."

The coffee was still too hot to drink, so they carried it upstairs with them. Rhys's bedroom smelled slightly musty, probably because of the damp problem the landlord never got around to fixing, but it was blessedly tidy. Coco perused the space, taking in the double bed pushed against one wall, the desk half-buried under piles of scribbled notes, and the dancing plastic cactus on the windowsill. Stacey had given it to him as a Christmas gift. Now, the batteries were as dead as their relationship, but he'd never quite been able to bring himself to throw it out.

"It's better than I was expecting," Coco said. "After I saw the lounge, I was worried we wouldn't be able to find the floor."

"That's why I keep the door locked. If the others can't get in, they can't trash it."

She wandered over to the window and gazed out at the patch of dirt the estate agent had called a garden. Since it faced north, it was perpetually cast in shadow, and even the weeds struggled to survive out there. The overcast sky threatened rain, and Rhys was glad they'd got home before the storm started. He didn't like driving in bad weather, not least because his car only had one windscreen wiper.

"I can take the floor tonight," Coco said, turning to face him. "I don't want to kick you out of your bed."

"You're not sleeping on the floor."

Coco huffed and went back to the window. Thinking of escape already?

"Fine."

The logistics would take some getting used to. In the end, Rhys headed to the bathroom to change while Coco borrowed another of his T-shirts and a pair of jogging bottoms. If this arrangement was to last two months, they needed to buy her pyjamas.

Oh, for crying out loud…

Rhys switched on the bathroom light and immediately wished he hadn't. The black ring of scum around the bath was bad enough, but the pedestrian crossing light lying inside the tub? That was ten times worse. Where had it even come from? The geek in him was tempted to wire it up and see if it worked, but the pragmatist overruled. He needed to get rid of the bloody thing. Was that classed as aiding and abetting? *Deep breaths, Rhys. None of this should surprise you.* Beyond the bath, the toilet seat was of course up, and also decorated with a dubious array of yellow stains. Stacey might not have worried about things like that, but no way would Coco be setting foot in this mess.

Rhys grabbed a scouring pad and began scrubbing, and when the bathroom suite no longer made him cringe, he went to find a screwdriver.

Two months, that's all he had to last.

Coco was sitting on the edge of the bed when he returned, hands folded neatly in her lap.

"You took a while."

What was he meant to say? She probably thought he'd been taking a dump or jacking off, but he could hardly admit he'd been breaking stolen property into its component parts, could he?

"Best if you use the downstairs loo tonight." That way, he could wait until she went to bed and then cart the remains of the crossing light out to the bin in the dark. He sensed another question on her lips, one he didn't want to answer. In moments like this, avoidance was the best tactic. "Let's make some dinner, eh? Then we can get some sleep."

It was going to be a long, long evening.

CHAPTER 8
RHYS

Was it normal to lie in the dark, listening to another person breathe? Rhys had never been tempted to do that with Stacey, although she *had* kept him awake with her snoring from time to time. Was Coco too hot? Or not warm enough? It might have been June, but nobody had told the weather that, and Gary-the-prick opened the windows every chance he got. Rhys was bloody freezing. They needed to buy an extra duvet tomorrow as well.

Make that today. He could just about make out the luminous hands on the clock above his desk, hear its steady tick over the noise from outside. His bedroom was farthest from the road, but one of the neighbours was having a party, the inconsiderate bastard. Who held a party that late on a weekday?

At least Coco seemed to be sleeping. Thank goodness for small mercies.

Rhys channelled the living dead as he dragged himself off the floor in the morning. Two hours' sleep didn't cut it, especially after yesterday's drive and the late-night cleaning session. Gummy eyelids weighed heavy, and his first stumbling steps reminded him of Jorge after he'd drunk one too many shots. Coco, on the other hand, looked as lovely as ever.

When her eyelids fluttered open, she gave him one glance and swung her legs out of bed.

"I'll make coffee."

"I can…" He couldn't. "Thanks."

Five minutes later, she put a steaming mug down on his bedside table.

"Are you sick? You look sick."

"No, just tired."

"You didn't sleep well?"

"Not really."

"Then why don't you rest? The bed's empty now."

Oh, if only. "I've just sat my final exams. I need to stop acting like a student."

And besides, if he didn't go out and buy some sort of mattress, he'd be spending another night on the floor.

"How do students act?"

"They go to bed late, get up late, drink too much beer, know the phone numbers of every takeaway within a five-mile radius by heart, and occasionally, very occasionally, they go to a few lectures."

"I'm not sure if I've ever been a student, but I don't think I could live on beer and takeout."

"I've always been a night owl, but being honest, I found there were better things to spend my money on than alcohol and pizza." Plus Rhys had gone to most of his lectures, which quickly earned him the status of "least cool housemate." Seriously—Hashim had presented him with a plastic trophy and everything. Best to leave that part out. "Do you want breakfast? I'll make us both breakfast."

"I could do with a shower first. Where is it?"

"Turn right out of the bedroom, and it's straight ahead."

Coco's soft footsteps padded along the hallway, and the bathroom door clicked shut as Rhys scalded the roof of his mouth on his coffee. Great start. How was he going to get through two months of this? Coco wasn't a bad roommate, but the sheer awkwardness of—

"Rhys? This may be a dumb question, but what should I do with the goldfish?"

"The...goldfish?"

"The two goldfish in the bathtub?"

Oh, for fuck's sake. Sharing a house with Gary, Jorge, and Hashim was like living in a zoo, and this morning, Rhys meant that quite literally.

"Jorge!" And it was pronounced like George, not the Spanish way—his parents just weren't great at spelling. "Why are there goldfish in the bathtub?"

The next door along the hallway clicked open. "Because they didn't look happy in the washing-up bowl."

Take a deep breath.

"I'll rephrase. Why are there goldfish at all?"

"Who knows?"

"Was beer involved?"

"Probably."

Coco giggled. "At least I'm not the only one with a memory problem."

"You can't leave the fish there," Rhys told him.

"Yeah, yeah, I'll fix it later."

Jorge slammed his door shut, and the pulse throbbing in Rhys's temple told him that he'd have a monster headache by the end of the day if he wasn't careful. Why him? Sober, Jorge was bearable, but drunk or hung-over? He was a real asshole.

"That guy's an idiot," Coco whispered. "How do you put up with him?"

A girl after his own heart.

"The rent's cheap, and I'll be leaving soon."

"Right."

Shit. "I won't see you stuck."

"We both know this arrangement can't last forever." Coco turned and headed towards the bathroom again. "Guess I'll skip the shower."

An hour later, Rhys browsed the aisles of the local pet store with Coco in tow. What did fish need? He picked out a basic aquarium, a tub of food, coloured gravel, and a filter, then Coco added a couple of fake plants and a mock cave.

"I don't want them to get bored," she said.

"Don't their memories last about seven seconds?"

"Who knows? But if they do, they can have seven seconds of happiness."

Such a tiny, innocuous comment, but it showed who Coco was, didn't it? She cared about others, even if that "other" was a damn goldfish. Rhys added a miniature pirate ship to the basket and went to pay.

Afterwards, they headed to the outdoor store to pick up an inflatable mattress, plus Tesco for groceries, a cheap duvet, and another pillow. In hindsight, they should have gone to TK Maxx instead.

"Oh, hell," he groaned as they walked out the door.

"What's wrong?"

"Not what, who." Rhys cut his eyes to the side. "That's Gary and Stacey."

And short of hightailing it back into the store and hiding in the cleaning aisle—because neither of them would ever find it—there was no way of avoiding the pair.

But Coco, it seemed, had a plan. Rhys jolted as she slid an arm around his waist and rested her head on his shoulder.

"What are you doing?"

"Helping."

As Rhys's blood headed south to his cock, he thought that was debatable.

"All right?" he asked through gritted teeth as Gary got within spitting distance. He didn't expect an answer, but if Gary had caught an incurable disease or his testicles had dropped off, that would be a bonus.

Stacey replied for both of them. "Never better. We're having a party at mine tonight, so you know... Gotta get the drinks in." At one time, Rhys had found her saccharine voice sweet, but now it grated. And was he imagining things, or did it also sound slightly strained today? "Who's your friend?"

"This is Coco."

Gary's slow perusal made Rhys want to knock the man's teeth out. But Tesco had CCTV, and he also didn't want to end up in jail.

"You from around here, Coco?" Gary asked.

"I'm staying with Rhys at the moment."

That gleam in Gary's eyes was almost predatory. Perhaps jail wouldn't be so bad?

"Maybe I could show you the sights, help you feel at home?"

The sights? In Uxbridge? There were two shopping centres, a handful of dodgy nightclubs, and a canal. It was hardly fucking Disneyland.

Stacey gave Gary a disgusted look, but Coco just laughed.

"No, thanks. I like to hang out with men, not boys."

Coco spoke the words so sweetly that it took a few seconds for the insult to register. Plus there was the fact that Gary was a bit slow in general. But he finally worked it out, and his face turned beet red.

"We're running late," he mumbled, then grabbed Stacey's arm and pulled her into the store.

Perhaps that was the moment when Rhys began to fall a tiny bit in love with Coco.

"I can't believe you said that."

"He deserved it. *I* can't believe he hit on me in front of his girlfriend."

"I don't think she could either. Did you see her face?"

"Yes, but she made her bed, so she can lie in it." Coco touched Rhys's arm with her free hand. "Sorry, that was insensitive."

"Forget it. I had a lucky escape."

And quite possibly a lucky find, in a greenhouse of all places.

CHAPTER 9

RHYS

"I'm sorry, babe. I'm so sorry."

"It's not your fault."

Coco sat cross-legged on the bed twisting a damp tissue while Rhys paced the room with his phone in his hand, plotting murder. Why did men have to be such arseholes? The caller had claimed to be a friend of Coco's, except he'd said her name was Janine. And the story had sounded believable. They'd met at the gym, gone out for coffee several times. She'd just split up with a boyfriend. So Rhys had handed the phone over, and the pervert had spewed such filth that Coco had run to the bathroom to puke.

And *that* was the best lead they'd had so far.

"I'll screen the next call better."

"What if there isn't a next call? It's as if I never existed." Coco blew her nose and sniffed a bit. "Or if I did, nobody cares enough to look for me. Am I that bad of a person?"

No. No way. Since Coco had no memories to guide her, what Rhys saw must be her natural personality, right?

Sweet with a little bit of sass. How could anybody not be fond of her?

"You're a good person. Perhaps you'd only just arrived in Wales? Maybe you didn't have a chance to get to know anyone?"

Those hints of an American twang had come back, stronger this time. The Welsh lilt she'd picked up had all but been replaced by a London accent. It was as if Coco were a blank canvas, learning as she went, but what if the US accent was natural?

"So what can we do?"

"I reckon we should try social media. It's got a further reach."

"I suppose."

"You don't like the idea?"

"I'm not sure what's worse—not knowing who I am, or having the entire world knowing that I don't know who I am. What if it brings even more crackpots out of the woodwork?"

"I can't think of any other options."

Coco slumped against the headboard, resigned. "Go on, then. Try it."

Rhys selected the best headshot from the photos he'd taken in Wales and composed a message to go with it.

"How does this look?"

Do you know me?

I was found suffering from amnesia in North Wales, and I'd like to go home. I may have a connection to the US. Please send a message if I look familiar.

"Okay, I guess."

"I haven't put too much detail on there, and any messages will come to me. I'll delete the ugly ones."

A shrug.

Rhys took that to mean acceptance because really, they had no other choice. A minute later, their plea for help was posted.

"Now, we wait."

A bad day only got worse when they went downstairs to make dinner. Originally, Rhys had planned to order food to eat upstairs because forking out for a pizza was more appealing than making small talk with Jorge and Hashim, but Uxbridge's answer to Laurel and Hardy had driven off somewhere in Hashim's Honda, which meant Rhys and Coco had the house to themselves.

Plus Coco wanted to cook. Earlier, she'd asked him what he did for work, and he'd fessed up about the apps he'd written, then sworn her to secrecy because if his housemates found out he had an actual job, they'd expect him to pay for all the groceries. Now that she'd realised he was the brain behind the Pan Friday app, she was determined to challenge it and him. Rhys didn't mind. Firstly, he knew the app would perform, and secondly, he liked seeing her happy. Hell, he'd even buy a set of bakeware if it made her smile.

"Okay, what can we make with walnuts, canned pineapple, and an egg?"

"Pineapple chocolate chip cookies."

"Uh, it says we need flour. Is there any flour?"

"I think so." Hashim had bought a bag to play a prank on Jorge last month. "Here it is."

"Okay, we have to—"

The back door crashed open, and Rhys swore under his breath.

"I thought you were throwing a party?"

Stacey shrugged and helped herself to a pineapple chunk. "We postponed it. Gary got a last-minute DJ gig at Toxic."

Sounded about right. Toxic was the skankiest nightclub in town—picture watered-down drinks, vomit, and music that left you with a headache. And even that place was scraping the bottom of the barrel with Gary. He thought he was going to be the next David Guetta, but his attempts at mixing sounded more like a chain-smoker having a coughing fit.

And of course, the tone-deaf twat headed straight for Coco.

"We haven't met properly yet." He grinned at her, showing off his cubic zirconia dental grill. Gary thought it made him look like Lil Wayne. Rhys thought it looked as if a toddler had glued glitter to his teeth. "I'm Gary."

"So I heard."

"You thought any more about my offer?"

"What offer?"

"To show you around town."

"I already said no."

"Hey, don't knock it till you've tried it. We'll have a laugh."

"I'd rather thread the needle on a sewing machine while it's still running."

The jibe went straight over Gary's head. "Sewing?

That's boring, man. Bet Mr. Life and Soul of the Party here hasn't taken you out once." He jerked his thumb at Rhys. "Am I right?"

"Oh, he's been keeping me quite entertained."

Gary snorted. "Well, when you fancy having some proper fun, let me know."

"Will that be before or after you've taken care of your girlfriend?"

Rhys glanced at Stacey. She'd paled a few shades, and he recognised that tight set to her jaw. She was pissed.

"Before, after, at the same time. Whatevs."

Rhys thought Stacey might actually take a swing at the philandering prick, but unfortunately, he was saved by a phone. Unintelligible rap music blared, and Gary fished a faux-diamond-encrusted monstrosity out of his pocket.

"It's my record producer. Gotta take this."

He ambled off, holding up his jeans with one hand. Hadn't the idiot ever heard of a belt?

Stacey didn't move.

"By 'record producer,' does he still mean that guy with an entry-level mixing desk and a computer in his bedroom?" Rhys asked her.

"I think so," Stacey mumbled, turning to Coco. "So, how long have you known Rhys?"

"Not long. A couple of weeks."

"And you've moved in with him already?"

Rhys could understand Stacey's surprise. Once or twice, she'd made noises about them getting a place together, but he'd always made an excuse not to. Had his subconscious known even then that the relationship was doomed to fail?

"I needed a place to stay."

Stacey's eyes narrowed. "And Rhys's bed was the only available option?"

"It was the best option." Coco headed for the door. "I have things to do."

Rhys hurried after her and caught up at the door to his room. Their room.

"You okay?"

Stupid question. The answer was obviously no.

"I hate being reminded of my lack of options."

"I understand this isn't easy, but something's got to give soon. You didn't materialise from thin air."

"I just want to know who I am."

A tear rolled down Coco's cheek, and Rhys reached out to wipe it away.

"We'll find out, babe. Why don't I order us a pizza, and we can bake those cookies tomorrow? Let's get an early night. Maybe some info'll come in on social media while we're asleep?"

Rhys had been checking the posts—they hadn't exactly gone viral, but the one on Twitter had a few hundred retweets.

"Okay."

On impulse, Rhys gave Coco a hug. After a second, she returned it, and damn, she felt good in his arms. Too good. This girl, she'd wormed her way into his heart, and he had no idea how to loosen her grip without damaging at least one ventricle. She was the wrong woman at the wrong time.

Wasn't she?

Then why did it feel so right?

Sleep still eluded Rhys, but by the early hours, he had made one important discovery: never buy a cheap air mattress. Not only had it damn near killed him to blow it up that afternoon, but the thing had half deflated already. As he rolled back and forth, trying to get comfortable, he was left with a feeling of mild seasickness.

With sleep a pipe dream, he gave up and read a book. By the time he'd got through twelve chapters, sunlight was spilling over the horizon and some inconsiderate bastard had started mowing their lawn. If Rhys ever saved enough money to buy a home of his own, it sure as hell wasn't going to be in a town. In fact, another fortnight at Woodside Lodge seemed remarkably attractive at that point.

"You're up early," Coco whispered.

"So are you."

She padded across the room and knelt beside him. "At least I slept. You didn't, did you?"

"Let's just say that whoever wrote the testimonial for this mattress was a dirty liar."

"Take the bed for a while. I can borrow one of your books and then make breakfast."

Rhys tried to protest, but his eyes began to close, and when he opened his mouth to speak, he ended up yawning instead.

"Maybe just for an hour."

Happiness was a beautiful woman carrying a bacon sandwich and a mug of freshly brewed coffee. At first, Rhys thought he was still dreaming, but then he realised that Coco had made good on her offer of breakfast. He could get used to this.

"Feeling better?"

"Yeah." He glanced at the clock. "But I've slept for six hours. Why didn't you wake me?"

"Because you needed the rest. Plus I started reading one of your spy thrillers and forgot about the time." She gifted him a soft smile. "I guess I like action and adventure."

Rhys was no James Bond. He couldn't offer much more than a roof over her head, but he smiled back.

"Thanks for breakfast."

"Anytime. Can you check the messages now?"

"Sure."

She'd even remembered to add ketchup and brown sauce to the sandwich. Yes, Rhys was beginning to like this cohabiting thing. He pulled out his phone and checked Facebook first. One single, solitary message, and yeuch... If Rhys's dick was that small, he'd at least have photoshopped it first.

His Twitter DMs yielded a whole array of dicks, both literal and metaphorical. Rhys had to concede that some of the equipment was impressive, but there was still no way he'd be showing it to Coco. Then he checked the other messages.

You have been selected to receive six million dollars...

Delete.

Scam artists like you make me sick, posting pictures of dead girls like that. You've got a problem, man. You should get help. Delete your account and stop digging up the past.

Dead girls? Could Coco have faked her own death? Rhys fired off a message just in case, but the internet was full of kooks.

Sir, I am a psychic...

Delete.

Does she have an OnlyFans?

Is she single?

She's hot—I'd do her.

Ah, finally, the common or garden internet trolls had arrived. Delete, delete, delete.

"Any news?" Coco asked.

"Sorry. But we won't give up. I'll call the police again this afternoon and see if they've got an update. Somebody might've filed a missing persons report by now."

"What if they haven't? I should find a job, but I have no idea what I'm good at. Or if I'm good at anything at all."

"That's not the biggest problem. If you want to work in the UK, you'll need identification showing you're allowed to."

"Oh. I hadn't even thought of that."

"This is why we need to focus on finding out who you are."

Easier said than done. Rhys tried calling the American embassy, just in case a US citizen had been reported missing. None had. Even the crank messages dried up, and all that was left was dick pics. The only notable thing to happen over the following week was the death of Stacey's microwave, which meant she'd come over for dinner every bloody night seeing as her oven had given up the ghost nearly six months previously. Rhys's room in the house on Cardon Street began to feel like a prison. At least his cellmate was easy to get along with.

Plus he'd worked out a possible solution to Coco's financial woes. She was a quick learner, and when she made herself useful by answering user queries and helping with marketing, Rhys found he could work twice as fast on the nitty-gritty programming parts of his job. If he could launch his new app earlier than planned and make a start on the next one, then maybe, just maybe, his little business could support the both of them.

His travel plans? Those would have to wait. No way

could he ditch Coco to backpack around Australia, not if he wanted to live with himself afterwards. There was always next year.

But every day that passed with no news, Coco asked the same question, and today was no different.

"What next?"

"Let's have dinner and sleep on it," he said, pushing his chair back and stretching. He'd been at his desk for hours, and his eyes ached from staring at the screen for too long.

"Do you want me to cook again?"

"I'll give you a hand."

Teamwork made the chores go faster, and if they worked together, there was a chance they could escape the kitchen before Stacey came over with her microwave lasagne.

Except when they got downstairs, Stacey was already in the hallway, backed up against the wall with Gary slurping at her tonsils. Hashim walked past and made a gagging noise, which saved Rhys the trouble. Honestly, this was taking the piss. Everyone knew Gary was shagging Stacey—was there really a need for him to keep rubbing Rhys's face in it?

When Stacey realised they had an audience, she pushed Gary away, but there was no mistaking the look of triumph on the prick's face when he saw who was standing there.

"Jealous, mate?"

"Why would I be jealous of you?"

"'Cause your girl won't put out."

What was Rhys meant to say to that? Deny it, and he'd be casting Coco as someone she wasn't, which he had no right to do. Admit it, and he'd probably get arrested for punching the smug grin off Gary's face. How did the jerk even know what they were or weren't doing in Rhys's bedroom?

"That's none of your business."

"So it's true?" Gary snorted laughter. "Thought so when I saw that packet for the blow-up mattress in the kitchen bin. Bet she's kicked you out of your bed too."

"Gary, shut up," Stacey told him.

"What do you care? You ditched him."

You know what? A night in the cells would be worth it if Rhys could just ram Gary's grill down his fetid throat. He balled up a fist, but before he could break a knuckle, Coco slipped her arm through his.

"We bought a camping mattress because we're planning to go on a camping trip, you idiot. Not that it *is* any of your business, but I'd give Rhys eleven out of ten in bed. Now if you'll excuse us..." She pulled Rhys towards the door. "We're going out for dinner. Rhys doesn't have the energy to cook after his efforts this afternoon, and I can barely walk." Coco fired a smile at Stacey. "Have fun 'putting out.'"

Rhys managed to hold it together until they got outside, but when the front door slammed behind them, the laughter started. Both of them bent double on the pavement, clutching each other for support, and a passing couple gave them a wide berth.

"I can't believe you said that," Rhys choked out.

"Neither can I, but what an ass. I'd feel sorry for Stacey if she hadn't cheated on you."

"Yeah, he's an ass, but thankfully, I only have to put up with him for a few more weeks."

Coco stopped laughing, and the sadness returned to her eyes.

Dammit. Why had Rhys reminded her of the time limit hanging over them?

"So, about dinner…" he started.

"Sorry I said we were going out. Maybe we could just pick up some chips? Like, British chips."

"Hell no. I'm taking you to a proper restaurant. After what you said to Gary, I owe you three courses and wine."

CHAPTER 10
RHYS

One bottle of wine turned into two, and it was almost midnight by the time Rhys and Coco stumbled along Cardon Street, arm in arm because neither of them could stand up on their own.

"Enough with that noise," a hunched guy pushing a shopping trolley full of cans griped, and Coco made an exaggerated sad face.

"Aw, he doesn't appreciate our singing."

"Can't imagine why not."

"But our harmonies are...hic...perfect."

The door lock kept moving, and it took Rhys four tries to insert the key. Coco tripped over the step on her way inside, and when Rhys tried to catch her, they ended up in a heap on the floor. Yeuch.

"Need...bed," she mumbled.

At that moment, the stairs looked as challenging as Mount Everest.

"We could sleep on the sofa?"

"Urgh, no way. The sofa has sex cooties. From *Gary*. His naked ass conti...contan...contaminated it."

She was absolutely right.

"Okay, so... I guess we'd better tackle the stairs."

After an ungainly scramble, they made it to the top, and a little crawling got them to the bedroom. With Coco and a dead woodlouse as his witnesses, Rhys swore he was never drinking expensive wine again. He'd never got this drunk from beer on his rare trips to the Students' Union bar. Probably because they watered all the drinks down, but...

"Aw, the air escaped from your mattress again."

"Fuck it."

"So I guess we're not going camping now?"

"Did you want to go camping?"

"No." Coco landed on the bed, arms and legs spread wide like a starfish. "I want to go to a tropical island and drink cocktails on the beach."

"Perhaps give the cocktails a miss, eh? Dammit, I need to blow this thing up."

"Need a hand?" Coco rolled over and reached for his belt buckle. "Maybe I'm good at blowing things? Who knows?"

Rhys hardened in an instant, but even in his drunken state, there was no way he'd take advantage of Coco like that. He peeled her fingers off, and she grabbed his hand instead.

"Not tonight, sweetheart," he muttered.

"Spoilsport."

"You've been drinking."

"So have you."

"Coco..."

She pouted, and it shouldn't have been cute, but it was. "If I'm not allowed to blow things, then neither are you. There's plenty of room in this bed for two."

Rhys's first instinct was to say no, but realistically, he'd probably puke if he tried to inflate that mattress tonight. The room was spinning already, and his head felt disconnected from his body. And the bed *was* a double. As long as he kept his hands to himself…

They were both adults. What would be the harm in sharing?

Hot… So hot…

Had Hashim turned the thermostat up again? Because they'd had words about this. Utility bills got split four ways, and if he wanted the house hotter than the tropics, he had to pay a greater share.

And what was that tickling Rhys's nose? Had the ants come back? He moved to swat the irritation away, but his hand wouldn't move. Why not? He forced an eyelid open, only to realise he had bigger problems than he'd thought.

Shit. So much for being a gentleman.

His body was curled around Coco's, her back to his front, and it seemed he'd been sniffing her hair in his damn sleep. Worse, the reason he couldn't move his hand was that after he'd curved it around her breast, she'd wrapped her own hand over the top of it, holding it in place.

This was… Well, awkward didn't even begin to cover it. He tried a gentle tug to extricate himself, but Coco only held on tighter and squirmed against him. Great. Now his dick was about to explode.

"Sweetheart…"

"Mmm?"

"You need to let go."

"But why?"

Because otherwise, Rhys would be tempted to do something they'd both regret later. He'd be lying if he said he didn't consider it, but then what? They didn't even know if she was single. A girl like Coco—sweet and smart, witty and pretty—would kick a guy like him to the kerb on any other day.

"I need to use the bathroom."

For a shower. A freezing-cold shower. Then he needed to find coffee, painkillers, and the common sense he'd mislaid last night. What had he been thinking? Oh, that's right—he hadn't. Alcohol had a lot to answer for, although he knew deep down that the wine didn't make him do anything he hadn't wanted to do already. This whole "roommate" thing was harder than he'd ever dreamed.

When he got back upstairs, Coco was sleeping peacefully, her hair spread out over his pillow. She looked so innocent. Did she realise she'd turned his entire world upside down?

As if she could sense his presence, her eyelids flickered open.

"She wakes. How's your head?"

She blinked a couple of times. "Ouch."

Rhys held out the packet of paracetamol he'd found downstairs. "Try these."

"Paracetamol?"

"Aceto...whatever you call it."

"Thanks." Coco shuffled up to a seated position, back against the wall. "Is that coffee?"

"Black. Someone finished the milk again, and most of our coffee granules too."

Our coffee. Rhys caught his slip of the tongue the moment the words left his mouth. Since when had there been an "us"? A "we"? His growing feelings for Coco scared him because how could this have a happy ending? There were too many unknowns.

If Coco noticed his overreach, she didn't let on. "Do we have any plans today? Apart from buying groceries?"

"We need to go to the outdoor store again. Buying the cheap air mattress was a false economy. I should have bought the deluxe one to start with, and a battery-operated pump as well."

"You're buying a new mattress? But I thought..."

"Thought what?"

"We shared the bed last night—I thought we'd carry on that way."

"That's not a good idea."

"Why?"

When Coco nibbled on her bottom lip, Rhys almost forgot the reason entirely. His dick began to twitch again. Dammit, he'd just taken care of that.

"It's just not, okay?"

"But you wanted me this morning." Coco shrugged one shoulder and glanced at his crotch. "It was pretty obvious."

At that moment, Rhys wanted to vanish as suddenly as Coco had arrived. He'd been hoping to hide the evidence of his dirty dreams.

"It doesn't matter what I want."

"What if I want the same thing?"

"Coco..." That wasn't even her name. "Babe..." No, that was worse. "Look, you can't possibly know what you want. Neither of us knows the first thing about you. You could have a boyfriend, or a fiancé. You could even be married."

"I wasn't wearing a ring."

"You weren't wearing *anything*."

"Thanks for reminding me."

She bit her lip, eyes filling with tears, and Rhys cursed under his breath. He'd hurt Coco with his words, and he wished he could take them back, but now she wouldn't face him.

"You're right, okay?"

"Right about what?" she mumbled.

"I do want you." Rhys stated the obvious. "And when we solve this puzzle, if it turns out you're available, then I'd like nothing more than to take you out on a proper date. But for now, I can't touch you. I don't want either of us to end up getting hurt."

Rhys walked to the window and stared out. Next door's cat was sitting on the fence, washing its paws. The bin was overflowing because Hashim had forgotten it was his turn to put the rubbish out, and two traffic cones had appeared from somewhere to give the yard a splash of colour. Just another day in paradise.

Coco let out a long sigh. "I guess I can understand that. I don't like it, but I understand it."

"We have to make the best of this."

Rhys tried to stay optimistic, but if he'd known what was to come, he'd have opened that window and jumped right out of it.

CHAPTER 11

RHYS

The keening wail cut to Rhys's core, and he knifed up in bed, his heart racing.

His first thought? A fox had caught next door's cat. His second thought? *Coco.*

As his eyes adjusted to the darkness, he saw her thrashing on the bed, the sheets tangled around her feet. A sliver of moonlight caught the sheen of perspiration on her forehead. *A nightmare.* She was only having a nightmare, but it sounded as if she were dying.

"No! No, no, no..." The last word dissolved into sobs, and she arched off the bed, her limbs stiff. Bloody hell, this was like a scene from a horror movie. Should he wake her? Call an ambulance?

"Help me," she gasped.

How?

Her body gave one last heave, and then she lay still, head and shoulders hanging off the side of the bed. Was she...alive?

Rhys crawled to her side and grabbed her wrist, his own breath coming in pants as he felt for a pulse. Faint, but there it was, powerful in contrast to her limp body. Thank goodness. Her hand felt cold and clammy, and when he touched her cheek, it was slick with sweat. And...something else. Tears. She'd been crying in her sleep.

"Coco," he whispered, then raised his voice and tried again. "Coco?"

Nothing. Rhys switched on the bedside lamp, bathing the room in a yellow glow, and risked shaking her shoulder.

"Wake up!"

Her eyes popped open. Their focus wavered at first, but when her gaze finally fixed on Rhys's, his skin prickled. Why? Because he'd never seen fear like that before. A second later, Coco threw herself into his arms, holding him in a death grip.

"It'll be okay," he soothed, empty words for empty promises. "Everything'll be okay."

Rhys's T-shirt grew damp as more tears fell, and she gulped in air as if tasting it for the first time. Desperate, hungry breaths. Boy, that must have been some nightmare.

"What happened?" he whispered. "Can you remember?"

"I...I was in the water. *Under* the water, and I couldn't get out. Something was keeping me down, and I couldn't...I couldn't *breathe*."

She'd dreamed she was drowning. How cruel a person's mind could be. First the amnesia, and now this.

"You're okay now. You're safe."

"But it was so vivid. So real."

"The only water in this place is in the bath, and if you want, I can come with— Ah, shit, now I sound like a right perv."

Coco choked out a laugh. "I think I was in the ocean. Or maybe a lake."

"Then you're safe here." Although she was in danger of catching a chill. Her pyjamas clung to her back, soaked through with sweat, and the heating was turned off. Gary again. "But you should change into dry clothes."

"This is my only pair of pyjamas."

Rhys had put off buying Coco more clothes on the assumption that she'd soon be going home, but since it seemed she'd be sticking around for a while...

"You can borrow one of my T-shirts tonight, okay? We'll go shopping again tomorrow."

Rhys rummaged through his closet until he found a new shirt, a promo item from a software company still in the cellophane wrapper. He'd never worn it because it was size XXL and he didn't want to hear Hashim's jokes about needing to go to the gym, but it would make a reasonable substitute for a nightie.

Coco's dreams had sapped her energy, so Rhys pulled her to her feet and held her steady while she swayed for a second.

"You all right?"

She nodded, but she didn't seem convinced. Neither was Rhys, but what could he do about it?

"I'll make us both hot chocolate while you change. Want to watch a movie when I get back?"

Another nod, this time more certain. "I don't think I'll be able to sleep again tonight."

That made two of them. As Rhys waited for the kettle to boil and for his heart rate to return to normal, he replayed the earlier scene over and over in his mind—Coco's wails, her tears, her sheer terror. Watching a woman he cared about scared out of her mind had left him feeling drained as well. And he *did* care about her. Far too much.

Tomorrow, he'd buy her all the pyjamas in the world because he didn't *want* her to go home.

"Want me to do the shopping while you work?" Coco offered, sounding more cheerful than she looked. "I might as well make myself useful."

On any other day, Rhys would have joined her, both for the pleasure of her company and to get away from his screen. But he'd just received a message from a make-up vlogger about a possible collaboration—he'd write an app, she'd provide the content—and the girl wanted a call this morning. A deal like that could net him thousands, and it was too good an opportunity to pass up.

"You know the way into town?"

"Yup. I'm good with directions. It's just everything else I can't remember."

Rhys raided the emergency stash of cash he kept hidden in his underwear drawer and gave Coco enough money for groceries and more pyjamas. He considered giving her his debit card so she could use the ATM as well, but they weren't quite at that point in their relationship yet.

Relationship.

Did they have a relationship? True, he'd knocked her back when she came on to him, but his chivalry had been reluctant. And there was no denying how close they were becoming. It was difficult not to develop feelings when they were living in each other's pockets.

Coco wasn't like any of the girls he'd gone to uni with. They'd been more interested in his ability to help them with their coursework than him as a person, and after being used one too many times, he'd begun to perfect his avoidance tactics. Stacey alone had managed to get through his defences, and look how that had turned out.

But Coco... Coco was different.

"Buy whatever you want. If this isn't enough cash, we can make another trip tomorrow."

She leaned in to kiss him on the cheek. "You're too generous, Rhys Evans."

Damn, he was in trouble.

Thankfully, the phone rang as Coco slipped out the door, and he was grateful for the distraction. At least, he was until he saw the name on the screen. This was the third call from Uncle Albert in as many days, and Rhys took the coward's way out and let it go to voicemail. He knew exactly what his uncle wanted—answers about his tree pod —and Rhys didn't have any.

That seemed to be a recurring theme in his life at the moment.

CHAPTER 12

RHYS

"We can't go on like this."

Rhys covered his mouth out of politeness as he yawned, but there was no hiding his exhaustion.

Two weeks after Coco's first nightmare, they'd both become zombies, and he looked back with fondness at the nights when Gary and Stacey had thrown their alcohol-fuelled parties because even those had been easier to sleep through than Coco's nocturnal shenanigans. They'd hoped the first nightmare was a one-off, but it turned out to be just the start. Every time she drifted off, the hellish dream came back, and she drowned over and over and over again. Meanwhile, Rhys was living in his own nightmare as he tried to comfort her, usually with limited success.

He managed a few hours of work each day, splitting his time between the fitness app and the make-up project. The latter wasn't difficult, per se, but keeping up with the whims of an Instagram "star" who changed her mind more often than he changed his underwear took every bit of patience he possessed.

Coco scrubbed her hands through her hair. "I know we can't go on like this. It isn't fair on you. I think... I think I should look for somewhere else to live."

How could she with no job, no money, and no identity? And that was only the logistics. Rhys didn't want her to leave; he just wanted her to sleep through the night without dying. They'd visited the pharmacy and tried five different over-the-counter remedies—everything from Nytol to valerian extract—but none of them made the slightest difference to Coco. Rhys had started taking them himself before his afternoon naps.

"That wasn't what I meant at all."

"What alternative do we have? The meditation app didn't help one bit, and Gary's still angry at me."

She'd woken the whole household with her screaming the night before last, and when Hashim made a crack about Rhys's horrifying performance in bed, only Coco's hand on Rhys's arm had stopped him from swinging a punch. The lack of sleep had left him with a short fuse.

"Let's see if there's somebody who can help. A doctor. Or a therapist?"

"They'll probably think I'm crazy."

"You can't be the only person with nightmares. Maybe sleeping pills would work?"

"I'll try anything." Coco's voice dropped to a whisper. "Sometimes, I wish I could fall asleep and never wake up."

"Don't talk like that. *Don't.* We'll fix this, I promise. We'll fix it."

Although Rhys had no idea how.

A trip to the doctor presented its own challenges. Luckily, the local GP's practice was taking new patients, but Coco still needed an identity.

"Coco? Just Coco? Are you a singer or something?" the receptionist asked, tapping away at her keyboard. "Nope, it says I need a surname. Even Madonna has a surname."

"I don't know it. I have amnesia."

"Amnesia? Sure you do, hun. Still gonna need a surname."

"We have a police report."

"My cousin made a police report saying he'd got abducted by aliens, but that don't make it true."

"Just put the surname down as du Ciel," Rhys told the receptionist. That was easier than trying to argue with a computer.

"You're gonna have to spell that."

"D-U space C-I-E-L."

"Du Ciel... Okay. And what's your nationality?"

Which part of "amnesia" did the woman not understand?

"She doesn't know."

"Well, I'll just note her down as 'refugee.' She'll be able to access GP and emergency care, but she's not eligible for hospital inpatient services."

The receptionist's words were another reminder of the need to find out Coco's history, otherwise she'd spend her whole life being treated like a second-class citizen. Rhys hadn't put quite as much effort into the search as he should have over the past fortnight, mostly because he'd been exhausted but also because he'd come to the realisation that he wanted her to stay. Despite trying to keep some distance between them, he'd developed feelings that wouldn't go away even if she did. The selfish part of him didn't want to get hurt.

"A refugee?" Coco murmured. "Is that what I am?"

"No, sweetheart, and we'll prove it, but not today. Let's focus on getting you healthy again, and then we can sort out the rest."

They left the surgery with a prescription for Zopiclone and high hopes. Twelve hours later, those hopes hadn't just been dashed; they'd been pulverised, stomped on, and flushed down the toilet.

Coco began thrashing around on the bed, and unlike the other times, Rhys couldn't wake her. A minute passed, two, and he tried shaking her, squeezing her hands, even slapping her when she seemed as if she were choking, but her eyes stayed closed as her subconscious tore her soul apart. When he tried to hold her still, she punched him, but the physical pain was nothing compared to the agony in his heart.

Finally, *finally*, she stopped flailing and lay limp on the mattress, her face white and cool to the touch.

Fuck, she wasn't...was she? Rhys scrabbled for her wrists and checked for a pulse, holding his breath for those terrifying seconds until he felt the faint flutter. Still Coco didn't wake up. Those damn pills...

Screw chivalry—he climbed into bed with her and gathered her close, one hand pressed against her chest so he could feel her racing heart. As long as it kept beating, they could fix this. He'd promised.

"Everything's gonna be okay," he whispered, but deep down, he knew he was lying. He was way, way out of his depth here. His degree was in computing, not psychology, and even if he magically knew what to say, how could they ever unlock the secrets of Coco's mind? Her past was a black hole. Even an astronomer would struggle to find its hidden secrets.

The sky had started to lighten when she finally stirred in his arms. She twisted around to face him, smiling at first, but that smile quickly faded when she saw his serious expression.

"What happened? Something happened, didn't it?"

"You had another nightmare. A longer one this time, and I couldn't wake you."

"Sorry, I'm so sorry. Did I disturb everyone again?"

"Just me. Hashim bought a pair of earplugs, and Jorge and Gary both drank too much last night."

Rhys tried to keep his voice light. Telling Coco that her refusal to wake up had been the scariest moment of his life would only make her feel worse than she already did. And considering Rhys had once accepted a lift with a guy who turned out to be not only tipsy but also a speed demon, that was saying something. Being a passenger as a nutcase drove the wrong way along a dual carriageway was no joke. He'd seen his life flash before his eyes several times that night, but now it was Coco he feared for.

"Sorry," she said again. "Do you think it was the pills?"

"Probably."

"I won't take them again."

Aaaaand...they were back to square one. "How do you feel?"

"Okay, I think. A little headache, but..." Coco screwed her eyes shut, then stiffened. "The nightmare went on for longer."

"The same dream? You were underwater again?"

"Yes, but this time, I remember walking along the shore. It was a lake, not the sea. Dark water, pine trees, a small boat tied to a dock... And somebody pushed me."

"What do you mean?"

"Into the water. Somebody pushed me into the water. I felt a hand on my back, then I lost my footing, and I couldn't get out. Something was holding me down."

Coco began to tremble, and Rhys hugged her tighter. "It was just your imagination. You're safe now."

"But what if it wasn't? It always feels so vivid. The chill of the water rushing into my lungs, the wisps of my hair wrapping around my neck, the panic when I realise I can't tell which way is up. I hear myself choking. And last night, every detail was crystal clear. There was a bonfire nearby. I smelled the woodsmoke before I fell into the water. Tasted it on my tongue. And then I drowned, and suddenly there was nothing. I was just floating in the dark."

"You didn't drown, sweetheart. You're still here." Rhys squeezed her hand. "You're alive."

"Am I? Nobody will admit to knowing me before the day I met you. What if I'm some kind of ghost?"

"Coco, I'm holding you in my arms, and I assure you, you're very real."

"So why is it like I never existed?"

That was yet another question Rhys couldn't answer.

CHAPTER 13
RHYS

ick, tick, tick...

Three weeks until Rhys's lease on the room on Cardon Street ran out, and the clock wouldn't slow just because he was knackered.

Over the past fortnight, they'd developed a system. Internet research had turned up a wealth of information on sleep phases and patterns, and by trial and error, they'd worked out that if Coco slept for seventy minutes at a time, she didn't reach the REM stage of sleep where she began dreaming. They'd set a timer and Rhys would shake her awake, then he'd take a turn at sleeping. Far from ideal, but it was better than the alternative.

Of course, that didn't leave many hours when they were both awake to house-hunt.

Rhys wanted to avoid another shared place if at all possible. Firstly, it wouldn't be fair to inflict their sleep experiments on a new set of housemates—tiptoeing around at four a.m. to make toast because their circadian rhythms were screwed up got awkward—and secondly, he was sick of having to be nice to people he didn't much like.

Gary was still being an absolute dick, and Stacey seemed to spend more time at their place than at her own.

With Uxbridge clinging to the end of the Metropolitan Tube line, housing in the area fetched London prices, and even the tiniest flat would be a stretch on Rhys's income. So they'd decided to look farther afield—Sussex, perhaps, or Wiltshire—seeing as neither of them had any need to stay close to the city. Fit4Life and Project Beautify were coming along as well as could be expected under the circumstances, and the make-up vlogger had kindly plugged Pan Friday, which resulted in a nice boost in sales.

"What about this flat?" Rhys suggested, turning his laptop screen for Coco to see. "Only one bedroom, but we could put a sofa bed in the lounge."

"Are you sure you want to do this?"

"We've already had this conversation."

"But going travelling was your dream."

Rhys could visit the most beautiful destinations on earth, but if he left Coco behind to fend for herself, they'd all be flat and grey. Tainted because she wasn't there to share the trip with him.

"It's my decision, and I'm staying. What about this place? Two bedrooms, but the kitchen's more of a closet."

"I'll live anywhere."

So Coco said, but after their first trip to Wiltshire, a whistle-stop tour where they viewed six properties in one day, she quickly rethought her words. One place had looked hopeful until the next-door neighbour stomped out of her door and yelled at them for parking outside her house—on a public road—and Rhys realised from the letting agent's sigh that the woman was a psycho. At least the agent had the good grace to apologise for wasting their time.

"How about a tent?" Rhys suggested as they turned

back onto Cardon Street, only half joking. "At least a tent wouldn't have mould on the walls."

"There's no possibility we can stay here?"

"I expect the landlord's already let our room to a new student."

And even if he hadn't, there was no way in hell Rhys would consider enquiring about staying, not after the conversation that took place downstairs fifteen minutes later. Coco had crawled into bed for a nap, which gave him a clear hour to make dinner. In hindsight, they should have picked up something to eat on the drive back, but the food at motorway services was always a rip-off.

He'd just started frying leeks to make a pasta sauce—some arsehole had nicked his last onion—when Stacey sidled in.

"Gary said you're leaving?"

"That's hardly news. I always said I wouldn't stick around in this place after I graduated, and the ceremony was last month."

Coco had come as his guest, and he hadn't missed the snide looks Stacey sent in her direction throughout.

"Yeah, but I figured you'd stay near here. You're going to, like, Wiltshire?"

"Maybe."

"With *her*?"

"Coco has a name."

"I thought her staying with you was a temporary thing."

"Well, it looks as if it may become slightly more permanent."

"But..." Stacey started. Her expression reminded him of the time she'd drunk too many shots and hurled on Jorge's new trainers.

"But what?"

"She's weird. I mean, who gets nightmares *every* night? And she acts like your maid."

Only because she felt guilty that she couldn't do anything else to help.

"Don't you have somewhere else you need to be?"

Stacey sucked in a breath. "Don't go."

"What?"

"I made a mistake, okay? I've realised that now. Gary's an idiot."

"Is that meant to be an apology?"

"Yeah, I guess. All I wanted was a bit of excitement, and you spent so much time on that bloody computer."

"How does that excuse you sleeping with my housemate?"

"I said I was sorry, didn't I?" Well, no, actually she didn't. "And I kind of hoped we could get back together."

"Are you kidding me?"

"Uh…"

"Nothing on this earth could convince me to give you another chance. You cheated on me."

Stacey's eyes began to glisten, and Rhys cursed under his breath. What was it with the women in his life? One was a nightmare when she was awake, and the other was a nightmare when she was asleep. A couple of months ago, his life had been on the dull side of normal, but now… Now he had Coco and all the joys and frustrations that came with her. Yes, the memory and sleep issues were a problem, but the rest of the time he loved her company, the sound of her voice, her smile, the little dance she did when something made her happy…

Maybe he even loved her.

Well, shit. That was a recipe for disaster. Perhaps he should add it to his app?

"But Gary doesn't mean anything to me." Stacey tried to take Rhys's hand, and he pulled it away. "It was a blip, that's all."

Rhys turned his gaze to the ceiling. *Give me strength.*

"Look, Stacey…"

Saved by the bell. Rhys practically ran into the hallway and fumbled with the lock on the front door. If this was a canvasser, he'd answer their questions all day long.

But it wasn't a canvasser.

And now he had an even bigger problem than Stacey.

CHAPTER 14
RHYS

"Uncle Albert? What are you doing here?"

That was his pristine old Jaguar parked at the kerb. He'd driven all the way from Wales today?

"Voicemail broken, is it?"

"I've been busy," Rhys mumbled. "I kept meaning to ring you back."

"I thought youngsters were glued to their phones nowadays? In more than a month, you couldn't manage five minutes for a call? Or even one of those text messages? Good thing I had to travel to London for the National Orchid Festival—it meant I could stop by to ask you what in heaven's name happened to my coco du ciel tree."

Uh-oh.

"All you had to do was water the plants, feed them, and check the lights were working as they should be. And yet somehow, you managed to knock my most cherished possession to the ground and break it. What on earth were you playing at?"

A soft voice came from behind. "It was my fault."

Ah, shit. Rhys turned to see Coco standing there in a pair of cartoon pyjamas, water bottle in hand. She'd sure picked the perfect time to get thirsty.

"No, it was an accident."

"But I was the only one in there. Whatever happened, it stands to reason that I must have done it, and I'm not letting you take the blame."

"What was this girl doing in my greenhouse? You didn't ask me if you could bring a guest."

"I didn't bring a guest. I just went in to check the plants one morning, and there she was."

Albert turned his gaze on Coco. "Why were you there?"

"I don't know, I swear."

"She doesn't remember."

"Why not?" Uncle Albert's bushy white eyebrows pinched together as he frowned. "Were you drunk? Honestly, young people these days, they've got no self-respect."

"She wasn't drunk, Uncle. She's got amnesia. The first thing she remembers is waking up under that tree the nut fell out of."

"Fruit, not nut. Well, technically, it's a drupe—pulpy on the outside with a hard shell on the inside that contains one seed, like a walnut or an almond." Did it really matter? "She has amnesia?"

"I took her to the hospital, and they said she didn't have a head injury, but there's nothing..." Why had Albert turned so pale? His complexion matched his hair. "Uncle, are you okay?"

"This can't have happened. No, no, not again."

"What can't have happened?"

Albert's voice came out as a whisper. "The legend... Son, I think I need a cup of tea."

"Legend? What legend?"

Coco took Albert's arm and led him towards the kitchen. As soon as Stacey saw them coming, she scuttled out the back door, which was one small thing to be thankful for. The kettle took forever to boil, and Albert settled onto a rickety wooden chair that was only one wobbly leg away from landfill.

"Perhaps my grandmother wasn't quite as cuckoo as I imagined," he muttered.

"Your grandmother? What's she got to do with any of this?"

"I suppose I should start at the beginning... Plenty of milk and two sugars, lad."

With the tea made, Rhys settled into a seat opposite his uncle with Coco at his side. The old man seemed more resigned than angry, and Rhys had to take that as a good sign.

"What's this legend, then?"

"You never met your great-grandmother Alice, but she was quite a woman. An adventurer. Always off on some trip or another with my poor long-suffering grandfather."

"Mum mentioned her once or twice." Rhys had always been under the impression that they didn't get along. "Didn't she lose a toe from frostbite after she visited Antarctica?"

"Indeed she did. And before that, she went to South America to hunt for the lost city of El Dorado and her pilot crash-landed in the Brazilian rainforest. Alice was the only person to survive the impact, albeit with a broken arm and several lacerations. A lesser woman might have given up."

"But Alice didn't?"

"Of course not. She salvaged what she could from the aircraft, found the nearest river, and set off downstream."

"Mum never told me any of this."

"Alice and your mother didn't always see eye to eye. Alice thought young women should get out and see the world, but all your mother wanted to do was sit at home and watch TV."

Not much had changed later in her life—Rhys's mum had always been a homebody with dinner on the table before *Coronation Street* started. The farthest she'd ever ventured was Bognor Regis, and even then, she'd been happiest sitting in the holiday park with a magazine. But despite her unadventurous streak, she'd been a wonderful mother, and nearly five years on, Rhys's chest still tightened every time he thought of her.

And what else had his mum said about Alice? Oh, yes, after Grandad Bert died, she'd lost the plot and spent her remaining days in a psychiatric hospital.

"Everyone gets to choose their own path in life."

"That they do. And Alice's took her into Karaza territory."

"Into what?"

"The Karaza are an indigenous people who live deep within the Amazon rainforest. They do trade with neighbouring tribes, but for the most part, they're hunter-gatherers who eschew contact with the outside world. Your great-grandmother came across one of their villages, and apparently, they were so fascinated by her blonde hair that she lived to tell the tale." Albert shook his head. "They've got a fierce reputation by all accounts."

"What do they do? Shoot people with bows and arrows?"

"I believe so. Grandma Alice said the chief kept a pair of skulls on posts outside his hut as a warning."

Rhys mentally crossed Brazil off the list of places he

might ever want to travel. "Okay, I get it—Great-Grandma was a badass. But what's that got to do with Coco?"

"Coco? You're calling her Coco?"

"I had to call her something."

Albert snorted. "Well, the name's certainly appropriate. Now, where was I? Ah, yes, the Karaza… They speak their own dialect of Portuguese, but there were enough similarities to Brazilian Portuguese that Alice could communicate with them."

"Where did they learn to speak Portuguese?"

"According to Alice, their lore said they were reincarnated from ancient souls to act as guardians, which is clearly codswallop, but I don't know the true answer. Maybe a few hapless missionaries joined their tribe? Anyhow, they put a splint on Alice's arm, treated her cuts with herbal paste, and let her stay with them until she was well enough to leave."

Great-Grandma Alice sounded like one hell of a woman. Rhys wished he'd been able to meet her, to hear her stories first-hand, and he was disappointed that his mother had barely mentioned Alice while she was alive. But at least Uncle Albert was willing to share.

"How did she get home?"

"Three tribe members paddled her down the Amazon in a dugout canoe and left her just outside the nearest settlement. A group of missionaries helped her from there."

"I still don't understand—"

"Hush, lad, I'm getting to that part. The botanist who accompanied Grandma Alice on the trip was short-sighted, and miraculously, his spectacles survived the crash intact. Alice took them with her in case she needed to light a fire with the sun's rays, but to the Karaza, they were magical. One small girl was so myopic she could barely see, so Alice gave her the spectacles before she left. And in return, they gifted her the most precious thing they had to offer—two of their revered coco du ciel trees. Just seedlings at the time, no more than six inches tall, but they grew into the specimens you saw in my greenhouse."

Okay, okay, Rhys got it—the trees were part of the family history. And now he felt even guiltier for not taking better care of them.

"Sorry about the fruit. I wish I could undo whatever happened that night, but I can't."

"No, you can't."

"Why are those trees so special? To the Karaza, I mean. I understand they're like a family heirloom for you."

"According to Alice, the tribe was sworn to protect the trees. They'd fight to the death for them, and the reason they'd do that so readily was due to their belief in the trees' ability to bring fallen warriors back to life."

"That's crazy. But didn't some of those ancient tribes believe in human sacrifice? The Incas worshipped the sun. And the Mayans thought that rainbows were the flatulence of demons and brought bad luck." A handful of random facts from GCSE history had stuck in Rhys's head. "I suppose magical trees are quite tame in the great scheme of things."

"Yes, yes, I scoffed at the story too. Until the Frenchman came, I treated the trees as a fascinating piece of my heritage and took pride in the fact that they were the only pair on this continent."

This was getting weirder and weirder. "What Frenchman?"

"Four years ago, shortly after I gave a lecture on South American flora at Kew Gardens, I was contacted out of the blue by a young botanist. At first, he wanted to talk about the coco du ciel trees, but then I mentioned that I had two *Santalum paniculatum*—Hawaiian Sandalwood trees—and he asked if he could study them."

"And you agreed?"

"I'm always happy to discuss my plants, and I don't get many visitors. Plus his research was funded by a big pharmaceutical company, and in return for access to the greenhouse, he negotiated a fee for me."

"Is that normal?"

"Well, no, but the heating bills don't pay themselves. My state pension's barely enough for me to live on. And I felt sorry for the chap. He'd lost his wife three years before —a mugging gone wrong—and he was still getting over the loss."

Coco picked at the edge of the laminate on the table. Nerves or boredom? It was hard to tell, but Rhys was beginning to wonder what the point of this story was.

"What does this have to do with Coco?"

"All in good time, lad... That's the problem with the younger generation—you kids have no patience." And the older generation had no sense of urgency. "I wouldn't say no to another cup of tea."

"I'll make it," Coco offered.

Good plan. Then Rhys could keep Albert talking.

"The Frenchman...?" he prompted.

"Ah, yes. Remi, that was his name. He was studying the effects of classical music on transpiration across different species. Fascinating stuff. Did you know that a walnut tree will literally weep for Bach?"

"I can't say it's a fact I've come across."

"What do teenagers study in biology these days? All that newfangled genetics? It was a sad day when botany disappeared from the curriculum. Anyhow, I was looking forward to reading Remi's thesis, but then the accident happened."

"Accident?"

"With the coco du ciel tree. The female tree bears fruit every four or five years, and it takes months to ripen. Did you see the specimen in the lounge?"

"Uh, that dark brown thing in the corner?" Rhys had figured it was some kind of wood carving. He'd knocked on it with his knuckles and it had been solid. How had its successor shattered when it hit the ground? A crack or two, Rhys could have understood, but not smithereens.

"Isn't it magnificent? Back when Remi was spending time in the greenhouse, there was another fruit growing. It was around a year old at that point, still green, same as the one that broke last month. And it suffered the same fate."

"It broke too?"

Albert nodded. "One night when Remi was alone in the greenhouse."

"So maybe it just happens, them falling from the tree? You know, like apples?"

That would actually be a relief. Perhaps the broken fruit had been nothing to do with Coco at all? Possibly she'd wandered into the greenhouse for some other unknown reason?

"I don't think so. I had to hack the first one down with a machete."

Good grief. The thought of Uncle Albert waving a machete around was quite terrifying.

"So what are you saying? That he sabotaged it?"

"At the time, I didn't know what to think. Remi left a note saying he was sorry, that it had just fallen down, but I never saw him again after that day. He simply vanished. I always feared he'd been involved in an accident—his phone was out of service, and when I wrote to the company that funded his research, they claimed they'd never heard of him."

"Did he finish his study?"

"I have no idea. If he did, he never published the results in any mainstream journal."

"Did you try looking on the internet?"

"Oh, I'm not good with that stuff. Email's about my limit."

That would explain the dust covering Albert's keyboard, and he seemed to have been using his DVD drive as a cupholder.

"I still don't understand what any of this has to do with Coco."

"When Grandma Alice told me about the legend of the coco du ciel trees, I thought it was a bunch of hogwash. So did she, truth be told. Trees that bring the dead back to life? That's something out of a storybook. But now…"

"Now what?"

"Now I'm not so sure."

A chill ran through Rhys, and it wasn't due to the temperature in the house because Gary had gone out and Hashim had turned up the bloody thermostat again.

"Why would you say that? I mean, it's crazy."

"Because that last night with Remi, I'd got up to use the toilet when I heard the side gate slam shut. Usually it's just the wind, but there'd been a few burglaries not so long before. Ragamuffins breaking into sheds, mainly, but Vera Dalrymple forgot to lock her back door and a thief swiped her handbag from the hall table while she was watching *Emmerdale*."

"*Was* it a burglar?"

"No, it was Remi. And he had a woman with him, all bundled up in a blanket."

The chill turned into full-on ice as Rhys processed his uncle's words. There'd been a second mystery woman in the greenhouse?

CHAPTER 15
RHYS

A woman bundled up in a blanket—now, that sounded remarkably familiar. Under the table, Coco crushed Rhys's hand in a death grip. The blood was being squeezed out of it, and one of his fingers made a cracking noise. Had they shared the same thought? Rhys managed to free his thumb, and he stroked it over her knuckles, trying to soothe her and think logically at the same time.

"You can't possibly think the legend's true?"

Uncle Albert sighed. "I'm saying I don't know what to think. Something strange happened in my greenhouse that night, and the only person who knows for sure what went on is Remi Leroux."

"Remi Leroux? That's the Frenchman's name?"

Albert nodded. "At least, that's what he claimed. Who knows whether he was telling the truth? All I know is that he's rich, because he paid me the money he promised for the study. Fifty thousand pounds."

Fifty grand? Flipping heck. "Are you serious? He paid you that much for playing music to plants?"

"To trees, and yes, it was very generous of him."

"You think I'm dead?" Coco whispered. She'd turned completely white.

"Clearly you're not dead now, my dear. But the legend…"

"It's bullshit, that's what it is." Rhys thought back to his mother's words about her brother: *Albert doesn't live in the real world, everything revolves around bloody plants. Half the time, he's away with the fairies.* She hadn't been far wrong, had she? The old boy had gone completely doolally. Or perhaps he'd been drinking? Rhys recalled the half-empty bottle of Scotch on his uncle's kitchen counter—Albert was fond of a tipple, despite his complaints about young people and their lack of self-respect. "Trees can't just create people out of thin air. It would go against every biological principle."

"I'm only telling you what I saw."

"Remi Leroux probably had a girlfriend who popped over." Given the right music on a moonlit night, a bottle of wine, and a blanket, a tryst in the greenhouse might be quite enjoyable. Risky, but if Leroux knew Albert went to bed early… "That's a far more likely scenario."

"Then how do you explain your friend here?" Albert waved a hand at Coco, and Rhys wished she'd stayed upstairs. Hearing the ramblings of a man who'd watched one too many episodes of *The X-Files* couldn't be doing her psyche any good. But Rhys was unable to answer the question.

"We're still looking for Coco's family, and they're human beings, not plants. Surely if Remi Leroux found some random woman wandering around in your green-house, the first thing he'd do would be to ask you if you knew her?"

"You didn't."

Touché.

"That was different. You weren't there."

"You could have phoned me."

True. "I figured you'd be pissed about the nut. Sorry, the fruit. The *drupe*."

"I was. I *am*. But if it fell because of the legend…"

Albert glanced at Coco, who hadn't moved a muscle in the last two minutes. What must be going through her head? Would she judge Rhys for being related to a conspiracy theorist?

"Wait… You don't honestly think…what, that Coco came out of the damn fruit?"

"Well, it was big enough."

Rhys put his head in his free hand. How was he meant to respond to that? Facts and logic didn't seem to be making much of an impression on Uncle Albert, unless… Rhys wriggled his hand free from Coco's and pushed his chair back.

"Where are you going?" she asked.

"To get my laptop."

Without thinking, he leaned over and kissed her on the head, a gesture that should have worried him because it felt entirely too natural. But he had bigger concerns today, like the fact that his only living relative had lost his fucking mind.

"Who's that old dude in the kitchen?" Hashim asked as Rhys hurried through the living room.

"Not now, okay?"

Upstairs, Rhys grabbed his laptop plus a sweatshirt for Coco. Her hand had been cold and clammy, and he didn't want her to catch a chill. Another visit to the GP was something they could both do without.

Albert was halfway through his second cup of tea when Rhys opened up a browser and typed in "Remi Leroux botanist." Half a dozen results popped up, but none of them were actually about a botanist named Remi Leroux.

"What was the company Leroux was affiliated with?"

"Hmm, I forget. It was years ago now. Bio-something?"

That didn't sound hopeful, but Rhys tried searching anyway. "Remi Leroux bio" brought up nothing useful. There *had* to be a way to find the man. Albert was right—Leroux was the only man who truly knew what had happened in the greenhouse that night, and Rhys needed him to share. How else would he stop Albert from filling Coco's head with nonsense?

"Let's assume Leroux lied about some things, if not everything," Rhys mused. "Given his sudden departure and subsequent disappearance, that doesn't seem an unreasonable position to take. Uncle, what do you know for certain about him? I mean, are you sure of his name?"

"Remi? Well, yes."

"Why? Did you see it on official paperwork? A driver's licence? A credit card?"

"None of those things, but he wore his wife's wedding ring on a chain around his neck, and their names were engraved on the inside. Remi and Cambria. I remember because it was like Cumbria, but with an A. Why would he lie about that? And he was certainly knowledgeable when it came to botany."

Rhys tried again with the search engine—Remi and Cambria. Nothing useful, but when he added "mugging," a slew of results popped up on the screen, all for the same story. He clicked on the first article, which was in French, but Google translated it for him.

•   •   •

Today, the town of Villance is in mourning after the death of a local philanthropist. Cambria Klein lost her fight for life after an altercation with an armed mugger outside Le Louvre. Police believe her killer was attracted by a Chanel watch and a diamond necklace, both of which were later found discarded near the scene. An eyewitness said Mrs. Klein attempted to kick the mugger, and then "all I heard was screaming."

The assailant has yet to be caught, but police are hopeful of apprehending the suspect. A large reward has been offered for any information leading to an arrest.

Cambria's husband, Remi, has been one of Villance's most generous benefactors, funding the construction of the new museum and the children's activity centre as well as tackling homelessness on our streets. The reclusive Kleins made their fortune as the major shareholders in RK Biotronix, the largest global pharmaceutical company still in private hands. A spokesperson for the family asked that they be allowed to grieve in peace.

A picture of Remi and Cambria Klein in happier times accompanied the article. Remi was in his early thirties, which probably seemed young to Uncle Albert. Handsome, Rhys supposed, but not particularly striking. Cambria, on the other hand, was beautiful. Smooth pale skin, a curtain of blonde hair that hung to her shoulders, high cheekbones, and an eye-catching smile. She'd certainly turn heads, and it seemed she'd done exactly that in Paris. Rhys angled the screen to face his uncle.

"Is this Remi?"

The colour drained out of Uncle Albert's face, and worse, he clutched at his chest.

"Are you okay?"

"I-I..."

"Do you need an ambulance?" Coco asked. "Does anyone in this house know first aid?"

"I-I-I'm fine, son. Just my angina playing up. But... but..." Albert leaned closer to look at the screen. "Yes, that's Remi. And I could swear that's the woman I saw with him outside my house."

"That's impossible."

"Well, it certainly looks like her."

"Wasn't it dark that night? How did you even see her face?"

"There was a full moon, and she looked right at me."

"Maybe she was similar, but it couldn't have been the same person." Was it creepy getting involved with a woman who looked like your dead wife? Yeah, it was a bit. "Cambria Klein died seven years ago, according to the date on this article."

"But the legend..."

"Forget the legend. It's a fairy tale. Next thing, you'll be seeing Little Red Riding Hood skipping through the greenhouse with Bigfoot."

"A fairy tale? Let's hope so, eh? Because if Remi had mentioned that he was interested in the coco du ciel trees, I'd have passed on Alice's warning."

Beside Rhys, Coco stiffened. Surely she couldn't believe this rubbish either?

"What warning?" she asked.

"The Karaza told Alice never to attempt a resurrection more than one lunar cycle after death. If Remi's wife died three years before I met him, then he should never have gone near those trees."

"And what did the Karaza say would happen if somebody didn't listen?"

"I forget the details. Something about mixed-up souls? Alice said it didn't much matter because she wasn't going to start playing around with the supernatural. To her, the trees were a souvenir from another adventure, nothing more."

"What if..." Coco's voice cracked. "What if my soul's broken?"

Rhys wrapped an arm around her shoulders. "Your soul isn't broken, sweetheart. It's just a silly story. Great-Grandma Alice probably made it up."

Magic trees? No wonder she'd been sectioned. Although the part about Remi Klein was interesting—what weirdo would spend fifty grand to visit a greenhouse? And why had he used a fake identity?

"Your great-grandma was fond of a good story, I'll give you that," Albert said. "Did your mum ever tell you about the dodo Alice saw in Mauritius?"

"Didn't dodos go extinct hundreds of years ago?"

"In the seventeenth century. Yes, yes they did."

"So I think we can all agree that Alice might have been adventurous, but she was also a few sandwiches short of a picnic. Do you have to drive back to Wales this evening?"

"Just to Herefordshire."

"What about the plants?"

"My regular girl finally got back from that sponsored bike ride, so she's taking care of them. I'm going to stay with my old pal Dickie for a night. He runs a market garden now, although his daughter's gradually taking the place over." Albert glanced at his watch. "I should get going."

"I'm sorry about the fruit."

"You and me both, lad, you and me both. Let's hope the next one fares better, eh? Although I might not be around to see it."

Rhys hated when people talked like that. His mum used to do it too, joke about her own mortality, but it had been no laughing matter.

"I'm sure that's not true. Do you want another cuppa before you leave?"

"Perhaps just the one…"

CHAPTER 16
RHYS

While Coco dozed fitfully that evening, Rhys couldn't resist the lure of Google. Remi Klein was nothing short of a genius. He'd started at Harvard two years early and aced his PhD in molecular biology by the time he hit twenty-one. His professors described him as "a prodigy" and "a young man with the power to revolutionise the field of genetics." At twenty-three, he'd taken the helm of RK Biotronix following his father's untimely death.

One life, two tragedies. How had the deaths of both his father and his wife affected Klein? And what the hell had led him to Uncle Albert's greenhouse? Had he been suckered in by myths about the trees as well? *Could* there be any truth to the story?

No.

No, no, no.

It just wasn't possible. At this rate, Rhys would turn into Hashim, who loved to hang out on the internet with the tinfoil-hat brigade. Even though Gary took the piss out of him mercilessly, Hashim still wouldn't make a call on his mobile without a "brain guard" he'd bought on eBay clipped to his ear. Hey, perhaps Rhys should ask him about the damn trees?

Speaking of which... He searched various permutations of "coco du ciel" and "Karaza." Crikey, those guys were bloodthirsty. Assuming Alice hadn't made up the entire story—and a total fabrication seemed unlikely because there was no denying the trees were in Albert's greenhouse —her survival had been a miracle. Most people who ventured into the tribe's territory never made it out. The Brazilian government had declared the place a no-go area, both to protect the Karaza from diseases brought by outsiders and to protect would-be explorers from having their heads mounted on pikes. Aerial footage on YouTube showed a long, narrow valley, a slash between two rainforest-covered peaks, and that valley was filled with the distinctive spiky foliage of coco du ciel trees. A dozen half-naked men gathered in a clearing, and as the plane flew overhead, they hurled spears at it. Nice.

Rhys watched Coco as she fidgeted in her sleep. Part of him wanted to find out everything about her, but the other part, perhaps the bigger part, just wanted to move on and enjoy the future together as best they could. What if there was some way of her officially claiming refugee status, as the doctor's receptionist had mentioned? It wasn't as if the authorities could send her home, was it?

Maybe the best option would be to put the past behind them?

It turned out that laying the past to rest wasn't quite as simple as Rhys had hoped. Over the next week, Coco became obsessed with those bloody trees. Every moment that Rhys wasn't using his laptop, Coco spent poring over search results and making notes. She'd even begun studying genetics. It wasn't healthy.

And Rhys could hardly stop her. Sure, changing the password would be straightforward, but that would break the trust between them, which was the last thing he wanted. She didn't have anyone else. Neither did he, really, only Albert, and the old man wasn't in his good books right now, not after he'd started Coco on this wild goose chase.

And when Coco finally looked at the information Rhys had saved about applying for leave to remain in the UK as a stateless person, she only wanted to know when she'd be able to apply for a passport.

"Where do you want to go?"

"Brazil."

"To look for those trees? Do you have a death wish?"

Wrong choice of words. Coco burst into tears.

"I don't know! I don't know anything! Who I am, where I'm from... Only that those trees were involved, and I'm the second woman to appear in that freaky greenhouse."

"Sorry, I'm sorry." Rhys took a step forward, and Coco took a step back. "I understand how difficult this must be."

"Do you? Do you really? I'm living in permanent limbo, and now it seems I might not even be alive."

"You're very much alive." This time when Rhys moved towards her, Coco stayed put. "I'll do everything I can to get to the bottom of this."

Which was why he found himself on the phone an hour later. Coco had fallen into an exhausted sleep, and Rhys snuck out to the garden so he wouldn't disturb her. Even after his mum died, he'd never really felt alone, but now, with nobody close to confide in, he became all too aware of his social isolation. Sure, he had plenty of acquaintances and he got invited to parties, but there wasn't a single person—not one—that he trusted to provide advice. Which meant he had to make do with Uncle Albert...

"I need to ask a favour."

"What kind of a favour, lad? How's that girl of yours?"

"That's what the favour's about. She can't get this nonsense with Great-Grandma Alice and the trees out of her head, and I think the only way to prove it's just a crazy myth will be to find out where Coco came from. I was wondering if you could ask around the village again? *Somebody* must know her."

"I already did that. For my own curiosity, like. Angharad Davis who runs the post office knows everything about everyone, and she says the only girl who's gone missing recently is young Candace McDade."

"Could Coco be Candace?"

Albert snorted a laugh. "Oh, heavens no. I'd have recognised Candace. I helped her with her gardening badge when she was a Girl Guide, which turned out to be something of a mistake because she got arrested for running her own cannabis farm a few years later. Her mother still blames me for teaching her about the benefits of hydroponics. And Angharad thinks she ran off to London with a boy."

"Dammit, I need to solve this mystery."

"Tsk-tsk-tsk. A gentleman shouldn't curse."

Good thing Rhys wasn't a gentleman. "I'd say cursing's warranted under the circumstances. Coco thinks she grew in a bloody tree, and you didn't help by telling her about the other woman in the greenhouse."

"I didn't say much. I don't *know* much. The only person

who does is Remi Leroux, Remi Klein, whatever his name is."

"Except he's denied everything. I tried emailing him, and his assistant replied and said he'd never been to Wales."

"Oh, hogwash. I had lunch with Branwyn Jeffries at the B&B in the village, and we looked up this Remi Klein on the internet. Did you know he gave one of those TED talks? Something fancy about genetics? Anyhow, Branwyn says it's definitely the same chap who stayed with her. He'd booked the room for two whole months, but after the incident with the woman, he left enough cash to cover his entire stay in an envelope on his bed, plus a note saying that he'd really enjoyed Branwyn's cooking and apologising for leaving in such a hurry."

"So he's a billionaire and a liar."

"Certainly seems that way, lad. Branwyn found an article on some lifestyle website, and he lives in a castle."

"I saw that story too."

The castle—or château since it was in France—had a tower with those tiny little slitty windows archers used to fire arrows out of, and even a bloody moat.

"Since we know where he is, maybe you should try speaking to him in person?"

"Are you kidding? I can hardly stroll over the drawbridge and ring the bell."

"He has to leave sometime. How does he buy groceries?"

"He probably has them delivered. Or gets his butler to go to the supermarket."

"Perhaps you could catch him at work?"

"You can't just make an appointment with a man like that."

Rhys knew because he'd already tried. He'd called RK Biotronix pretending to be a journalist looking for an interview, only to be told that Mr. Klein didn't see anybody, ever.

"Well, use your imagination, lad. Or don't young 'uns do that anymore? Every time I see someone your age, they're fiddling with one of those fancy smartphones. What's wrong with good old buttons?"

"I have imagination, but what I don't have is time. If we don't find a new place to live in the next fortnight, me and Coco will both be homeless."

"What's wrong with the place you're living in at the moment?"

"The lease runs out."

"Don't you have letting agents in London? I'm as curious about Remi's motives as you are."

"I'll make the trip when I'm able, but it'll probably be a waste of time."

"You never know. Remember what Arthur Conan Doyle said: 'Once you eliminate the impossible, whatever remains, no matter how improbable, must be the truth.'"

"There's a perfectly rational explanation for all this."

"I'm just saying."

"Please, just don't."

CHAPTER 17
RHYS

Klein's home town of Villance lay south of Limoges in north-western France. Home to fifteen thousand people, it was renowned for its art exhibitions as well as the ornate water feature in the town square. A bit of a tourist trap, it seemed, judging by the number of souvenir shops clustered around the fountains. According to Google Earth, Klein's castle was five miles away on a quiet, leafy road, although it might as well have been on the moon. The security around the place was no joke. Guards, cameras, warnings of dogs on patrol...

Rhys might have lied to his uncle when he'd said he had imagination. Right now, he saw no way of getting within a hundred yards of Remi Klein. And he couldn't stop wishing that Coco was there with him. Not only did he miss her company, but she was also the more devious out of the two of them. After all, it was she who'd had the idea of removing the back panel from Gary's beloved bass speaker and inserting a little leaving gift—two haddock fillets and a dozen peeled prawns.

But instead of having his partner in crime at his side,

Rhys was stuck in France with only a hired Renault Clio for company, while Coco was trapped in a dingy bed and breakfast on the outskirts of Uxbridge with three alarm clocks and—thankfully—a landlady who was hard of hearing. Better still, the lady had offered a twenty-five percent discount as long as Coco didn't need fresh linen and towels every day, and she'd also agreed to the goldfish staying at no extra charge. They couldn't leave them behind with the three imbeciles. Everything else Rhys had wanted to keep from the house on Cardon Street had fit into two suitcases —including the tiger-print onesie, which Coco had insisted on keeping if only to laugh at—and those were tucked into a corner of Coco's room, awaiting his return.

They'd spent three weeks planning this trip, but in the end, the only part that had mattered was the goodbye. Coco's murmured words, her confidence that he'd get to the bottom of the mystery, followed by *that* kiss. A kiss that Coco had started, but which Rhys hadn't stopped. He'd been about to walk out the door when she'd pulled him back, shoved him against the wall, and pressed herself against him. Their gazes locked. Every atom in him screamed "bad idea" as she leaned in and touched her lips to his, but he couldn't bring himself to regret kissing her back. Those breathy little gasps... In that moment, the past didn't matter and the future didn't matter, only the present. Rhys had gone from relaxed to rock hard in the time it took her to slide her tongue into his mouth, but she'd been polite enough not to mention the state of his dick when she finally stepped back and reminded him not to be late for his train.

And now here he was.

In France.

At his wit's end.

Tourists were welcome in Villance, it seemed, but nosy foreigners weren't. Any questions beyond *"Où est la fontaine?"* and *"Y a-t-il une boulangerie près d'ici?"* were met with suspicion by the locals. Rhys pretended to be a writer struggling for inspiration as he penned his latest novel—the tale of a medieval lord who had the power to rewind time by twenty-four hours and made his serfs relive each day over and over until they got it right—but he wasn't sure the townsfolk had bought the story. Shame. He was quite proud of the idea, even if he hadn't worked out the ending. Perhaps he should start writing it for real?

Oh, the French were friendly enough most of the time, despite snickers at Rhys's attempts to murder their language, but they quickly brushed aside any probing questions. Remi Klein was a town hero, and nobody would hear a bad word said against him. Did he actually visit the town? Not often, but when he did, he spent a ton of money. And he'd donated all the benches around the fountains. Had Rhys seen the fountains yet? Because if he hadn't, he really should. And did he know there was a son et lumière every evening at eight?

Back when Rhys used to have free time, he'd watched a lot of mystery shows, but he'd never look at those amateur sleuths in the same way again. You know the ones—dramas where Joe Average invariably discovers he has a natural flair for detective work, solves the problem within a week thanks to his blinding deductions, and everyone lives happily ever after. Except for the murder victims, obviously.

At least nobody had died in this episode.

"I might as well come home," he told Coco over Skype. He'd bought her a cheap smartphone before he left, so at least they could stay in touch. Their nightly conversations were the only thing that kept him going at the moment. "Klein might as well be a ghost."

"Who did you speak to today?"

"The hotel owner's son, the waiter at lunch, a couple of shopkeepers, a guy walking his dog near the castle, and three teenagers with skateboards."

And quite honestly, trying to solve this puzzle was trickier than knitting a sweater out of spaghetti while wearing mittens.

Coco sighed. "They're all men."

"So?"

"Try asking women your age. If I were them, I'd talk to you."

Hmm. Rhys shuddered at the thought. He'd always had a tendency to get tongue-tied around women he didn't know, so he avoided speaking to them wherever possible. He'd only ended up with Stacey because *she* kept talking to *him*.

"I'm not sure that's a good idea."

"It's a great idea."

"But what would I say?"

"Simple—just start with an easy question they'll definitely know the answer to, like is there a cinema nearby or where's the nearest art gallery? Then notice something they're wearing and compliment them on it."

"Won't that seem creepy?"

"Not if you do it right. I mean, don't say that you love their sweater because it looks like one your mom knitted. Perhaps admire their necklace and ask where they bought it because your sister would love one just like it?"

Okay. Right. That sounded straightforward enough. Could it really be that easy?

"That's it?"

"If they like you, they'll start talking. Sure, you might crash and burn a few times, but you have to keep going. Just put on your English charm."

"What charm?"

"Yeah, exactly like that. It's cute when you act self-deprecating. And smile. You look handsome when you smile." On-screen, Coco rolled her eyes. "I can't believe I'm giving you tips on how to pick up women. You'd better not find one you like."

"I already did."

Her face fell. "Oh."

"I'm talking about you."

"Oh," she said again, but this time it was followed by a smile. Rhys traced the outline of her lips with a finger.

"I miss you."

A tear rolled down her cheek, and he wished he'd kept his mouth shut because he couldn't be there to wipe it away.

"I miss you too."

CHAPTER 18
RHYS

Coco was right—Rhys crashed and burned on his first few attempts. One girl laughed at his pitiful attempts to speak and walked away, and another called her boyfriend over. The guy started off hostile, but he soon realised Rhys was no threat and drew him a map to the nearest hostel. Only the thought of Coco stopped Rhys from skulking back to his hotel room to nurse his wounded pride. Failure wasn't an option.

His reward came at lunchtime when he struck gold, quite literally. Breakfast had been a solitary croissant and a cup of coffee, and by noon he was starving. He chose a tiny backstreet café to eat in, not because it looked nice, but because it looked cheap. Anywhere within sight of those bloody fountains charged a premium. Surely he couldn't go wrong with a cheese baguette? Or a croque-monsieur? Or one of those mini quiches? Maybe a—

The waitress appeared from nowhere. Well, a door to the left, but Rhys still didn't see her coming. *Oof.* Her tray clattered to the floor, and cream cakes splattered all over the tiles.

"I'm so sorry!"

"*Je suis désolé*," the waitress said at the same time, beaded bangles clinking as she stooped to clear up the mess. She wore more costume jewellery than a QVC host.

"Here, let me help."

Bad move. Rhys slipped on the remains of a chocolate eclair and landed on his arse. At least the girl was laughing—he had to take that as a positive.

"Sorry."

"You are helping by cleaning the floor with your...?" She patted her own behind.

"Well, not quite..." Now what was he meant to say? "Uh, I like your necklace."

Was it possible to sink right through the floor? Even if he ended up in hell, it couldn't be worse than the current situation.

"Oh, thank you." The waitress beamed at him. "I made it myself."

"Really? I was going to ask where you got it. It's my sister's birthday soon."

"I 'ave an Etsy store. Let me get this mess cleaned up, and I will write down the details."

"Uh, *merci beaucoup*."

She let out a peal of laughter.

"*Quoi?*" he asked. What?

"Your pronunciation's terrible," she said, her English perfect. "You just told me I 'ave a nice ass, and I don't think you meant to."

Rhys's cheeks burned. "No! No, of course I didn't. Not that your arse isn't lovely, but... I'm going to stop talking now."

The girl giggled. "At least you tried. Most of the tourists, they just shout louder in English."

"I apologise on behalf of my fellow countrymen. I'll try to keep the volume down."

Another giggle. "You're on vacation in Villance?"

"Not exactly. I'm writing a novel, and I thought I'd take a trip to France for inspiration."

"*Très excitant!*" she said as he scrambled to his feet. "Chanté."

"Chanté?"

"It's my name."

"Ah. Yes, of course." Even dealing with Coco naked in the greenhouse had been less awkward than this. "Rhys."

He held out a hand, Chanté leaned forward and offered a cheek to kiss, and he ended up jabbing her in the chest. *Please, somebody kill me now.*

"Sorry."

"Ah, the 'andshake. It's very English." She did shake hands, hers soft and dainty, his hot and sticky. Fuck. One thing was certain—he'd be leaving her a massive tip. "Sorry, the *hand*shake. Always I am forgetting my 'aitches.' And I should find a mop."

Rhys managed to gather his wits enough to scoop the cakes into the bin while Chanté washed the floor. He was the only person in the café, which surprised him since the proprietor was so friendly. The food looked better than he'd expected as well. He ordered a croque-monsieur and an opera cake, plus a cup of coffee.

"Have you worked here for long?" he asked Chanté when she brought his lunch over.

"Two years. But maybe..." She looked around, and her smile dropped for the first time. "But maybe not for much longer."

"Why not?"

"I had...how do you say...a fell-out?"

"A falling-out?"

"Yes, a falling-out with the mayor's daughter, so local people don't come 'ere anymore. And the tourists, they stay by the fountains."

It was none of Rhys's business, but he couldn't help asking anyway. "What did you fall out over?"

"At the Fête du Travail cake-decorating contest, somebody covered her cake in paint, and she told everyone it was me."

"And nobody found the real culprit?"

"Nobody looked. I think she did it 'erself."

"She sabotaged her own entry?"

A shrug. "*Oui.*"

"But why would she do that?"

"Because for Nicolette, it is better to cause a scene than to come second." Chanté's smile returned, but this time it looked forced. "I shouldn't be bothering you with my problems. Tell me, what 'ave you found in Villance that inspires you?"

She'd given him an opening, and he had to take it, didn't he?

"I've visited both of the art galleries, plus of course there're the fountains." He crossed his fingers. "And the other day, I drove past what looked like a castle just outside town. Are people allowed to visit it?"

She shook her head. "Oh, no, no, you can't go there."

"Shame. It looked interesting."

"*Oui*, it is. When I was young, it was an abandoned ruin, and we were able to visit then. My papa took my little brother and me on the weekends, and I used to hide behind the rocks and jump out at him. Even now, my brother still believes it's haunted. Many people do. At night, you can hear strange footsteps and sometimes a woman wailing."

Chanté shuddered, but Rhys struggled to keep the grin off his face. At last, somebody was talking to him about the castle. Who knew splattered cream cakes and terrible French could be such a great conversation starter?

"So who rebuilt the place? Surely that must have cost a fortune if it was a ruin before?"

Chanté's voice dropped to a whisper. "We don't talk about him."

"Why not? Is he a criminal or something?"

"A criminal? No, not at all. But Monsieur Klein is very private, and he gives a lot of money to the town. There is a… I suppose an unspoken rule that if we don't ask questions, he will donate more. And he hates visitors."

"Ah, a reclusive billionaire?"

"*Oui*. Like the 'ero out of a romance novel, except his love, she died." Chanté clapped a hand over her mouth. "Probably I shouldn't tell you that."

"I couldn't imagine spending my life locked away in a castle. Does he come out often?"

"I've never seen him. My father has once or twice, but not for years. Mostly he comes and goes by helicopter."

Rhys's heart sank. If Klein rarely left the castle grounds, how would he talk to the man?

"Maybe *he's* a ghost?"

"*Non*, I don't think so," Chanté answered in all seriousness. "He likes flowers, and I don't think ghosts 'ave a sense of smell."

"Flowers? How do you know that?"

"My friend Adele, she runs the florist." Chanté waved her hand to the right, so Rhys assumed it was somewhere nearby. "Every Friday, she delivers six bouquets to the gatehouse. Always roses, in every colour."

Interesting, but short of hiding himself inside a bunch

of flowers, Rhys couldn't see how that snippet of information helped him. He was trying to think of another question when the bell over the door tinkled and Chanté's face lit up in a smile.

"Another customer! *Excusez-moi.*"

Would she come back to carry on the conversation? Rhys hoped so, but Chanté dragged a chair up to the newcomer's table and began chatting. They obviously knew each other. With no further progress to be made, at least today, he tucked into his lunch. He'd come here again for sure, even if it did nothing for his waistline. The diet would start as soon as he got back to England. But for now, he left enough cash on the table to cover his meal, all the cakes he'd ruined, plus a tip, and headed out to the streets.

"At least she spoke to you," Coco said that evening when Rhys recounted his visit to the café. He might have omitted to mention the part about sitting in cakes. "Maybe you could go back for lunch tomorrow?"

"I'm planning to, but I'm not sure it'll help much. Klein hardly ever leaves the castle."

"Then you need to get in."

Sometimes, Coco could be the tiniest bit exasperating. Still beautiful, even on a low-res video call when she was obviously tired, but exasperating nonetheless.

"What do you expect me to do? Swim across the moat? Scale the walls? It's a castle—it was designed to withstand an invading army."

"How about hiding in a delivery truck?"

"Deliveries go to the gatehouse. There are guards."

They probably had guns. Were guns legal to carry in France? Rhys considered looking it up, but then he decided he'd rather not know.

"What about tradesmen? Plumbers? Electricians?"

"You want me to get a job as a tradesman's apprentice in a country where I barely even speak the language?"

"A gardener? What if you got a job as a gardener?"

"It would be easier to parachute in."

Coco totally missed the sarcasm. "Do you think? How much do parachuting lessons cost?"

"Too much, and did I mention I hate heights? We need a better idea."

Coco fell silent for a long moment, and then she snapped her fingers. "Okay, I have a better idea."

Now what? Did she want him to snorkel through the moat with a grappling gun?

"Okay, let's hear it."

She explained her plan, and Rhys had to concede that it wasn't actually that bad. Maybe, just maybe, it even had a chance of working...

CHAPTER 19
RHYS

As soon as Rhys walked into the florist, he began sneezing. Damn lilies. He scanned the shop until he saw the culprits, a dozen white blooms in a metal vase complete with their stamens of doom. He'd been allergic to lily pollen since he was a kid, which was a shame because they'd been his mum's favourite flower.

"*À vos souhaits.*"

"Huh? I mean, *pardon.*"

The girl behind the counter giggled. Adele, Chanté's friend, according to her name tag.

"It is what we say when you sneeze."

"Ah. Right." Thank goodness she spoke English. "I'd like to order a bunch of flowers."

"We have plenty of those. What kind?"

"A dozen white roses. And could you put some of those palm fronds with them?"

"Palm fronds? With roses?"

Her expression said they definitely didn't go together, but Rhys nodded. Just another British guy with dubious taste.

"Yeah, I think they'd look nice. Can you deliver them tomorrow?"

"In Villance?"

"Do you know the castle on the outskirts? Uh, to the…" Rhys pictured the map in his head. "To the west."

Until that point, Adele had been smiling, but now her lips pursed. "You want to have flowers sent to Le Château de Villance?"

"If that's what it's called." He'd rehearsed the story with Coco last night, and he kept his fingers crossed that he wouldn't trip over his big fat lying tongue. "I was cycling past the place yesterday when my bike got a puncture. I didn't have a spare tyre, but somebody pulled out of the driveway and stopped to help."

Adele folded her arms, grim-faced. "The people from there, normally they are not helpful."

"Then I guess I got lucky. The lady works there as a maid. Perhaps you know her—she said her name was Coco?"

"I don't know anyone who works there."

Thank goodness. "Well, she saved me from a long walk. When I couldn't repair the puncture, she was kind enough to drop me and the bike off at my hotel."

Adele still looked sceptical, so Rhys tried a smile, clasping his hands behind his back so she wouldn't see them shaking.

"We talked all the way. She said she wanted to practise her English, and my French needs work. Apparently, I've been telling women they have nice arses instead of thanking them very much."

Finally, Adele's smile came back.

"I'm sure she'll be very happy to receive flowers. I

deliver to the château every Friday, so I can take your gift along too. Do you want to write a card?"

Most definitely he did. That was the whole point of the exercise. Sure, he could have tried the postal service, but there was a greater risk that the message would get filed in the bin by an overzealous secretary. If Remi Klein—or his female companion—was fond of flowers, there was a better chance of them seeing the note if it was attached to a bouquet.

Rhys selected a card from the rack by the register, a print of a seemingly innocuous tree silhouetted against a blue sky. Adele lent him a pen, and he scribbled out the words Coco had suggested last night. Go big or go home, right?

I know your secret.

He signed the note from Coco du Ciel and included his phone number, and before Adele could get curious and read it, he shoved it into an envelope and sealed the flap. On the front, he addressed it to Ms. C Karaza. Was the mystery woman still living with Klein? Why else would he hide away like a hermit, sealed off from the world? Rhys only hoped that the thought of his secret getting out would elicit a response from the mysterious billionaire.

But as he handed over cash to pay for the flowers, doubt crept into his mind. What if he and Coco were wrong? What if this whole trip was a wild goose chase and they never found out her origins?

He didn't even want to think about that possibility.

Rhys spent most of Friday pacing his tiny hotel room. Twice he cracked his shin against the bed's wooden frame when he got distracted by his thoughts, and twice he let out a string of curses that would make a hip-hop artist blush.

He stared at the phone in his hand, willing it to ring. Had the flowers been delivered yet? And if they had been, had anyone read the card? What if it had been thrown away unopened? Or fallen off in transit?

A bead of sweat rolled down his forehead. This stress... He wasn't cut out for it. Even his final exams had been a walk in the park compared to the agony of waiting for Remi Klein to act. Should he call Coco? Rhys longed to, but the last thing he wanted to do was stress her out as well. Every time he saw her, she looked a little more ragged around the edges.

And while Rhys fidgeted in a one-star hotel in France, his heart was in England with the girl who'd stolen it. Despite the difficulties of the last few months, he'd never regret meeting Coco.

Daylight turned into darkness, and the phone remained stubbornly silent. Should he go out for dinner? The hotel didn't have a restaurant, and he'd eaten nothing since the cheese-and-ham baguette he'd picked up from Chanté at lunchtime.

"Ring, dammit."

The phone rang, and Rhys looked at it in shock. *Blocked number calling.* Shit, shit, shit! He'd been running through what to say since dawn, but now his mind had gone blank.

"Hello?"

If this was someone asking about an accident, trip, or fall, they were going to get an earful.

"Coco du Ciel?" The speaker was male, his accent French.

"This is her, uh, representative. She can't come to the phone right now."

"When will she be available?"

"She's in a different country. There were some, uh, problems with her passport."

"I bet there were," the voice said dryly.

"Is this Remi Klein?"

"Let's just say it's his representative."

Rhys's thoughts were a jumble. In truth, he hadn't quite believed that anybody would call. "I'm not sure where to start."

"How about you lay out whatever crazy theory it is you have, and I'll laugh in the appropriate places."

"I-I-I won't speak to anybody but Mr. Klein. This isn't a story I'd feel comfortable telling anyone else."

Rhys feared the caller would simply hang up, but instead, he heard a long sigh.

"Be at the gates of Le Château de Villance at ten o'clock sharp tomorrow. You get fifteen minutes."

The line went dead, and Rhys stared at the screen for a second. Then he pumped a fist in the air. It had worked.

Their crazy, crackpot, wing-and-a-prayer plan had worked. Holy fuck.

Now he had to call Coco.

CHAPTER 20

RHYS

At a quarter to ten the next day, Rhys drew to a halt outside the huge metal gates of Klein's castle. Imposing. And that was just the outer perimeter. Through the bars, he saw the moat glistening in the sunshine, and behind that, a stone wall that had to be twenty feet high. The château itself was visible on a small rise in the distance, beyond an archway with an honest-to-goodness portcullis raised to let the lucky few inside. Or possibly keep them there. He shuddered at the thought.

A guard emerged from the gatehouse and peered through the driver's window.

"*Qu'est-ce que vous voulez?*" What do you want?

The man's stance was designed to be intimidating, and an equally hulking clone stood behind him, arms folded. Nothing like being welcoming, eh?

"I-I-I'm here to meet Mr. Klein. He said to come at ten o'clock."

The guard gave a curt nod. "*Garer là-bas.*"

What did that mean? The guard waved at what appeared to be a parking space beside the gatehouse. He wanted Rhys to leave his car? That was good, right? At least if he disappeared, there'd be evidence on show for the police to find. If Coco didn't hear from him in the next twenty-four hours, she knew to contact the authorities.

The guard motioned him through a small pedestrian gate and into the back seat of a golf cart, and a moment later, they trundled up the driveway to a fate unknown. The castle rose imposingly in front of them, its weathered stone walls casting ominous shadows. Dark. Jagged. Somehow cold despite the September sunshine. The place had a malevolent feel, almost as if the gloomy forests were pressing in from either side. Perhaps Chanté had been right and the place *was* haunted?

Rhys jumped as his escort hammered on the château's huge wooden door. The *crack* of metal on metal was loud enough to wake the dead, and somebody must have watched their arrival because Rhys barely had time to inhale before the door swung open on silent hinges. The man on the other side might have dressed as a butler, but his muscles and bearing screamed ex-military.

"*Suivez-moi,*" he commanded.

Rhys followed as ordered, trotting along like an obedient child as he was led into the bowels of the castle. When they reached a wood-panelled library, the man pointed at an uncomfortable-looking leather chair.

"*Maintenant, vous attendez.*"

Wait? How long for? The hands on the grandfather clock in front of him ticked around to five past ten, a clock that looked remarkably similar to Uncle Albert's. Would Remi Klein deduct that wasted time from Rhys's allotted quarter-hour?

Finally, footsteps sounded outside the door, the *click* of heels on the bare stone floor. Rhys half hoped they'd carry on past. Then he wouldn't have to face a bona fide genius ruthless enough to become a billionaire by the time he hit thirty. Klein probably had his own dungeon as well as staff who'd throw Rhys into it at a snap of their boss's fingers.

The footsteps stopped.

Brilliant.

Rhys scrambled to his feet as Remi Klein walked towards him. The man was easily recognisable from the pictures Rhys had seen, but he'd aged, and not only that, he had a weariness about him that an expensive suit couldn't hide. Plus he needed to visit a barber. Unless, of course, shaggy hair was the fashion in France, which was a distinct possibility judging by some of the chaps Rhys had come across in Villance.

"Uh, bonjour?"

Klein didn't return the greeting, nor did he proffer a hand. Instead, he studied Rhys the way a person might peer at a pesky beetle before they crushed it with their shoe. Rhys did his best not to wither. What on earth had made him think coming here was a good idea? He was no match for a biotech magnate.

"Your name?"

"Rhys. Rhys Evans."

"So, Rhys... You think you know my secret?"

"Well, uh..." Gee, that was a good start. "Uh..."

Klein held Rhys's gaze, unblinking. A lion sizing up its prey.

"So you see, the thing is... You went to Wales, didn't you? A few years ago? And on your last night there, you left my uncle's greenhouse with a woman."

Did that even make sense? Maybe not, but Rhys was sure he saw Klein give an involuntary start when he mentioned the word "greenhouse."

"And who is your uncle?"

"Albert Evans."

"I've never heard of him."

"Really? That ring on the chain around your neck says otherwise." And so did Klein's eyes. That fleeting flicker of fear gave him away. "My uncle remembers you wearing it. The inscription says 'Remi and Cambria,' right?"

"Let's say I was in Wales. Leaving a greenhouse with a woman is hardly a crime."

"Perhaps it is if she just fell out of a tree." Okay, so the North Wales police hadn't seemed too concerned about Coco's origins, and also Rhys sounded like a lunatic, but what else was he meant to say? "How does the coco du ciel thing work, anyway? Do you chant in the moonlight or something?"

Rhys waited for the explosion, for the sputter of incredulity, but it never came. Instead, Klein stepped back and let out a thin breath.

"You have no proof of anything." So it *was* true? "If you're trying to blackmail me, it won't work. I don't give in to criminals."

"Blackmail you? I'm not trying to blackmail you. No way." Rhys didn't want to end up shackled in the dungeon. "But that thing with the trees... I think it might have happened again. There's another girl."

Klein's eyes widened. "What's your uncle trying to do? Turn this into a commercial venture?"

"Of course not! He wasn't even there when she appeared. I was house-sitting, and when I went out to water the plants one morning, there she was."

"Coco? That was the name you used on the note."

A lump forced its way into Rhys's throat as he nodded. "Yes, Coco. And she doesn't know who she is or where she came from. I promised I'd help her find out, and that led me here."

Klein walked over to the window and stared at the grounds. "And how do you think I'd be able to help?"

"By telling us what you know. Right now, we have no idea whether it's a simple case of a missing person or... something more."

"And if I gave you information, then what?"

"Then...nothing. We'd walk right out of your life. We don't want anything else from you, but you've got all this..." Rhys waved a hand at the castle. "And Coco's got nothing. I want to help her to rebuild, not just her life but her soul, and this is eating away at her. She tries to stay positive, but how can you get on with day-to-day living when you don't even know your own name?"

"*Merde.*" Klein tugged a hand through his hair as he cursed under his breath. "Your Coco... Does she have any issues sleeping?"

"Nightmares. She has terrible nightmares." A chill ran through Rhys's veins. "But how do you know about that?"

"Celine, she has them too."

"Celine?"

"You may know her as Cambria."

Holy fuck. Was Klein saying what Rhys thought he was saying? This whole time, he'd secretly thought there must be a rational explanation for Coco's existence, that he just needed to dig deeper and find it. But if Cambria was alive... Or reanimated... What did you even call it when a person was resurrected from the dead?

"Then it's true? The legend?"

"*Oui.* It's true."

An involuntary gasp escaped Rhys's lips. Klein sure looked as if he meant what he was saying, and nothing in

Rhys's research had suggested the man was a kook. But even so... How the hell did a tree replicate a human?

Klein strode over to a leather couch, one of three arranged in a U shape around a low table. A crystal decanter sat on a tray with four tumblers, and he poured a generous measure of amber liquid into one of them.

"Cognac?"

Why not? Day-drinking seemed like the appropriate response in this situation.

"Thanks."

The clock's minute hand ticked past three as Rhys took a seat opposite Klein. Hmm. The strict time slot wasn't quite as important as Rhys had been led to believe.

"So," Klein said, holding out a glass. "What do you want to know?"

CHAPTER 21

RHYS

Everything. Rhys wanted to know everything. He had a thousand questions, but one was more intriguing than the rest.

"What do the trees do? I mean, how can they create a person?"

"You've asked the one question I'm unable to answer. That perhaps nobody will ever be able to answer. The trees have been alive for millennia, but nobody's studied them in any depth."

"Why not? I mean, surely it'd be the discovery of the century? We could bring back Einstein, Newton, and Faraday. The advances they could make... And the arts... What if Van Gogh were alive to paint again?" Rhys paused, his mind working overtime. "We could even bring back Amy Winehouse."

"Amy Winehouse?"

"Underrated musical genius."

Klein rolled his eyes. "You think I haven't thought of the possibilities? For years, I tried to study the trees in their natural habitat, and I have the scars to prove it." He rolled up a trouser leg to reveal a bumpy white line on his calf. "The Karaza are fierce fighters. You know about the Karaza? You must, since you addressed your note to them."

"Just a little."

"They're fond of arrows. Plus disturbing them is against Brazilian law, and the more people you bribe, the more questions get asked. And could you imagine what would happen if I did study the trees and wrote a research paper? Either I'd get laughed out of the scientific community or the trees would go extinct. There are fewer than three thousand specimens, and they're very slow growing. It takes over forty years for them to mature. If their powers became widely known, they'd be decimated through greed. Far better for them to remain a myth."

Rhys had to concede that Klein had a point. "If nobody's studied them, how did you find out what they could do?"

"By chance. Your uncle may have told you I suffered greatly after Cambria's death?"

Rhys nodded.

"I became obsessed with finding a way to bring her back. With the advances we've made in science in the past few years, I refused to believe it was impossible. I kept Cambria's body cryogenically preserved at my company headquarters, waiting for a breakthrough, but every avenue I tried was a dead end. Cloning, reanimation, gene splicing —they all failed." Gee, that wasn't creepy in the slightest. Rhys wasn't sure what was worse—that the man kept his dead wife on ice or that he could speak so casually about it. "I hunted through every resource from scientific journals to the theories of madmen to ancient texts, searching for a miracle. Then I found it."

"Where?" Rhys asked.

Klein put down his glass, stood, and walked over to the

wall. A moment later, an ugly old painting of a horse slid to the side, revealing a safe hidden behind it. What did it hold? Cash? Gold? The elixir of life? No, a pile of musty papers.

"In this." He placed the papers on the table. "Are your hands clean and dry? This manuscript is almost three thousand years old."

"Seriously?"

Forgers could do clever things with fakes nowadays.

"I had it carbon dated. The goatskin it's written on is older than most religions."

"Uh, my hands might be sweaty."

"Then please don't touch."

"Shouldn't you be wearing gloves?"

"We're not in a movie. Gloves can snag on the edges and lead to more problems than they solve."

Rhys stuffed his hands into his pockets, just in case he got tempted to reach out. "Where did you get it?"

"It was at the bottom of a box of papers I bought on Victorian medicine."

"And what is it?"

"Think of it as an instruction manual."

He carefully turned to the first page. A drawing showed a bearded figure emerging from a dark opening—an oval with a flat bottom and pointed top—carrying two small trees in his arms. The rest of the page was taken up by strange symbols, a cross between Morse code and hieroglyphics.

"What does that mean?"

"I think it's an artist's impression of how the trees arrived in Brazil. There's a ruined temple with a door in the shape of that portal in the Mala Valley, although I've only seen it in drone footage."

"I don't understand—is it saying the trees came from another world? That they're some kind of alien being?"

"Not a being, more of a biological machine. And why is the idea of coming from space so far-fetched? There are billions of planets out there. It stands to reason that we're not the only life forms."

Thank goodness Rhys was sitting down because his legs would have given way otherwise.

"You think Coco came from another planet?"

"Not at all. The trees merely use human DNA as a blueprint to build a replica, and it's delivered via a seed pod."

"That's...that's *insane.*"

"*Oui*, I agree with you. But it happened. I'd almost given up hope by then."

Klein turned the page, and it was like looking at an ancient comic strip. In the next scene, a figure poured something onto the roots of a tree—a coco du ciel judging by the shape of the leaves. The following page was torn, half of the illustration missing, and Klein let out a heavy sigh.

"Are those planets?" Rhys asked.

"Yes. This is the page I wish I'd understood before I did what I did."

"What do you mean?"

The Frenchman didn't answer, just kept flipping the pages. The drawing of the tree's giant fruit was remarkably similar to the actual fruit in Uncle Albert's lounge. On the last page, a crude sketch showed a figure sitting on the ground under the trees, surrounded by pieces of smashed fruit.

Holy fuck.

"Surely you couldn't have worked out everything from these pictures?" Rhys asked.

"The process was surprisingly simple. And fast. A mature coco du ciel tree can grow a fully formed adult female body in less than two weeks. Compared to these ancient instruments, our current cloning technology is still in kindergarten."

"You really think they came from outer space?"

"Truthfully, I don't know. While I was waiting for the trees to work their magic, I happened across Albert's grandmother's journal in his study one evening. She'd written notes from her stay in the Mala Valley."

"You read Great-Grandma Alice's diary?"

"*Oui*, Alice. She was quite a woman. But unfortunately, it was too late by then."

"Too late for what?"

"To stop the process. Perhaps I should have cut the fruit down, but I just couldn't bring myself to do it."

Rhys's blood turned icy. "Something went wrong?"

"The trees are biological machines. Feed them DNA, and they'll build you a living body. But the soul... That turned out to be an issue."

"I don't understand."

"To work, the trees must be paired, and a regeneration must be performed within one lunar cycle of a person's death or there's no guarantee that their original soul will be reunited with their body."

The ice became liquid nitrogen.

"So what are you saying?"

"I'm saying that I recreated Cambria's body, but the person who now inhabits it? She isn't the woman I married."

Now Rhys broke out in a cold sweat. He'd come to France searching for answers, but now that he'd got them, he wished he could turn back the clock and live in blissful ignorance.

"Then who is she?"

"I don't know, but we decided to call her Celine. They're essentially two different people. Her new soul, well, it was as if somebody wiped the hard drive. Memories are funny things. There are many different types, did you know that?"

"Types of memory?"

"*Oui*. At the top level, there are short-term and long-term memories. For our purposes, we're only concerned with the long-term memories. Those can be further divided into explicit and implicit memories, or conscious and unconscious if you prefer. In the case of Celine, it appears that her unconscious memory remained with her body. She recalled how to speak French, how to use cutlery, how to brush her teeth, how to ride a bicycle. She didn't have to relearn everything from scratch as a child would. And sometimes, I see glimmers of Cambria in the way she does things."

Rhys sensed a "but" coming.

"But her explicit memories, those are a problem. She retained a little general knowledge, such as the grass being green, for example, but for the most part, her semantic memory's a blank. And her episodic memory—of personal events and feelings—is non-existent while she's awake."

This got worse and worse. "So to use your computer analogy, the operating system's installed, but the files have been deleted?"

"Yes, exactly."

Was it too late to walk out of the château and pretend today's meeting never happened?

"And while she's asleep? What happens then?"

"She relives her murder. Tell me, what does Coco dream of?"

Rhys's throat went dry, and he had to force the words out. "She thinks she's drowning."

"Then that's how she died."

"But I don't understand—how did her body end up in the coco du ciel tree?"

"Her DNA must have found its way into the soil at the base of the trunk. That's how it worked with Celine. I amplified her DNA using a polymerase chain reaction, mixed it with distilled water, and poured it in the right place." Klein turned the pages of the manuscript back to the picture of a three-thousand-year-old stick figure doing precisely that. "Several millennia ago, I suspect they'd just have poured blood."

"That explains the logistics, but not where Coco's DNA came from in the first place. I never poured any blood on the trees."

"I can't help with that question."

Rhys thought back to his days in the greenhouse. Albert's instruction manual, the red-slash-pink pot with the fancy label, mixing the plant food into a can full of water, sprinkling it around the trees. What the hell had been in that tub?

Only one person knew the answer.

"I think I need to call Uncle Albert."

Klein gestured towards a cordless phone in a cradle on a side table.

"Be my guest. I'm as curious about this as you are."

CHAPTER 22

RHYS

The phone rang once, twice, three times. Ten times. Fifteen times. It was gonna go to voicemail, wasn't it? At the last second, Uncle Albert answered, sounding breathless. Had he been out with those bloody trees?

"Albert Evans."

"Uncle, I have a question for you."

"Rhys?"

How many other nephews did he have? As far as Rhys knew, he was the only child of Albert's only sibling.

"Yes, it's Rhys."

"Good to hear from you, son. Did you ever make it to France? What was the place called? Villance?"

"I'm there at the moment. That's why I'm calling."

"Excellent! How's it going over there?"

"Could we discuss that later? I don't have much time right now."

"Same, same. I'm meant to go over to Branwyn's for lunch, and one of the frangipani plants is covered in red spider mite. I don't suppose you happened to see the neem oil when you were here?"

"The what oil?"

"Never mind. What was your question?"

"The coco du ciel trees—what have you been watering them with?"

"The hosepipe?"

"No, I mean what have you been putting in the water? Your notes told me to use the powder in the red tub?"

"Ah, yes, the blood meal. Some of their lower leaves were looking slightly yellow, and I was worried about a nitrogen deficiency. That new additive seems to have done the trick, though."

"B-b-blood meal?"

"It's perfectly normal. A slaughterhouse by-product. I use bonemeal too, although that's a source of phosphorus rather than nitrogen."

Rhys collapsed into the nearest chair. Coco had been turned into plant food? Or rather, her previous body had? Did *she* have a different soul? Fuck. What was he supposed to tell her?

"Are you okay?" Klein asked softly.

He shook his head. How could he ever be okay again? Because Coco most definitely wouldn't be okay, and in the past few weeks, his happiness had become linked to hers. Perhaps he could just...not tell her? *Oh, great move, asshole. Lie to the woman you love.*

That he loved? Yeah, he did.

"Where did the blood meal come from? Where did you buy it?"

"Hmm, no, I didn't buy it. That particular tub came in my goody bag at the Chatsworth Flower Show a few months ago. All the presenters got one. Pricey stuff, as I recall, and I'm not sure it's much better than my usual brand from the local garden centre."

"What brand is it?"

"From the garden centre? Supagro. You can't go wrong with Supagro."

"No, the expensive one."

"I forget. Why? Is that important?"

"It might be. Could you go and look?"

Albert grumbled a bit, but he grudgingly agreed. "Give me a minute."

Rhys put his phone on mute just in case his uncle was still listening, then cursed liberally. Klein leaned against the wall, watching him.

"There's a problem?"

"Hell, yes, there's a problem. Coco came from a bloody slaughterhouse."

While Albert ambled out to the greenhouse—which would take him a lot longer than a minute—Rhys filled Klein in on the latest developments. It felt weird sharing with a virtual stranger, but the Frenchman was the one person in the world who might understand.

"So you believe Coco's DNA came from this blood meal?"

"Well, it makes sense, doesn't it? If you're right and she dreams of her death, then somebody drowned her and disposed of her body in a slaughterhouse. Part of the remains got made into plant food, and fuck, how am I meant to explain this to her?"

"Take one step at a time. I doubt her killer transported the body far, so by finding out which slaughterhouse supplies the plant-food manufacturer with raw ingredients, you'll be closer to finding out your girlfriend's original identity."

Rhys didn't bother to correct Klein on the "girlfriend" part. He was sick of fighting his damn feelings anyway.

"Her *original* identity? What if she's got another soul now?"

"What if she does? Unless she turns out to be a chess grandmaster or a concert pianist, the chances of finding out her new soul's origins would be slim. Once I accepted that, I learned to love Celine too. Not in the same way as my wife, but I'd be devastated to lose her."

"When was the Chatsworth Flower Show?"

Rhys opened up a browser to find out himself, but Klein was faster.

"The second week in June. When did Coco appear?"

"June twenty-sixth."

"And the incubation period is two weeks, give or take. So the fate of her soul depends on how long the manufacturing process took. And how long the product was sitting on the shelf. Ask your uncle for the batch number."

"Do souls get assigned at the beginning of the incubation process or the end?"

"That I do not know."

"Rhys?" Albert was back. "The brand's Eastlake. From the United States, it seems—there's a flag on the front."

So Coco *was* American? That explained the hint of an accent he thought he'd heard right after they met.

"Is there a manufacturing date on the label?"

"Let me fetch my glasses... Okay, it says to use by the end of June next year."

"But it doesn't say when it was made?"

"No, but this stuff lasts a year or two as long as you keep it cool and dry. Otherwise it starts to smell funny, and I don't suppose the trees would like that."

What would the mutant trees do with defective DNA?

Create their own version of Frankenstein's monster? It was the stuff of nightmares.

"Does the label have a batch number?"

"In the bottom right-hand corner."

"Could you read it out?"

"N-V-4-2-8-9-3-2-5-0. Or that last zero could be an O, I'm not sure. Say, did you ever find Remi?"

"I'm with Mr. Klein right now."

Klein took the phone out of Rhys's hand and hung up.

"Hey," Rhys started, and then remembered who he was talking to. "Sorry."

"I don't appreciate being gossiped about. And call me Remi, for goodness' sake. I'd say we've gone beyond formalities now."

True. They weren't friends, but with their shared secret came a weird intimacy that left Rhys twitchy.

"Right, yes, I understand. On both counts." He glanced across at the clock. So much for fifteen minutes—he'd been there for over an hour. "I've got the batch number. I guess I should try contacting Eastlake now?"

"Precisely."

"I don't suppose you've got any idea what to tell them? I mean, if I just come right out and ask which slaughterhouse their product came from, they'll send the message straight to the trash folder."

"Pretend to be a disgruntled customer. Tell them there's an issue with the product—that it smells strange, or it has lumps, or it's an odd colour—and question its origins." Remi fell silent for a moment, then blew out a long breath. "On second thought, forget that. Give me the batch number, and I'll have one of my people look into it."

"Your people?"

"I keep a security and investigations firm on retainer. They're less likely to me— Less likely to arouse suspicions."

He'd been about to say "mess this up," hadn't he? Rhys wasn't sure whether to feel grateful for the help or insulted. After all, he'd tracked Remi down to Villance *and* pushed him into a meeting. But since Rhys didn't have a private investigator at his beck and call, he swallowed his pride and nodded.

"Thank you. I'd appreciate that."

"I'll have him call you, but it might take a week or—"

"*Remi, le repas est prêt,*" a woman's voice interrupted, high and melodic. Rhys turned to see Celine Klein in the doorway. Her hair was different to that in the pictures he'd found—dark brown instead of blonde, and with a long fringe that swept over her eyes—but the face was the same. "*J'ai fait...*" Her hands flew up to cover her features when she realised Rhys was in the room, and she tripped over her feet as she backed away. "*Je suis désolé.*"

"Celine, it's okay. Come back."

Her confusion was all too clear as she took one hesitant step forward. Did she ever leave the castle? Who did she speak to apart from Remi? Just the staff?

"Celine, this is Rhys."

She stopped ten feet away, her gaze switching between her husband and the stranger in her home. Rhys got the impression she'd run if he made any sudden movements.

"*Bonjour?*" she tried.

"Rhys is from England."

"Hallo?"

"Celine understands English, although she rarely gets the chance to speak it," Remi explained. "She likes to watch American movies."

"It's good to meet you," Rhys said, careful to keep his words slow and clear.

"*Je ne comprends pas*," she whispered to Remi.

"It's a long story, but you have a lot in common with Rhys's girlfriend. She appeared one morning beneath the coco du ciel trees in his Uncle Albert's greenhouse."

Celine gasped and focused on Rhys. "This is true?"

"Yes, but unlike you, she doesn't have any links to her past. I'm helping him to find out where she came from."

"That...that might be impossible." Celine looked around. "Where is she? She is here?"

"No, she's in England."

Celine's face fell. "How did her DNA get into the tree? That is where to start."

"I'll explain later," Remi told her.

"Over lunch? There is enough food for three. I like to cook," she explained. "Always I make too much, but the staff eat what's left."

Judging by Remi's sour expression, a cosy lunch for three definitely hadn't been on his agenda. But rather than showing Rhys the door, he sighed and smiled at his sort-of wife.

"Of course, *chérie*. We can talk over lunch. Unless Rhys has pressing business elsewhere?"

The note of hope in Remi's voice suggested he'd have preferred his unwanted guest to drive straight to the train station without looking back, but curiosity got the better of Rhys. He'd never have this chance again, and he wanted to find out more about Celine-slash-Cambria. Aside from the obvious—namely being a prisoner in her own home—did she lead a normal life?

"Perhaps I could stay for a quick bite to eat?"

Celine beamed at him. "I'll ask the staff to set another place."

The table in the formal dining room seated twenty-two, which seemed a waste if Remi and Celine kept to themselves. Remi took his place at the head of the table with Celine to his right, then waved Rhys to sit opposite her while a maid bustled around setting out more crockery.

"Why such a big table?" Rhys asked. "I mean, if you're not keen on guests."

Remi rested his chin on steepled hands. "An illusion of normality."

Normality. Right. They lived in a bloody castle.

"*Le déjeuner sera servi dans cinq minutes, monsieur,*" the maid said before hurrying out of the room. She spoke French, but her accent was more guttural. Eastern European?

"Aren't you worried the staff might spill your secrets?"

"We don't hire staff locally, and they all abide by a strict confidentiality agreement. None of them can afford to breach it."

"Money talks," Rhys muttered.

"Quite the opposite, actually."

While Remi fussed with his napkin, Rhys took a moment to study Celine. In the pictures he'd seen of Cambria, she'd always looked sleek and polished, the epitome of a billionaire's wife in her designer clothes and jewellery. Today, the second Mrs. Klein was dressed casually in leggings and a long T-shirt, her thick hair tied into a topknot. To Rhys's untrained eye, she didn't appear to be wearing any make-up apart from something shiny on her lips.

Was her new look down to her new personality? Or just because she never went out anymore?

"How long ago was your girlfriend reborn?" Celine asked.

"Almost two and a half months. But she's not exactly my girlfriend."

Remi raised an eyebrow. "Really? You're going to a lot of trouble to help her."

"I didn't want to fall in love and then find she was already involved with somebody when she got her memory back."

Except it was too late. He'd managed to fall in love anyway. The warmth whenever he thought of Coco, the niggle of fear that he wouldn't be able to help her—they were there to stay.

Celine spoke softly. "If she's like me, her memory won't come back. It's gone for good."

"But what if she finds out who she used to be? You fell in love with the same man again."

"Falling in love was the easy part. Staying in love, that's much harder."

"What do you mean?"

"To be with Remi, I have to remain hidden from the world. He's too well known for us to go out in public. So yes, I have the man I love, but I'm also lonely. Remi too. We can't make friends, we can't take a vacation together, we can't hold a dinner party. It would be far easier if I moved to the other side of the world and started afresh, but then..." She glanced over at her husband. Remi was watching her closely now, and she slipped one hand into his. "I can't. I just can't. But it's okay—the château is beautiful, and the staff are friendly. I'm learning to play tennis. Do you play tennis?"

"Not very well."

Rhys understood now that the castle wasn't only a

home; it was a fortress. A prison. Suddenly, he was glad he was a nobody and that Coco's reappearance had flown under the radar. It meant they'd managed to avoid a plethora of awkward questions.

A chef walked in followed by a pair of kitchen staff, each carrying a serving dish. Silver covers were lifted with a flourish, and the staff melted away again. Lunch was cottage pie—although Celine called it *hachis parmentier*, which sounded far posher—with a selection of steamed vegetables. It tasted pretty good, and Rhys wished he had more of an appetite.

"So, how did you two meet?" he asked to break the silence.

"The first time?" Celine asked.

Think before you speak, idiot. "Sorry, that was insensitive."

"I met Cambria while I was at Harvard," Remi said. "She worked in a coffee bar just off campus. I ran in there one morning to take shelter from a rainstorm, and there she was. Until that day, I thought love at first sight only happened in movies, but now I know differently."

"So you started dating?"

"Not right away. She'd been through a bad break-up and swore she'd never date again. But I went back every morning just so she'd serve me coffee, and I hate coffee."

"Imagine that," Celine cut in. "A Frenchman who hates coffee."

"We're rare creatures, but we do exist. Two months passed before Cambria realised I wasn't a *connard*, and then she asked me out on a date. I booked tickets for the theatre, but my car broke down on the way and we ended up walking to a restaurant instead. The food was terrible. But we talked for hours, and that was the night I knew she'd be my wife."

"I've seen pictures of our wedding day, and I looked so happy. Now I know why." Celine smiled at Remi, a private moment in front of a stranger. "And even though life is harder now, I'm glad to be here. Now, tell me more about your friend. How is she coping?"

"Not all that well," Rhys admitted. "I get the feeling she was quite self-sufficient before, and now she's got no choice but to rely on me. We've been living in one room in a shared house, and I love being with her, but there are times... Times when some space would be nice."

"Cambria was the same. Independent. Adjusting isn't easy."

That wasn't the only similarity they shared. Celine and Coco both had an underlying vulnerability about them, a chink in their armour that no amount of money could hide. Fear for the future? The influence of their past? Probably both, but from that flaw, their sweetness seeped, sticky tentacles that wrapped around a man's heart and held it prisoner.

Coco had done that to Rhys, but he didn't care. He'd willingly give her everything he was able to. And right now, he needed to get back to England and update her on the situation. What he'd learned wasn't the sort of news you broke over the phone. If he left straight away, he could be back in Paris in four hours, catch the next Eurostar, and have her in his arms that evening. If Remi was correct, then nobody was looking for her and they never would be. The apathy of the Welsh police had proven to be a blessing in disguise. Plus Rhys had hastily scrubbed his social media profiles of any mention of her mysterious reappearance before he sat down for lunch, which meant all that remained were a few faded posters in Gwynedd. Coco's first body was dead and buried. Or perhaps cremated.

Gone, anyway.

Which meant that maybe Rhys stood a chance with her. Those niggles of guilt that had been plaguing him over their growing closeness faded into the distance. Even if she'd left a boyfriend behind, she could hardly just waltz back into his life, could she? Rhys began to eat faster.

"I've made macarons for dessert," Celine said. "Three different kinds. And we're having salmon en papillote for dinner. Do you want to stay here tonight?"

"Thanks for the invite, but I need to get home." Or back to England, at least. The "home" part was still somewhat uncertain. "Coco's on her own."

"Could I meet her, do you think? I don't often have people to talk to."

"That'd be tricky. You don't travel, and she can't."

"Why not?"

"Because she doesn't have a passport, a birth certificate, or any other kind of identity documents."

"Remi?" Celine asked, her tone pleading.

"You know it's not a good idea to leave the château, *chérie*."

Celine kept her eyes fixed on her husband, and Rhys knew that look. When Coco used it on him, he'd do anything for her.

Remi sighed. "What if I had Coco brought here? Would that work?"

"Without a passport?"

"Privacy and silence aren't the only things that money can buy."

CHAPTER 23
RHYS

Twenty-four hours later, Rhys paced the massive entrance hall at Le Château de Villance, the no-doubt-expensive rug soft under his feet. Remi hadn't been thrilled at Celine's invitation—or rather her insistence—for Rhys and Coco to stay with them, but he'd indulged his wife and grudgingly offered up a guest cottage in the grounds. The place was immaculate, and it still had that new-paint smell. Rhys would bet good money that nobody had ever slept there.

Staying with the Kleins promised to be awkward, but logic said it was the best short-term solution. Not only would it save cash, but Celine seemed happy at the prospect and Coco might be glad of the company too.

Now he was waiting for her to arrive. He hadn't told her much over the phone last night, just that somebody would be coming to pick her up, and although he'd kept his tone light and tried to frame it as a nice vacation, she'd seen right through the ruse.

"What's wrong, Rhys? What is it? What did you find?"

"I'll tell you everything tomorrow, I promise."

"So it's bad? It must be if you won't tell me today."

"Please, just pack your things."

"What about your stuff? Should I leave it here?"

"Bring that too. And the goldfish."

Remi had rolled his eyes at the mention of the fish, but he'd promised luggage space wouldn't be an issue, and this morning, Celine had let slip that he was sending a private jet. *A private freaking jet.* Not for the first time since that fateful morning in Wales, Rhys had pinched himself to make sure he wasn't dreaming.

"The plane has landed," Celine called from the doorway to one of the many living rooms. "The pilot called Remi."

"Where *is* Remi?"

He hadn't been at breakfast that morning. Celine had brought fresh pastries over to the cottage, and they'd eaten them on the terrace with coffee as she peppered him with questions about Coco. What foods did she like? Did she have a favourite colour? What type of music did she listen to? And movies, did she watch those? Was she fond of horses? Because Celine had a purebred Arabian that Remi had bought her last Christmas. Rhys hadn't been able to answer most of the questions, which was kind of embarrassing, but Celine had seemed happy just to talk.

"Remi's working. Most of the time, he works from home now, and always he is on the phone. He has an office in the tower and a lab in the basement."

"A lab?"

"Science is his first love. I'm his second. If you ask him, he'll say otherwise, but I know the truth."

Celine seemed okay with that, but Rhys suspected she was wrong. Remi had upended his whole life to care for her. She definitely came first in his eyes.

"He studies genetics?"

"Yes, genetic engineering. Biotronix has been at the forefront of genetic research for fifty years. Did you know Remi took over the company from his father?"

"I read it on the internet."

"So did I. Remi doesn't much talk about him. They... how do you say it? Headed butts?"

Rhys swallowed a laugh. "Butted heads."

"*Oui*, that." The *crunch* of wheels on gravel made them both snap their heads around. "Ah, they are here."

"Huh? But the airport's an hour's drive."

"*Non, non*, there's a private airfield ten minutes away."

Rhys practically ran to the front door and wrenched it open before the driver had a chance to knock. Coco's eyes went wide, and then she threw herself into Rhys's arms.

"I missed you," she sniffed, burying her face against his shoulder.

"Missed you too, beautiful."

"It's a castle. A real castle." Coco stepped back to look around the hallway, and when her gaze settled on Celine, all the colour drained out of her face. "*What?*" she whispered.

"Coco, meet Celine Klein. She was once known as Cambria."

"But... But... But Cambria *died*."

"She did. Now do you see why I wanted to speak to you in person?"

"The trees...? The legend...?"

"Yes."

Rhys took Coco's weight as she sagged against him, holding on until Celine leapt forward to help him carry her over to a red velvet loveseat in one corner. There were random chairs everywhere in this place, and he had to be grateful for that.

"Should I fetch Remi?" Celine asked.

"I think she's okay. Coco?"

Her eyes flickered open. "What about me?" she whispered. "Did I die too?"

All he could do was nod, and Coco dissolved into tears. Thank goodness they hadn't done this over the phone. Celine squashed onto the seat beside her and wrapped her up in a hug, two ghosts come to life. Nothing in this world made sense anymore, and Rhys had no option but to go with the flow. At least he no longer had to bear the burden of Coco's secret alone.

"She isn't crying for the person she is now," Celine explained. "She's crying for the person she once was. I did it too."

"What can I do to help?"

"Only time can truly heal, but you can create new memories to replace the ones she lost."

And he would. For as long as Coco would let him, he'd do exactly that. Rhys knelt beside her and squeezed her hand. Her slender fingers were cool to the touch, and he kissed her knuckles, trying to offer a little more comfort.

"H-h-how do you cope?" Coco blurted to Celine. "How do you deal with the fact that you died?"

"I won't lie and say it's easy. Most people would see a second chance at life as a blessing, but they don't realise it's also a curse. Just try to focus on the good things. I have Remi, and you have Rhys."

Coco looked down at him, and he used his free hand to wipe away her tears.

"Do I?" she asked. "Do I have you?"

"Always. You'll always have me."

"Why don't you show Coco the cottage?" Celine suggested. "Take a walk around the grounds, and then we can meet for dinner? There's still so much we need to talk about, but she looks tired."

"I didn't sleep much last night," she admitted, yawning. "Or any of the other nights you weren't there."

Rhys pressed a kiss to Coco's forehead as he helped her to her feet. "Celine's right; you should get some rest."

They still had a long evening of questions ahead of them with little prospect of getting the answers Coco needed.

"This place came out of a fairy tale," Coco whispered as they headed towards the dining room. Or at least, Rhys hoped they were going in that direction.

"Do you remember any fairy tales?"

"I've been listening to the *Grimm* podcast in between sleeps."

"Well, this place is an improvement on Cardon Street, that's for sure."

Remi showed up for dinner, and this time, he sat opposite Coco rather than at the head of the table. Out of curiosity or etiquette? Rhys had no idea of the rules.

"Do you feel better now?" Celine asked Coco.

"I got an hour of sleep. The cottage is beautiful. And so peaceful after the house in Uxbridge."

"If you don't like any of the furniture, we can change it."

How long was she planning for them to stay?

"No, it's perfect. Thank you for letting us borrow it."

"*Pas de problème.*" Celine waved a hand. "If I'm honest, it's a relief to talk to someone who isn't being paid to be here. And also someone like me. Remi's wonderful, but at times, it's…difficult."

"At least you know your past."

"Not quite. Wait—Rhys didn't tell you?"

Coco turned to him and narrowed her eyes. "Tell me what?"

"*Je suis désolé*! Forget I mentioned anything."

"Tell me *what*?"

Uh-oh. Now they had shrill, and that had never been a good sign with Stacey.

While Rhys froze, Remi did the honours. "I've studied Celine extensively over the years. The trees rebuilt Cambria's body perfectly, and her DNA is an exact blueprint of who she was before. But she's not the same person."

"What? I don't understand."

He laid it out—the details of the legend, the lunar cycle, the fact that when Coco was reborn, she might very well have been assigned somebody else's soul. The different kinds of memories. The way she relived her death in her dreams. Thankfully, the staff had left the room, but the food went cold on the table. And Coco turned deathly pale again.

"So you're saying I could be two people now? A mess of insides and outsides?"

"Not a mess. Just different to the person you were before."

"How do I find out? How the hell do I find out?"

"Does it matter?"

"Yes!"

"Sometimes, it's easier to just live in the moment," Celine said. "Grab your new life with both hands and make the best of it."

Remi chipped in again. "Even if you have the same soul, you won't be exactly the same person. Think nature versus nurture—your lived experiences shape you into the person you become, and all those have been lost."

Coco closed her eyes. Sighed. "But if what you say about my nightmares is right, then I was murdered, and I don't even know if the guy was caught."

"They never caught the man who mugged me either, did they, Remi?"

"Sadly not, *chérie*."

Remi's words said one thing, but his eyes said another. His expression was a challenge in itself. *Dare you to suggest otherwise.* Did money also buy revenge?

"What if the person who killed me kills someone else?" Coco asked. "How can I get on with my life if they're still walking free?"

Rhys tried to soothe her. "I'm sure the police are investigating."

"But what if they're not? What if my body was never even found? It could be rotting in a swamp somewhere."

"It's not."

Now she turned on him. "And how do you know that?"

Ah, shit. "We may have found a clue as to where you came from."

"Where? Tell me."

"It's in hand," Remi told her. "I instructed a private investigator to look into the matter yesterday."

"That's not a proper answer."

Remi looked as if he regretted sending the plane, and Rhys was having second thoughts too.

"It's a sensitive issue."

Celine folded her arms. "If you know something, you should tell her. It's not fair to keep her in the dark."

Oh, brilliant. Now they were getting tag-teamed by both women. Remi raised his eyes heavenwards and sighed.

"The decision is Rhys's to make."

Gee, thanks. But Celine was right—Coco deserved to know the truth, no matter how unpalatable it might be.

"The way the trees seem to work is that you have to feed in a DNA sample for them to use as a template. And the only thing fed to the trees in the weeks before you appeared was a certain brand of plant food, ergo..."

Ergo? Now Rhys sounded like a pompous ass. This damn castle was rubbing off on him.

"Plant food? You're saying I got made into *plant food*?"

"Uh, it seems to be the most likely possibility at the moment."

Coco fell silent, biting her lip. Fighting away tears? Celine shoved her chair back and ran to Coco's side, something Rhys had to be thankful for because he didn't know a whole lot about comforting emotional women. Or tact, it seemed.

"Is there any wine?" Coco asked. "I think I need wine."

In a heartbeat, Remi shoved a full bottle of red and an empty glass in Coco's direction, but she ignored the glass and drank from the bottle instead. Remi sucked in a breath but didn't say anything. If Rhys had to hazard a guess, he'd say that the wine with its posh gold label probably cost more than he earned in a month.

"Plant food," Coco muttered. "My whole damn life is a nightmare."

"Remi can help with the nightmares," Celine said, doing her best to sound upbeat. "Mine are almost gone now."

"How?"

"He runs a pharmaceutical company."

"You mean pills? I tried sleeping pills already. They only made things worse."

"The same happened with Celine at first," Remi said.

"But I created a protocol that alters her brain activity overnight. The dreams still come occasionally, but when they do, they're not as intense. I'd have to adjust the treatment for you—it took me six months to optimise Celine's—but even a low dosage should help."

That alone made the trip to France worth it. Without sleep, it was difficult for Coco to think rationally, which was far from ideal in the present circumstances. Plus Rhys was exhausted from monitoring her all night.

"I'll try anything," she said.

"Then I'll give you some medication to try after dinner. Please, eat. Don't let the person who killed you ruin your new life as well as your old one."

CHAPTER 24
RHYS

Coco gripped Rhys's hand as they walked to the cottage. A full moon shone from the cloudless sky, and the dim light cast eerie shadows on the ground. Was that the sound of footsteps behind them? Rhys glanced back, but they were alone on the path. Being honest, he found the castle grounds a bit creepy at night—earlier, he could have sworn he heard a baby crying somewhere—but he also knew the guards worked around the clock to keep the place secure. And he hadn't seen any of the ghosts Chanté had mentioned.

The cottage opened with a keypad, six digits, and they stepped into the hallway. Thick stone walls kept the place cool even on a warm September evening. In actual fact, "cottage" was something of a misnomer—the guest house was bigger than the entire house on Cardon Street, bigger than anywhere Rhys had ever lived. Two spacious bedrooms, two bathrooms, a living room, a full-sized kitchen, a separate dining room, even a small study... It would make a generous family home but was still cosy enough to be comfortable, not like the vast palace next door.

Coco nodded towards the study as Rhys checked the front door was locked.

"You can work in peace now. As long as there's Wi-Fi. Is there Wi-Fi?"

"Yes, and it's fast. You can have your own bedroom if you want."

"What if I don't want?"

Thank goodness. "Sharing works too. Are you feeling sleepy yet?"

"Not really. No more than usual."

Remi had given her three pills just before they left the castle, and she'd washed them down with more wine. Probably not the best idea, but Rhys hadn't been stupid enough to point that out.

"Maybe it would be sensible to go to bed before whatever was in that concoction Remi gave you takes effect?"

"I've got a better plan."

Uh-oh. "What plan?"

Coco curled her fingers into Rhys's shirt and pulled his mouth down onto hers. Okay, perhaps that wasn't so awful. And what was stopping them from being together now? Even if Remi's investigator found out who Coco had once been, she couldn't go back to her old life. Rhys was no saint, either. Coco tasted of good wine and the chocolate tart they'd had for dessert—delicious and moreish. He wrapped his arms around her waist and kissed her breathless.

"Celine said I should grab my new life with both hands," she gasped when they came up for air. "So..."

"No complaints from me."

Although in hindsight, their make-out session on the couch wasn't the best idea. Coco passed out in his arms with a smile on her face, and although he was happy that she was happy, how the hell was he meant to get her upstairs? Hauling her by her armpits seemed decidedly unromantic, plus he'd probably do his back in. In the end, he compromised by fetching a quilt from the spare bedroom and tucking it around her where she lay. He could set up his laptop in the study and monitor her while he caught up on work. Apps didn't write themselves.

That was Rhys's plan, anyway, but he quickly got distracted by the internet. Eastlake Horticultural was headquartered in Las Vegas, Nevada, according to Google, and had a manufacturing plant on the outskirts of the city plus another near Fernley in the north-west of the state. Had Coco come from Sin City? That seemed odd—she'd drowned, and wasn't the whole area basically desert?

Hmm, there were actually a surprising number of rivers in northern Nevada. And streams, and lakes. So much for narrowing down the location of her death. Rhys searched for meat processing plants, and there were a good number of those too. Perhaps if he cross-referenced...

But how would a dead body get processed like a side of beef? Wouldn't an employee, you know, say something? Or call the police? Or was the whole process automated? Wonderful, googling the inner workings of a slaughter-house was the perfect thing to be doing at one o'clock in the morning. At this rate, Rhys would be having nightmares too. Twenty minutes later, he fell into a rabbit warren of an animal rights website, and the videos...ugh. Tomorrow, he'd turn vegetarian.

Would it be worth emailing the animal rights group with a few questions? They'd recently managed to get a slaughterhouse in Fallon closed down after one of their members worked undercover there. If management had been merrily overlooking health violations left, right, and centre, maybe one or two of the staff might have been willing to go a little further in terms of illegalities?

The contact form on the website was broken, but the organisation did have an active Twitter account. Rhys clicked to send a message. Should he, shouldn't he...?

Then a different message caught his eye. One that had arrived weeks ago, soon after he and Coco first met. A warning to "delete your account and stop digging up the past."

The past.

The writer never had replied to Rhys's message asking for more information, and his finger trembled as he clicked onto the user's profile. The guy was a youth football coach from Lark's River, Nevada, his dogs were called Lucky and Chance, love was always the answer, and Go Cardinals! Rhys was still stuck on the "Lark's River" part. Was that anywhere near Fernley? A quick search told him that it was, and what's more, the town seemed to have grown up around the Larkspur Reservoir. Either that or the reservoir had been created for the town—did it really matter? Either way, there was a bloody great lake nearby.

Rhys held his breath as he typed in the next phrase: "Lark's River drowning."

And there she was.

Holy fuck.

CHAPTER 25

RHYS

Would it be rude to wake Remi in the middle of the night? He'd given Rhys his number "for emergencies," but did this count? It wasn't exactly life and death, more...a miscarriage of justice. Rhys paced the study, pausing to watch Coco breathing steadily on the sofa. Except her name wasn't Coco, was it? It was Jocelyn. Every so often, her face screwed up as she fidgeted, but at least she hadn't woken screaming yet. Remi's pills were definitely an improvement on the remedies they'd tried so far.

Perhaps a text message would be sensible? That way, if Remi was awake, he could answer, but Rhys wouldn't risk disturbing him.

Rhys: I found Coco's old identity. Not sure what to do now.

Her *old* identity. The face matched, but did the soul? He did some frantic calculations. Coco had been reborn on the twenty-sixth of June, and according to Remi, the incubation process for Celine had taken around two weeks. Jocelyn Bordeaux's body had been found on the twenty-first of May this year, three days after she'd last been seen. So it all depended on whether souls were assigned at the start of the rebuilding process or the end, and that was one thing they didn't know.

Rhys's phone buzzed.

Remi: Is this a joke?

Oh, please.

Rhys: As if I'd joke about something like that.

He attached the news article from the *Daily Lark* that he'd just read, the one that had sent chills through him.

Yesterday morning, a local fisherman spotted the body of Jocelyn Bordeaux in Larkspur Lake, bringing the three-day search by police and volunteers to a devastating end. Jocelyn was first reported missing by her sister, Rochelle, after she failed to return from a walk to "think about things."

Rochelle is said to be distraught by the discovery, and the girls' mother has asked that the family's privacy be respected at this difficult time.

Of course, it wasn't only Jocelyn's life that ended in this tragedy, but that of her unborn child as well. A friend who wishes to remain anonymous reports that Jocelyn was nervous about impending motherhood. "She wasn't looking forward to the birth of her baby," the source said. "She was worried about the future." A neighbour also raised concerns over Jocelyn's state of mind, saying that she'd grown more withdrawn in recent months.

Coco had been pregnant. The news came out of nowhere and hit Rhys like a right hook, leaving him reeling. Of all the things he'd considered, that hadn't even entered his mind. Who had the baby's father been? There was no mention of him in the article. The accompanying picture of Coco with her sister had clearly been taken in happier times. They were sitting in a rowing boat, possibly even on the lake where she'd died, laughing at something off camera.

Rhys's phone vibrated.

Remi: I'm coming over.

He must have run because there was a soft knock at the door thirty seconds later. Thankfully, Coco didn't stir.

"None of the beds were good enough?" Remi whispered. He'd thrown a dressing gown over a pair of silk pyjamas, neither of which matched the Nike trainers on his feet.

"She fell asleep there, and I didn't fancy my chances carrying her up the stairs. We'll have to talk in the study."

"How did you find her identity?"

Voice low, Rhys gave Remi a brief précis of the initial search for Coco's family and the message he'd at first written off as a crank.

"I guess we don't need your investigator after all."

"Are you sure? If Coco's body was found by a fisherman and reported to the police, how did it end up in a slaughterhouse?"

Ah. Shit. "I...don't know?"

"So perhaps we'll let the investigators do their job?"

"Uh, yeah. I mean, thanks. But how am I meant to explain this to Coco?" Rhys jabbed the screen with a finger. "She's already freaked out enough by her own death. And now there's a baby?"

"Might I suggest wording things very carefully?"

"Maybe I could just not tell her at all?"

"You may be willing to risk Coco's wrath by keeping secrets, but I'd rather avoid Celine's."

"So you think I *should* tell her?"

"I think if she finds out later that you kept this from her, that'll hurt her more than if you told her the truth in the first place."

"I suppose," Rhys said, but deep down, he knew Remi was right. Coco would want to know. However bad the story might be, she'd be furious if he kept her in the dark.

"Did they catch the person who killed Jocelyn?"

"I haven't got as far as looking yet."

No, Rhys had been too busy freaking out about the whole Lark's River discovery. But now he searched again and found another article dated two months later.

The inquiry into the tragic death of local woman Jocelyn Bordeaux was today concluded when the coroner determined her drowning in the unpredictable waters of Larkspur Lake to be an accident.

Despite the ruling, some locals believe her death was more likely to have been caused by suicide. Wade Gibbons, who lives near the Bordeaux house, tells us that the waters are shallow in the area of the lake where her body was found. "If she wanted to live, then she coulda turned around and walked right out. Ain't nothing that woulda stopped her," Mr. Gibbons said. "That girl hadn't been right in the head for months. She needed professional help."

The sheriff's office has refused to comment, other than to say the case is now closed.

Ms. Bordeaux was buried in a family ceremony at the end of May, and a memorial service will be held at Our Lady of Peace Chapel on Sunday at three o'clock. A request has been made for donations to the National Alliance for Mental Illness in lieu of flowers.

. . .

Rhys was beginning to fear that he'd bitten off more than he could chew. Jocelyn Bordeaux hadn't been suicidal, he knew that much, but if Coco's mental state had been fragile before, finding out the truth about her death could be devastating. The only people who'd shown any inclination to help were a mercurial billionaire and his once-dead wife, and Rhys wasn't sure quite how far that help would go. Would the Kleins kick them out if things got difficult?

And there was another problem, a more personal one—what if Coco's heart still belonged to another man?

"*Merde*," Remi cursed under his breath. "They wrote her murder off as an accident?"

"Seems that way." There was a killer walking around in Lark's River, living their life while Coco had lost hers. "Do you think there's any way we could convince them to reopen the case?"

"Not without new evidence."

"Well, we can hardly have Coco tell the cops what really happened."

"Especially because if she shows up, there will have been no murder in the first place."

Rhys leaned back in the leather swivel chair and sighed. "Why didn't I just leave the past the hell alone?"

"That's a question I've asked myself many times."

"You didn't know what you were getting into with the trees."

"Neither did you when you promised Coco that you'd look into her origins. At least you were honourable enough to keep your word."

There was a lot to be said for dishonour. And possibly lying too.

"That still leaves the question of how I break the news to Coco."

"I'd suggest keeping a box of tissues to hand. Celine cried constantly in the beginning."

"Tissues. Got it."

"And perhaps I should speak with Celine first? That way, she can help with the aftermath. One of her strengths is that she's an excellent listener, credit where credit's due. Cambria tended to focus on offering practical assistance rather than hugs."

"I'd appreciate that. It's the baby that worries me. How's Coco going to react when she finds out about the baby?"

"What baby?" she whispered from the doorway.

Oh, fuck.

Rhys looked at Remi, and Remi stared back, wide-eyed.

"I think Coco's dosage might need adjusting," he said.

No bloody kidding.

"What baby?" Coco asked again. "And what's Remi doing here at this time of night?"

Probably regretting ever calling Rhys in the first place. If he'd just ignored the note attached to the flowers, Rhys would have given up and gone back to England after a few days. Guilt hit like an intercity train. Rhys had upended not only his own life but the Kleins' too. Right now, he should have been sitting in a crappy bedsit writing code while Coco sweated her way through yet another nightmare, all of which would have been far preferable to the situation he found himself in at Le Château de Villance.

"Uh, while you were sleeping, I ran a couple of internet searches, and I kind of stumbled across a picture of you."

"A picture? From those posters we put up?"

"No, from your previous life."

"*What?*"

"I'm sure it's you. The timeline fits, and you used to live in America, and you drowned, and…"

"What baby?"

Rhys opened and closed his mouth like the goldfish swimming in the tank on his desk, but no words came out.

"Perhaps you should sit down," Remi suggested.

"Just tell me."

With a dead woman as his witness, Rhys was never house-sitting again. "You were pregnant when you died."

At least Rhys was close enough to catch Coco when she collapsed. With Remi's help, he got her back onto the sofa, but that was only the start. Next, they had to unravel the life and death of Jocelyn Bordeaux. And Rhys had a feeling that the twisted tale was just beginning.

CHAPTER 26

RHYS

Jocelyn Bordeaux had been popular in high school, a member of the photography club as well as a keen horse rider. She'd worked at a ranch on the weekends, helping to look after the animals, and in the evenings she'd been a leading lady in the Lark's River community theatre group. After she graduated from the architecture program at Western Nevada College in Carson City, she'd spent three years working at 4D Associates, an architecture firm near Reno. Either her Facebook posts had tailed off in the months before she died, or she'd worked out how to use the privacy settings, because there wasn't a single mention of the baby or any boyfriend either.

"I don't understand," Coco said for the hundredth time. "Why didn't I say anything about being pregnant? It must have been such a huge event in my life, and yet there's nothing. *Nothing*. And who was the father?"

She'd spent most of the night and the whole of the morning searching for her former self on the internet. On the two occasions Rhys had suggested she might want to take a break, she'd ignored him and snapped that she was "fine" respectively. The three mugs of coffee Celine had brought her sat cold at her elbow, as did the plate of croissants and the poached eggs on toast.

"Remi has investigators trying to find out about your past," Celine reminded her.

"But they can only look at facts. How can they tell if I'm still me? You know, inside?"

Celine didn't have an answer for that.

"I'm sure they're very good at what they do," Rhys tried. "I can't see Remi hiring a bunch of cowboys."

Nothing.

Click, click, click.

It was painful to watch as Coco devoured every article she could find, rereading the ones she thought were important. Occasionally, a tear would trickle down her cheek and Celine would hand her a tissue. Rhys stayed too, checking out the links on his phone as he puzzled over the mystery. Had Jocelyn Bordeaux got herself into some sort of trouble? Or was it merely bad luck that she'd gone for a walk and never come back? And how the hell had she gotten into the plant food? According to a note from Rochelle Bordeaux on Jocelyn's Facebook page, Jocelyn had been buried in the church cemetery. Unless the casket was empty, of course, but how would they find out? They could hardly request an exhumation.

Outside, night fell, and Celine began to fidget. Rhys couldn't blame her. His own arse cheeks had gone numb hours ago.

"Sweetheart, you need to get some food and some rest."

Coco dragged her eyes away from the screen for a brief second. "Are you crazy? How can I eat? I feel sick."

Click, click, click.

"The internet will still be here tomorrow."

"That...that *executioner* is still walking around free." She rubbed her face. "My head hurts."

"It's probably eye strain."

"Why don't you just take a tiny break?" Celine suggested. "We can walk over to the stables and see my horse. At least we know you like horses now."

Coco hesitated for a moment, and Rhys thought she was going to refuse, but then she nodded.

"Maybe fresh air would help." She tried to stand. "My legs have gone weird."

"That's normal when you've been sitting for seventeen hours straight."

"Are you sure?"

"It used to happen to me when I started building apps." In the end, Rhys had set a timer to remind himself to get up and move around every thirty minutes. "Here, take my arm."

Celine's suggestion of visiting the stables turned out to be a good one. Coco seemed to know instinctively how to handle the horse, and Rhys kept well out of the way as the girls brushed its fur and combed its hair. *Her* hair. Apparently, the huge white beast was female. It had a little friend too—a Shetland pony that was as wide as it was high. The Arabian was called Azizah, which meant "beloved one," and the Shetland had the unfortunate name of Al Capony.

"Remi bought him for our first Valentine's Day together," Celine explained.

"That was very thoughtful."

Celine giggled. "Not really. He'd travelled to England on business, and suddenly he remembered the date and realised he should buy a gift. It was late, and his business associate mentioned that his wife was happy with anything horsey, so Remi sort of...panicked?"

"And bought a tiny pony?"

"We were still getting to know each other, but he knew I liked animals." Another giggle. "Remi walked Cappy right into the house, and he pooped in the living room."

Coco smiled, just a tiny twitch of the lips, but it was there. *Thank goodness.*

"Don't get any ideas," Rhys warned her. "We don't have a paddock."

Celine waved a hand. "We have plenty of paddocks. Do you want to try riding Azizah tomorrow?"

Coco nodded, and Rhys breathed a sigh of relief. If the two women were outside, then Coco couldn't drive herself crazy staring at a computer screen. The thought gave him hope—maybe in time, they *could* get through this darkness and find the light.

Coco barely said a word as Rhys led her up the stairs in the cottage. There was no repeat of last night's kiss, no groping each other on the sofa. But at least she was in bed. Remi had given her different pills tonight, and Rhys thought she might protest about taking them, but she'd merely nodded and swallowed them down with half a glass of Chablis. Whatever they contained, it was heavy stuff because she was sleeping soundly by the time he'd finished brushing his teeth.

Rhys turned out the light and climbed into bed beside her, and tonight, it was he who couldn't sleep. Things had gone so, so wrong. *Would* they ever find their way back from this? Watching Remi and Celine offered another ray of hope, although Remi's foray into the coco du ciel trees' warped world had been planned, even if the outcome had been somewhat unexpected.

Rhys had fallen into this mess due to pure dumb luck.

Good luck or bad luck? The jury was still out on that. When things were good with Coco, they were amazing, but when they were bad? Oh, man… He wouldn't even wish that on Gary.

But giving up on her wasn't an option. Coco was his now, for better or for worse.

What time was it?

The sky was still dark when Coco woke Rhys with an eerie wail. His first thought? *Not again.* His second thought? *Fuck.* Her hand slammed into his gut as she thrashed away, and he doubled over in pain. While he tried to snatch a breath, she caught him under the jaw with her other fist, sending shooting pains up the side of his skull. He dove off the side of the bed as his self-preservation instincts kicked in.

What the hell was he meant to do? She was flailing like a madwoman, and even the *crack* of her arm hitting the iron bedstead didn't wake her. He tried to catch her hands, but all he got for his trouble was a black eye.

Then she began to retch, gulping in air, clawing at the mattress as she struggled to breathe.

"Coco! Wake up!"

The only response was the agonising sound of a woman

dying all over again. This was worse than the episode with the Zopiclone.

Then she went limp. Rhys poked her, shook her, but there was no reaction. Was she still breathing? If she was, the rise and fall of her chest was too shallow for Rhys to tell. He searched for a pulse and found a frantic fluttering. What did that mean?

He grabbed his phone and dialled Remi's number. Should he call an ambulance instead? What was the emergency number in France?

"It's four o'clock in the morning." Remi sounded groggy and more than a tiny bit pissed off.

"Coco's gone weird."

"Weird in what way?"

"All floppy, and she might not be breathing."

The grogginess disappeared. "I'm on my way."

Rhys didn't wait for Remi to arrive. A combination of desperation and fear helped him to drag Coco down the stairs and out the front door into the garden. Gravel from the path shredded his bare feet, but he hardly noticed. Still Coco didn't stir.

A minute later, Remi skidded to a halt beside them in a golf cart. Did he even play golf? Or was this just a billionaire's daily transport?

"What happened?"

"She had another nightmare, and I can't wake her up."

Remi knelt down and checked her vital signs himself. Did he have any kind of medical training? At least he looked as if he knew what he was doing.

"She *is* breathing, but her pulse is fast. Let's take her to the château."

"Not the hospital?"

"Do *you* want to answer those questions? Because I

don't. If necessary, I can get a doctor to come here, but at the moment, we don't need that."

"Are you sure?"

"Celine reacted this way several times while I was adjusting her medication." Remi scooped Coco up and laid her across the back seat of the golf cart. "The human body is more resilient than we think."

In the château, Remi stopped halfway along the corridor to the kitchen and opened a panel in the wall that Rhys had never noticed before. A second elevator? He expected to go up, but instead, they went down to the basement. Or was it a hospital? The white-walled room was set up with a railed bed and a bank of monitors.

"What is this place?"

"I installed the equipment so I could monitor Celine's sleep patterns."

Remi clipped something to Coco's finger, and her pulse scrolled across one of the screens, jagged and erratic. But it was there, and it was strong. Probably slower than Rhys's if he was honest. He gripped her other hand and whispered a prayer for her to wake up.

"Terrifying, isn't it?" Remi said.

"That's an understatement."

"Do you realise your nose is bleeding?"

"What? Is it?"

Remi passed him a tissue from the box on the night-stand, and sure enough, it came away bright red.

"Your eye is also bruised."

"She caught me with an elbow."

"An occupational hazard, no?"

"Yeah, this is my dream job."

There was only one chair in the room, and Remi slumped into it, so Rhys lay alongside Coco on the bed, hoping her subconscious would spare her from another nightmare. Remi was right—going to the hospital would be awkward, doubly so if Rhys had to explain a swollen nose as well. Together, they kept a vigil until Coco's eyes flickered open almost four hours later.

"Where am I?" She reached out and traced a fingertip across his cheek. "What happened to your eye?"

"At the château. You had another bad dream."

"Did I do that to your face?"

"It was an accident."

She sagged back against the pillow. "I'm so sorry." Her voice lowered to a whisper. "It's coming back now...worse than before."

"The dream?"

"Yes."

"In what way was it worse?" Remi asked.

"Longer. It was longer. He... I saw more of him than the other times. His arms...they were hairy."

"Light or dark hair?"

"Dark. Even underwater, I could see it. And he was wearing a watch. A fancy watch. And..." Her eyes widened. "He had writing on his skin."

"A tattoo?"

"I think so. Although you take notes on your hands, don't you?"

Remi shoved his ink-covered hands into his pockets. "Bad habit. Can you remember what it said?"

"I..." She screwed her eyes shut as she thought. "Not the words. But the writing was all curly. Like script."

"Why don't you try drawing what you saw? That worked for Celine when we needed to identify... Never mind."

Yes, Remi had definitely caught up with the man who

mugged his wife. Where was he now? In a shallow grave somewhere? Or had Remi made the death look like an accident?

"I guess I could have a go," Coco said.

"And you like to sketch," Rhys reminded her. "Remember all those doodles of buildings? Maybe there's something of your old self left."

She perked up a little. "Do you think? What if it's just a coincidence?"

"It would be a pretty big coincidence."

Remi headed for the door. "I'll find a pencil and paper."

Could Jocelyn the architect really be lurking inside Coco's subconscious? Only time would tell.

Five minutes later, Remi came back with a sketch pad and a whole box of pencils, plus a sharpener, an eraser, and a selection of pastels.

"Celine likes to draw too," he said as he handed them over.

Coco turned to a blank page and scratched a few lines with the pencil. Rubbed them out. Tried again. Wadded up the paper, threw it across the room, and huffed.

"Everything's fuzzy."

"Close your eyes for a moment," Remi suggested. "Relax."

She glared at him. "Relax? Seriously?"

"Let's settle for 'cogitate.'"

"I don't even know what that means."

Why was she looking at Rhys? He had no idea either.

"It means 'think,'" Remi said, rolling his eyes.

"We didn't all go to Harvard."

But Coco thought, and this time, she drew an actual arm. She was right—it belonged to either a man or a very butch woman. There were muscles, and the attached hand wasn't wrinkled, exactly, but there were definite age lines.

"Not bad," Remi murmured.

Coco added a watch, an old-fashioned one with a numbered face. To Rhys, it looked expensive and boring—if you had that much money, why not get a smartwatch?—but Remi leaned forward and peered more closely at the paper.

"Are you sure about the shape of that watch hand?" he asked. "Or did the pencil slip?"

"The second hand? It seemed wavy, but maybe the water distorted it?"

"And what about that open mechanism at the top?"

"All the little cogs? That's how it looked. Is that normal? I've never seen a watch like that before."

"I have. It's a Blancpain Villeret Carrousel. If what you've drawn is accurate, it could narrow down the search considerably. Few men can afford a hundred-thousand-euro watch, and even fewer would wear it to push a woman into a lake."

Rhys glanced at his own twenty-quid Casio. "What kind of idiot would pay a hundred thousand euros for a watch?" Then he realised who was standing next to him. "Ah, right. Sorry."

"I don't wear mine anymore. Not since a Rolex and a pair of diamond earrings cost Cambria her life."

Coco closed her hand over Remi's. "I'm so sorry you lost her that way."

"Money can't buy happiness. Life is a series of lessons; I learned that the hard way." Remi stroked a thumb over Coco's knuckles. "But if we're lucky, vanity will lead to your murderer's downfall."

"Life is a series of lessons..." Coco said, almost to

herself, then she snatched up the pencil and began scribbling frantically. "Life is...an experiment. All life is an experiment."

What was she talking about? "Huh?"

"The tattoo. I remember! 'All life is an experiment'—that's what it said."

She drew it out, five words on pale skin, the flowing script running along the man's forearm. If he wore short sleeves, he'd see it every time he checked his watch.

"'All life is an experiment. The more experiments you make the better,'" Remi said. "It's a quote by Ralph Waldo Emerson. If one venture fails, try a new one. Walk a different path. Judging by his watch, the man we're looking for had a number of successes."

"He picked a pretty daring experiment when he decided to try murder."

Remi nodded his agreement. "He did. But some experiments are doomed to fail from the start. Both the tattoo and the watch are distinctive, and we know the culprit was in Lark's River. It's only a matter of time before we catch him."

"But how do we convince the police to reopen the case without evidence?"

"An excellent question. Thankfully, finding answers has always been a strength of mine." Remi smiled down at Coco. "We'll get you justice. But first, let's get you some sleep."

CHAPTER 27

RHYS

Over the next two weeks, facts trickled in from Lark's River, but it was slow going because Remi had to withhold information from the investigators. Telling them that new leads came from the woman whose death they were looking into clearly wasn't an option, so he'd made up a tale about a reluctant witness, a friend of his who'd seen a man acting suspiciously by the lake and, when she later read the story of Jocelyn's death in the newspaper, began to wonder whether the two might be connected. Sixth sense had made the imaginary witness duck behind a bush when the man approached, and as he walked past, soaking wet and with his sleeves pushed up, she'd been close enough to notice his watch and tattoo.

"Do you think the investigators believed the story?" Rhys had asked.

"Probably not, but with the amount I'm paying them, they're not going to question it."

"I don't know how I'll ever afford to repay all the costs."

Remi waved a hand. "Forget about it. Your presence here is payment enough."

"What do you mean? We've done nothing but cause you problems from the moment we arrived. Celine's practically babysitting Coco."

"Exactly. I love Celine, make no mistake about that, but being the only person here she can truly talk to is…tiring. My work suffers. Having the two of you around takes some of the pressure off. Plus Celine is a caring soul. She's happiest when she has someone or something to coddle, and she's fond of Coco."

"Even so…"

"If I can't use my money to buy justice, then what's the point in having so much of it? Somebody needs to make the man who killed Jocelyn Bordeaux pay." Remi chuckled. "Bordeaux. I suppose there's a certain irony that she ended up in France."

And that was the end of the conversation. It seemed that Remi thought of Rhys and Coco as amusements for his wife, and if he was happy to provide room and board in return for dinner conversation and mediocre attempts to play tennis, then Rhys couldn't afford to turn the offer down. Plus they were in the best place for Coco. Once she'd recovered from the initial shock of the Lark's River revelations, she'd settled into a grudging acceptance of her new life. Her internet searches had reduced to an hour or so in the evenings, and with further adjustments to her medication, she'd begun sleeping through the night. She even remembered how to horse ride, or at least her body did.

"Is there an update?" Celine asked over dinner.

They all knew there would be. The investigators—a small team in Lark's River and another in Las Vegas—were under orders to provide a report every day, no matter how brief.

"There is," Remi replied, as he did every time. "Some

good news, actually." Then he grimaced. "Okay, not *good* news, but progress."

"There's a suspect?"

"Not yet, but one of the investigators in Lark's River spoke to Rochelle Bordeaux today. A *female* investigator. Rochelle gave her a manicure."

Coco stiffened. She'd been worrying about her sister since she found out Rochelle existed. They used to share a house, a small duplex, and making the rent was most likely a stretch on a beautician's salary. The pair had moved in right after Jocelyn finished college. Rochelle didn't have a degree—she'd started training as a massage therapist right after she graduated high school before branching out into hair and nails. Neither of their parents lived in Lark's River —their father had hightailed it out of town when the girls were young, and their mother remarried and moved to Delaware when Rochelle turned sixteen, leaving the girls behind. According to the PI, that technically wasn't allowed in Nevada without a degree of emancipation, but the former Mrs. Bordeaux had gone anyway, and Jocelyn supported Rochelle until she finished high school and got a job of her own. Remi was hoping Rochelle would advertise for a roommate so he could have an undercover PI move in.

"What did she say?" Coco asked.

"Apparently, they bonded over a shared love of scented candles…" Remi rolled his eyes. "And Monica—the lead investigator—confessed that her sister had got involved with the wrong type of man last year and ended up pregnant. Rochelle opened up after that."

"She lied," Coco said. "To my sister."

"Sometimes it's necessary to bend the truth a little, and she said that Rochelle seemed keen to talk. Probably she doesn't have many people to listen."

Coco gave a quiet sniff. Everyone had taken to carrying tissues now—better to be safe than sorry—and Celine held one out.

"Th-thanks. I just hate the thought of hurting Rochelle more than she's been hurt already."

"Ultimately, we'll be helping her. And it was a useful chat. She believes Jocelyn was murdered, although the sheriff wouldn't listen to her."

"Why does she think that?"

"Firstly, because that lake isn't easy to fall into—the shoreline slopes gently, so Jocelyn couldn't have tumbled in accidentally. And perhaps more importantly, she said that her sister believed all life was sacred. She was terrified of becoming a mother, but she still did everything she could to make sure the baby had the best start—took vitamins, went to prenatal classes, read every book on parenting she could find."

"Then why did other people say I'd gone crazy?"

"I'm not sure 'crazy' is the right word. Rochelle said you'd changed. It started over a year ago. The two of you had always been close, but suddenly you wouldn't tell her where you were going in the evenings or who you were going with. You began staying out late, and she got worried."

"With good reason," Rhys said. After all, Jocelyn had ended up dead. But that was the wrong thing to say. Coco glared at him.

"Why would I have done that?"

"Because you had a secret boyfriend."

Coco gasped as the bottom dropped out of Rhys's world. He'd long suspected she hadn't been single, and she'd obviously been pregnant, but secretly, he'd hoped the baby was the result of a one-night stand. If she'd been involved with a man for over a year, that was considerably more serious.

"Are you sure? I mean, how did Rochelle know if I didn't tell her?"

"Because she followed you one evening and you got into his car."

"That could have been anyone. A friend, a colleague…"

"You kissed him, and it wasn't a peck on the cheek by all accounts."

"Well, who was he? What did he look like?"

"Rochelle only saw him in silhouette. The car was red, and…" Remi checked his phone. "Fancy-ass, probably cost an arm and a leg."

An expensive car that went with an obscenely pricey watch? Rhys saw from Coco's horrified expression that she'd had the same thought. Had Jocelyn been killed by her secret boyfriend, who was possibly the father of her baby too?

"Didn't…" The word came out as a croak, and Coco swallowed, then tried again. "Didn't Rochelle ask me about him?"

"Yes, and you had a huge fight. You told her to butt out, said that whoever you got involved with was your business and not hers, and then you stormed out and slammed the door. Rochelle was angry, not to mention hurt, and the two of you barely spoke for months."

"Then what?"

"Monica's nails were finished, and the next client had arrived already, so she had to leave. Rumour says the owner of the salon is a real dragon. But Monica's booked in for a pedicure at…" Remi consulted his phone again. "At eleven o'clock next Tuesday."

"Next Tuesday? That's almost a week away."

"It was the first available appointment."

"But—"

"Sometimes, the wheels of justice turn slowly, but they *are* turning."

"I was such a bitch to my sister. How could I have said those things? What was I thinking?"

Rhys caught Coco's hand as she paced the bedroom, but she shook him off and stopped in front of the window instead. He'd hoped that if he went to bed, she might join him, but so far, her pills hadn't taken effect and she was more upset than he'd ever seen her.

"You were under a lot of stress, sweetheart. You were pregnant, and it sounds like the baby's father wasn't giving you any support."

"But I had no right to treat Rochelle that way. How can I ever make it up to her?"

"You can't."

"But..."

"No buts. You don't exist anymore."

"Maybe I could write her a letter? You know, an apology?"

Bad, bad idea. "You died, remember?"

"But if I backdated it... I could tell her that I left it with someone else to mail after my...oh."

"Exactly. That would have meant you knew you were going to die, either by suicide or by another person's hand. And if you'd suspected you were in danger, you'd have contacted the police, not arranged for a posthumous apology. Plus you don't even know what Jocelyn's handwriting looks like."

"It might just come naturally."

"We're not even sure that you *are* Jocelyn."

"But I *have* to be. I like horses, and I draw buildings, and...and..."

"Thousands of women like horses. And yes, you draw buildings, but you also draw squirrels, cars, desert islands, flowers, people..."

She'd sketched Rhys the day before yesterday and then blushed when she caught him looking. He wasn't sure why —the picture was really good. Like, gallery-worthy.

"Did Jocelyn?"

"There were no drawings on her Instagram account." Just photos of Lark's River and a handful of herself with her sister. The posts had stopped over a year ago. "You might be a completely different person to the girl who fought with Rochelle."

"But how will I know for sure?"

Coco was starting to slur her words now, which under the circumstances was a good thing. They'd still done nothing more than make out, mainly because of the medication, but Rhys didn't mind waiting. Coco's health was more important. She fell asleep in his arms every night, and they were closer than they'd ever been. For now, that was enough.

"Give it time." This time when he took her hand, she sighed and slid under the quilt. "We'll find the answers eventually."

"Then I guess..." Coco covered her mouth as she yawned. "I guess I'll just have to be patient."

CHAPTER 28

RHYS

That was what Coco said, but it wasn't what she did.

The following Wednesday morning, Rhys woke up groggy. The sun was shining right in his face because he'd forgotten to close the curtains, and his limbs felt too heavy to drag out of bed so he could fix the problem. Why was his head full of cotton wool? He'd only drunk one glass of wine last night—he shouldn't have a hangover.

"Coco, you awake?"

No answer. And the bed felt strangely cold. He rolled over and found the other side empty, but the door to the en-suite bathroom was open. Was she downstairs? Rhys stilled to listen, but the cottage was silent apart from his breathing. Maybe she'd gone to see the horses? She'd taken to walking Cappy the pony like a big fluffy dog.

Then the hammering started.

"What on earth...?"

Rhys staggered out of bed, hung onto the door frame for a moment while he got his balance, then nearly fell down the stairs. Had he drunk a bottle of Remi's cognac and somehow forgotten about it?

When he yanked the front door open, he found Celine standing there in her riding gear.

"Where's Coco?" she asked, waving a piece of paper. "Is she here?"

"I thought she was with you."

"I haven't seen her today. And I found this note in Cappy's treat bucket." Celine thrust the paper at him. "Why is she sorry? What has she done?"

"I've got no idea."

But she'd been quiet for the last few days. Withdrawn. Miserable ever since the investigators had reported seeing Rochelle crying on the sofa during one of their evening checks. As yet, they didn't know what the problem was, so nobody had been able to fix it. Remi had offered to pay Rochelle's rent if they could find a way of funnelling the money to her anonymously. He'd made the suggestion to Rhys last night while Coco and Celine went to give the horses their supper, but neither man had been able to come up with a suitable plan at that hour. Remi had promised to work on it with his team.

But what was this note? Rhys unfolded the paper and began to read.

I need to start with an apology: I'm sorry. Sorry for turning your lives upside down, sorry I can't settle when you've all done your best to make me feel wanted, and sorry that I can't embrace the future without first putting the past to rest. Sorry that I can't pretend any longer. I've tried so hard to be happy as I am, but maybe that's not my destiny? Just know that I'm more grateful to the three of you than you'll ever believe, and Rhys, I love you. You

have the kindest soul. I only wish we could have met in another time and another place.
But for this life, please forget about me.
Jocelyn.

Coco loved him? No, not Coco. Jocelyn. She'd signed the note "Jocelyn." The flush of warmth in Rhys's chest quickly faded, replaced by a snake of dread that coiled around his guts. What the hell had she done? People who knew Jocelyn said she'd been suicidal, and although Coco had denied it, this note said otherwise. And the chances of forgetting about her were zero. Had she lost her mind in a different way this time?

"We need to find her."

"Remi can have the guards search the grounds."

He could, but there was no need.

A guard who'd worked the late shift reported that Coco had left via the main gate at ten o'clock last night, which he'd thought was kind of unusual, but he was paid to keep people out, not in, so he'd just waved her off as she climbed into a cab. She'd told him she planned to meet a friend in Villance for the late-night performance of the son et lumière at the fountains, and since Remi had recruited the guard from Poland in keeping with his "no local staff" policy, the chap didn't realise that the only show of the evening finished at eight thirty.

Further investigation revealed she'd also taken the credit card that Celine had lent her to do some online shopping, her fake passport complete with a bunch of realistic-looking visas because Remi's forger was nothing if not thorough, five thousand euros in cash that Remi kept in his desk drawer "for emergencies," plus a backpack with spare clothes. Oh, and Remi suspected she'd slipped last night's sleeping pills into Rhys's wine instead of swallowing them, which would explain why he felt so bloody awful this morning.

"I can't believe she did that," Rhys muttered, head in his hands as Remi paced the living room.

"At least she's still alive," Celine pointed out.

Remi paused for half a second. "*Fantastique.*"

Rhys wasn't sure whether to be relieved that Coco wasn't lying in a ditch somewhere or absolutely furious because she'd betrayed him, the man who she claimed to love, plus Remi and Celine, who were meant to be her friends. One thing was for sure—he felt absolutely mortified for bringing her into the Kleins' lives. All he wanted to do was slink off into the sunset, but that wouldn't fix the mess Coco had created.

"Maybe we should have taken her to a therapist?"

Remi huffed. "Or provided her with a padded cell and cut out the middleman."

"We can't just leave her to fend for herself. The trauma..."

"Of course we can't. Celine, she has your credit card. She used it to purchase a plane ticket. If she gets caught doing whatever it is she plans to do, then they could trace her back to Villance."

"I'm so sorry—" Rhys started.

"Those damn trees. In Brazil, the locals say the Mala Valley is cursed, and now I understand why." Remi pulled out his phone. "Claude, prepare the jet."

"The jet?"

"We all know where she's heading, don't we?"

Yes, they did. Coco, Jocelyn, whoever she was now—she was on her way to Lark's River, and she had a fourteen-hour head start.

COCO

"Ma'am, are you feeling okay?"

Coco—at least, that was the name on her passport—nodded and forced a smile for the flight attendant. The truth was, she didn't know how she felt. Scared, guilty, fatigued... As if she wanted to turn around at LAX and take a flight straight back to France. But she wouldn't be welcome there either, not anymore. She'd well and truly burned that bridge.

Another tear rolled down her cheek, and this time, she turned to face the window so the cabin crew wouldn't see her crying again. Crying for everything she'd lost twice over. But it wasn't only herself she had to think about. Jocelyn's past might have been destroyed, but Rochelle was suffering right now, and Coco was the only person who could make things right. There was a connection between them, an invisible thread reeling her in. She needed to apologise, to give Rochelle the money she'd taken from Remi, and then she needed to disappear.

Disappear where? She wasn't sure. Maybe she really would walk into Larkspur Lake this time. At the moment, she wasn't sure what the future held; she only knew that she had to stop Rochelle from crying over and over and over in her head, a movie that played on a loop. Did that happen to other people? Celine said that after she was reborn, she'd been a blank canvas, that she'd had an insatiable appetite to learn, but Coco just felt hollow inside. An empty vessel that only the past could fill. She'd tried to remember, to rewind back beyond that night in the greenhouse, beyond the moment in the darkness when she'd woken damp in the dirt, so confused and lost in a virtual jungle. But there was nothing. Only a vast, yawning hole.

And then she'd seen Rochelle, and in Rochelle's face, she'd seen her own.

Remi would never have let her go to Lark's River. Sure, he'd promised to help, and he'd kept that promise in his own way, but his way meant throwing money at the problem. Investigators and daily reports. He liked control. To be the king of his castle, and to keep that castle fortified so the outside world couldn't get in. Celine deserved more. A beautiful prison with horses and gardens and a tennis court was still a prison.

Rhys wouldn't have let Coco come to America either. From the moment they met, he'd cared for her and protected her, perhaps even loved her. She knew she loved him. But she didn't *deserve* him. He needed a partner, not an empty shell of a woman who'd left her previous life in ruins. What if she screwed up again? How could she learn from past mistakes if she couldn't remember them?

No, this was the best way. By giving up her own future, she'd free Rhys to thrive in his. He was smart, so smart. Coco, broken, messed-up Coco, would only have held him back if she'd stayed.

Damn these tears.

The plane landed at LAX, and Coco, Jocelyn, whoever she was, wandered the transit lounge aimlessly, waiting for the second leg of her flight to Reno. If that wasn't a metaphor for her life, then what was? Surrounded by people yet alone, dependent on others for the next step of her journey. She used some of the time to research bus routes. It wasn't as if she could hire a car—she didn't have a fake driver's licence, and she had no idea if she even knew how to drive. If she'd stayed in Villance, would she have turned into Celine, destined to trundle around immaculate gravel paths in a golf cart for eternity?

Outside the Reno-Tahoe airport, she tossed the last remnants of her temporary life into a trash can—her smartphone, her passport, and Celine's credit card. When she was found, she didn't want to be carrying anything that could cause problems for Rhys or the Kleins. Jocelyn's problems were hers to fix and hers alone. Maybe Coco and Jocelyn were the same person, and maybe they weren't? Maybe the girl walking towards the bus needed a new name? Jojo? She laughed, perhaps slightly shrilly, and a businessman wheeling a suitcase gave her an odd look.

Look all you want. She'd borrowed one of Rhys's hoodies and chopped bangs into her hair before she left France—there wasn't much of her face visible to see.

The bus ride to Lark's River seemed to take forever. Stop, start, stop, start, stop, start... Exhaustion set in. Coco hadn't slept since she waved goodbye to the château—she hadn't dared—and although the sludgy feeling from the pills had faded, it had been replaced with a bone-weary tiredness that left her fidgeting to stay awake. *Just a little longer.* Once she'd spoken to Rochelle, her soul could rest, either temporarily or permanently. She'd leave that up to fate.

The stop nearest to Rochelle's duplex left Coco with a half-mile walk through the quiet neighbourhood. She'd hoped she might recognise the place, that visiting might dig up buried memories, but as she hurried past the houses like a bargain-basement wraith, there wasn't so much as a tingle of familiarity. She even managed to take a wrong turn at one point.

As she approached the house, she ducked into the service alley. Remi's surveillance team would be watching at the front—that's what their reports said—so she'd have to use the back door. But when she knocked softly and waited, there was no answer. Had Rochelle gone out? A dim glow came from inside the house, and fear began to gnaw at Coco's insides. There was a killer on the loose, after all, and Rochelle didn't go out in the evenings. She worked, she came home, she cooked dinner, and then she read a book or watched TV. And cried.

Coco tipped up the flowerpot to the left of the door without thinking about it. The husk of a plant had died long ago, but the silver key was still underneath. Wait. How did she know that? *Did* she know that? Or had it just been a lucky guess?

No matter, she didn't have time to waste. The key turned with a quiet *click*, and Coco crept inside. The house lay in silence. No TV, no radio, no running water. Just the faint tick of a clock somewhere and the squeak of a floor-board as Coco checked the place for her sister. She wasn't there. Hmm. So she *did* go out sometimes. That was a good thing, right? Or maybe not. Coco spotted a note stuck to the fridge, block letters picked out by a streetlight.

Lost Souls Support Group - Thurs 8 p.m. - my turn to take cake!!

Coco choked out a sob. That was Rochelle's idea of a social life? Grief therapy? Jocelyn had failed as a sister in every way possible. And she felt even worse when she went upstairs. Her old bedroom was empty, completely empty, while Rochelle's was filled with photos of the two of them —on the walls, the dressing table, a chest of drawers. One side of the room was filled with cardboard boxes, each of them labelled in black marker. *Joss's clothes. Joss's drawings. Joss's shoes. Joss's random stuff.* She'd kept everything. Coco picked up a framed photo from the nightstand and traced Jocelyn's smile.

"You were happy once."

And now? Now she was just lost.

CHAPTER 30

COCO

Coco was woken by screaming, and for once, it wasn't her own.

Her eyes flew open, and glass smashed when the precious photo of her old self slid off the bed and fell to the floor. But that wasn't the worst part.

Rochelle had come home.

She was pressed into the corner by the door, and when Coco sat up, Rochelle's hands flew in front of her face, defensive.

"K-k-keep away from me."

Oh, shit, shit, shit.

"Sorry! I'm so sorry! I can't even manage to apologise without messing it up."

Rochelle squeaked in fear as Coco reached for her bag, and when she pulled out the money, she lost her grip and five thousand euros flew into the air, floating down like confetti as Rochelle began hyperventilating.

"Dammit! I only meant to bring this and then leave. And say I was sorry. Twice. Now I'm sorry twice because I fell asleep in your room and…" She swiped at her eyes with a hand. "I should go."

Mess, mess, mess. Such a mess.

She got to her feet and headed for the door, but Rochelle screamed again. And what was that in her hand? Rochelle thrust it in Coco's direction, and an arc of blue light crackled between metal prongs. A stun gun?

"Don't come any closer! I'm calling the police."

"There's no need, I swear. I'm leaving right now."

"W-w-who are you?"

"Honestly, I don't even know anymore."

"Y-y-you died."

"Jocelyn died. And I might be her, but I might not. I'm just not sure."

"You're a ghost? Is this some kind of joke? Cosmic revenge because I always refused to believe in ghosts, but you thought they existed, and so now you've come back to haunt me? It's not funny, Joss. Not one bit."

"No, I'm real. Well, the outside part is. I got…rebuilt? Reborn?"

"Like a mutant science project? That's not even possible. I was the one who studied science, remember?"

"I don't remember. That's the whole problem."

"Coco!" The shout came from downstairs, then footsteps thundered towards them. Rhys appeared in the doorway, hands on his knees as he fought to catch his breath. "What the hell are you playing at?"

"Rhys? How did you get here?"

His mouth set into a thin line. "In an aeroplane, the same way you did. What, you thought we'd just let you go?"

"I…"

"Who exactly are you?" Rochelle waved the stun gun in

front of her as if it could create an invisible force field. "And how did you get into my house?"

"The back door was unlocked," Remi said from behind Rhys. Double oops. Celine was there too, staring wild-eyed.

Make that triple oops.

"I always lock the back door. *Always*."

"You hid a key," Coco said. "Anyone could have found it. Like the man who *killed me*."

Rochelle had been pale already, but now the last of the colour drained from her face, and the hand holding the stun gun began trembling. Good thing it wasn't a proper gun with bullets.

"I-I-I don't understand."

"Funny, you look like I felt when I first found out," Rhys said. "The story's a doozy."

"Who *are* you people?"

"I'm Coco's boyfriend."

"And I'm a geneticist," Remi said.

"Wait, wait. Who the heck is Coco?"

Rhys pointed, and Rochelle's forehead creased in confusion. "Then she's *not* Jocelyn?"

"The jury's still out on that. Truthfully, we have no idea."

"Then what...?"

"How open-minded are you?"

"What sort of a question is that? Why are you here? I should call the police." She fumbled in her pocket, and her phone flipped out and landed on the floor beside the money. "Shit."

"And what would you tell them?" Remi asked. "That your dead sister and her friends have come to visit? They won't send a squad car; they'll send a psychiatrist."

"What do you want from me?" Rochelle whispered.

"An excellent question. Coco, what on earth possessed you to come here?"

Remi's voice was tight. He was *pissed*. Which was quite understandable and not at all unexpected, but Coco had planned on him being pissed in France, not the US.

"Uh, I just wanted to apologise."

"With *my* money?"

"Sorry." Coco stooped and began scooping up the cash. "You can have it back, I guess."

"If you'd asked, I'd have given it to you."

"Oh."

"And what did you plan to do after you'd terrified your sister?"

"I hadn't really thought that far ahead."

"Vintage Jocelyn," Rochelle muttered. "You never did think things through. No wonder Mom always said I was the sensible one."

Coco burst into tears. Despite all the fear and the screaming and the questions, Rochelle had called her "you" and not "she."

"Y-y-you believe I'm your sister?"

"I don't know! I don't know what to think! I identified your body in the freaking *morgue*. But you look like Joss, and apart from your weird accent, you sound like Joss." Rochelle turned on Remi. "You said you were a geneticist—what the heck did you do? Clone her? Isn't that illegal?"

Remi sighed. "I suppose now that she's here, we'd better fill you in on the details. But understand that if any of this information goes beyond this house, then Coco will be in danger."

"Why do you call her Coco? And what kind of danger?"

"The name is part of the story. And if anyone else finds out she's alive, she'll be locked up in a lab for the rest of her unnatural life while scientists try to work out how on earth this miracle happened."

"But you know?"

"I know the bare bones. The exact details of the process are still hazy."

"She...she really is my sister?"

"I believe so."

Rochelle's tears fell harder, and she dropped the stun gun in favour of throwing her arms around Coco. Of all the things that might have happened, Coco hadn't expected this. She should have been wading into the damn lake by now, and instead, she had her sister back and possibly Rhys as well. Celine gave her a shaky smile. Remi scowled, but that was quite normal. Maybe in time he'd forgive her.

And Coco had one more thing too: hope.

"You said somebody killed you?" Rochelle asked. "I *told* the police it wasn't suicide, but they wouldn't listen."

"The only thing I remember about my old life is someone pushing me into the lake and holding me under the water."

"Who?"

"I don't know, not yet. But I want to find out. I *need* to find out."

"What can I do to help?"

Coco screwed up her face because that was something else she hadn't thought through. "Uh..."

"Let's talk," Remi said. "I hope nobody was planning on sleeping tonight."

Remi ordered a pizza, then complained bitterly because the dough was too thick and there wasn't enough cheese. It seemed that living without a personal chef was tough when you were a billionaire. Celine, on the other hand, was fascinated with dinner, the house, the street outside, everything. Probably when a girl didn't get out much, she was easily pleased.

Rhys, well, he kept one arm around Coco's shoulders while he ate pizza with his free hand. She wasn't sure whether he'd turned a little possessive or was just making sure she didn't run off again, but it felt…nice. More than nice. She'd forced herself to keep her distance from him for the last few weeks because if she'd given in to her emotions, then she'd never have been able to walk away from him, but now she didn't have to hold back anymore. It felt natural to lean her head on his shoulder as Remi talked—first about the greenhouse, then the coco du ciel trees, and then about their time in France. Coco noticed that he didn't mention Celine's origins. He'd clearly decided that some things were on a need-to-know basis and Rochelle didn't need to know. And no way was Coco going to breach his trust a second time. She was already on shaky ground.

"Trees? You're telling me that trees can bring the dead back to life?"

"Only very specific trees under very specific circumstances. And if that secret gets out, how long do you think the trees would last?"

"I'm not going to tell anyone. But how did Joss's DNA get into the trees?"

"There's an investigator working on that problem as we speak. You're certain Jocelyn's body was buried? It couldn't have, say, been switched?"

"She had an open casket. The mortician was one of those conveyor-belt places, but they did a real nice job."

"Then we'll let the investigator in Las Vegas carry on with what he does best." Remi cut his eyes in Coco's direction. "Don't you get any ideas about visiting the funeral home."

"I'll behave, I swear."

Coco had her sister. What more could she ask for? Of course, moving back to Lark's River was impossible, but just to be able to phone and email Rochelle would be a blessing. Her tiny circle of friends had increased by one tonight. Or was it morning now? Celine yawned, and Remi squeezed her hand.

"We should find somewhere to sleep. Tomorrow, we can talk about the next steps."

"I have a spare room," Rochelle offered. "But there's no furniture. You strike me as the type of people who'd want furniture."

The idea of Remi roughing it was laughable.

"We'll find a hotel."

"Uh, the only hotel in Lark's River got closed down by the health inspectors last week." Rochelle grimaced. "Bedbugs."

"Airbnb?" Rhys suggested.

Remi crinkled his nose. "Anything's better than bedbugs. What happened to the furniture?"

"I sold it to pay the rent last month."

"Would it not have been easier to get a roommate?"

"When I tried that, I woke up in the middle of the night and found the creep sniffing my feet."

Urgh. "Chelle, I'm so sorry I left you on your own."

"It wasn't your fault. And I guess... I guess I still blame myself for it."

"What? Why?"

"Because I should have stopped you from going to the lake that day. Handcuffed you to the radiator or something."

"You weren't to know. I mean, why would you have stopped me from going for a walk?"

"Joss, you never, ever went out for a walk. If you could have driven from the sidewalk to the front door, you would have. You loved to go horseback riding, but walking? No way. I had a feeling you were heading out to meet someone."

"Who?"

"I figured the baby's father, seeing as you'd lied to me."

"I'm so, so sorry."

"The past is the past." Rochelle sounded like Celine. "I thought you'd tell me in your own sweet time."

"What about anyone else? Did I have other friends I might have confided in?"

"I doubt it. You quit your job and shut yourself in your room for months. You even ate in there. Gummy bears dipped in Marmite, packages and packages of them."

"Are you serious? That's disgusting."

"Yes, but would you listen? Of course not. I tried phoning Mom, but she just said that as long as you were eating, you wouldn't starve, and then she hung up on me. She's only called once since the funeral. *Once.*"

Coco was kind of glad she didn't remember her mother now.

"What did I say about the baby?"

"Not much. You didn't even tell me you were pregnant until the bump got too big to hide. I offered to help, but you said the person who should be helping was the one person who didn't want to know."

"The baby's father?"

"You were scared. That's why you lashed out at me. But you were tough as well, and I couldn't understand why you'd take your own life. Plus you said more than once that life was precious."

"Thank you for believing in me."

"I still believe in you. I'll always believe in you. And I'll do whatever it takes to catch the man who tried to steal my sister from me."

CHAPTER 31

COCO

Remi being Remi, he opened the Airbnb website, filtered the properties within a twenty-mile radius, sorted them in order of cost, and five minutes later, they had themselves a mansion. It wasn't as lavish as the château—*nothing* was as lavish as the château—but the agent was a night owl and agreed to meet them with the key.

At two o'clock in the morning, she was brimming with curiosity, but Remi just ignored her questions in the way that only rich people could and offered a bonus if she could arrange to have groceries delivered. *Cha-ching.* Coco could practically see the dollar signs in the woman's eyes as she promised to shop for anything Remi wanted *personally.* Anything at all, any time.

She did have the sense to back out the door when Celine glowered at her, though.

What would the sleeping arrangements be? There were four huge bedrooms, and Coco would have understood perfectly if Rhys wanted to sleep alone after the way she'd betrayed him. But following a moment's hesitation at the top of the stairs, he held out a hand.

"You look exhausted."

Warmth flooded through her as she slipped her hand into his. Maybe, just maybe, they stood a chance?

"In every possible way." Coco was physically and mentally shattered. "But I can't sleep for long. I don't have any pills."

In France, Remi had constantly adjusted the dose depending on how she felt each morning. Every breakfast had turned into a question-and-answer session. He'd bring the pills to dinner and she'd wash them down with wine, wondering if tonight would be the night that the memories of drowning would finally disappear. So far, they'd always been there, lurking at the edge of her subconscious.

"He gave them to me. Not literally. I mean, I didn't swallow them. They're in my pocket."

"I'm really sorry I drugged you. If I'd thought there was another way…"

"Desperate people do desperate things. I'm only sorry I didn't realise how much you were hurting inside. How do you feel now that you've met Rochelle?"

"Better, I think? Relieved. And I'm more and more sure that I'm Jocelyn the whole way through. All those mannerisms Chelle said were so familiar, the way I felt at home in the house even if I don't remember it, the timeline… Plus Joss loved Marmite and I do too."

"With gummy bears?"

"*Not* with gummy bears. I was *so* messed up."

They reached the bedroom door, and Rhys took Coco's other hand in his. "Promise you'll talk to me in the future? Please? The thought of you running again…"

"I'll talk to you." It was hard, opening up. Yet another

thing she had in common with Jocelyn, according to Rochelle. But Coco understood now that she had to try. Jocelyn's secrets had hurt so many people, not least herself. "I'm still processing everything, you know? The baby… Is this grief? This weird, hollow feeling?"

"It might be. Grief…it can hit you in different ways. When my mum died, the emptiness was in my heart. Some days, it would take a moment after I woke up to remember she was gone, and then I'd get angry. Angry that I'd forgotten and angry at myself because I wasn't there at the end. Angry at the universe in general. I miss her smiles. I miss her hugs. I miss being able to pick up the phone and talk to her. Grief…it feels like nothing, and it feels like everything. If you let it, it'll eat at you from the inside out, and every time I felt those teeth, I'd look at my mum's picture on my phone and remind myself that she wouldn't want me to mope. And each day I kept busy, my chest grew just a tiny bit fuller."

"How long did it take?"

"A while. Everyone's different."

"I don't feel angry, more confused. Does that make sense? I never even met my baby, but I think…I think I loved him."

Rochelle said he would have been a boy. A baby boy. A sob welled up in Coco's throat, and at first she tried to swallow it down, but when Rhys squeezed her hands, she gave in and let the tears come.

"I'm s-s-so sorry."

"None of this is your fault, sweetheart. You're the victim."

Was he right? For weeks, she'd been trying to convince herself that she was the lucky one. How many other people got a second chance at life? But honestly, it felt more like a sick supernatural joke. It would have been easier if she'd simply stayed dead, but each time she had that thought, she'd look at Rhys and feel a tiny glimmer of...hope?

"I don't want to be a victim. And I don't want to be weak, but I'm not sure I have much strength left at the moment."

"You'll get stronger in time. Right now, you have four people who care about your future—let us carry you for a while until you can walk by yourself."

Rhys gave the best hugs. He had strength, and he didn't mind sharing it. Or his kisses. And she'd take all of those that she could get. It was so easy to melt against him, to surrender the stresses and just *be* for a moment. Had it always been this way? Had she felt as comfortable with the baby's father? No. No, she couldn't have. Not when the asshole had left her to sit in her room night after night with only stress and gummy bears for company. He hadn't cared. Rhys had dropped everything and flown halfway across the world to find her. From what Chelle had said, the jerk who'd knocked her up hadn't even managed a phone call.

Aaaaaaaaand there was the anger.

"You okay?"

"You said that it helped to stay busy. I think I need to stay busy."

Jocelyn had been something of a magpie. She'd loved shiny things. One of the boxes in Rochelle's room had been filled with craft materials—cord and glue and beads and silver findings. In the evenings, pre-asshole anyway, she'd loved to watch old romance movies and make jewellery. For every on-screen smooch, there was a necklace, or a pair of earrings, or occasionally a bracelet. Chelle had dug through her jewellery box this evening and gifted a necklace to

Coco, turquoise and wooden beads on knotted yellow cord. Happy colours.

She fingered the beads, wondering how Jocelyn had come up with the design. So pretty. Once upon a time, tying those knots had sated her soul. Would she ever be happy again? Maybe. Each one of Rhys's kisses was like stringing another bead onto the cord. One day, the project would be finished and her heart would be whole again.

"If you want to stay busy, I could teach you to code? Simple apps aren't that hard to design."

Coding? No. "I actually had something else in mind."

When he didn't get the message, she stood on tiptoe and kissed him, praying he'd kiss her back again. If he rejected her, well, she'd want to run and hide, but you lost one hundred percent of the chances you didn't take.

He did kiss her back, but only for a second.

"Promise me you won't disappear again."

It was the easiest promise she'd ever had to make. At least, she thought so. "I'll stay by your side for as long as you'll have me. Close by your side. Nothing whatsoever between us. Not even clothes," she added, just in case her intentions weren't clear.

Rhys's eyes widened. Then he stiffened, and not in a good way. Shit. Too much, too soon. *Way to go, Joss. You've fucked up yet again.*

Instinct took over and she turned to bolt, but Rhys still had hold of her hand.

"Where do you think you're going?"

"Uh, to the bathroom?"

"We have an en suite. Don't you dare run."

"But—"

He silenced her with a kiss, and this time there was nothing tentative about it. Sparks shot through her lips and sizzled in her veins until she was a fizzing mess in his arms. Was it normal for your knees to go weak? For that spot between your thighs to pulse and throb?

Rhys ran the tip of his tongue along the seam of her lips, and they parted on a moan. Coco wasn't in control of her own body anymore, but it didn't matter. Rhys would take care of her. He always took care of her. If it hadn't been for the baby, maybe she'd even have been grateful for the ending in Larkspur Lake because surely what had come before couldn't have been as good as what she had now. Her killer still deserved to be punished, though.

"I didn't bring a condom," Rhys whispered when they finally stopped to take a breath. "We left France in kind of a hurry."

"It's okay."

"We'll have to wait. Neither of us wants to...you know..."

"Repeat the mistakes of my past?"

"I wouldn't have put it quite so bluntly."

"It's okay; I screwed up in so many ways, I realise that. And I'll wait as long as it takes. As long as I have you, I'll wait."

Rhys feathered soft kisses across her cheek. "You have me, sweetheart. And there's plenty we can do without going all the way. I want to taste every inch of you."

"Tonight?"

"Tonight, we sleep. Once we solve your mystery, we've got all the time in the world, but we can't hang around in Lark's River for long."

"I love you," Coco blurted. "I don't expect you to say it back, not now anyway, but I need you to know."

A lock of hair fell across her cheek, and Rhys tucked it behind one ear. Always so sweet. Jocelyn might have made a mess of her life, but she wasn't the biggest idiot in the world. No, that prize went to Stacey. She'd had Rhys and then chosen a douchebag who wore a retainer as a fashion accessory and had graduated from the Helen Keller school of DJing. Barely.

Wait a second... How did she know who Helen Keller was? Had Celine mentioned her? Or were there stray remnants of memories washing around in Coco's skull?

Did it honestly matter?

The past was the past, and the future stretched out ahead like a path to paradise. All she had to do was put one foot in front of the other, slow and steady, and she'd finally find happiness.

CHAPTER 32

COCO

"You changed in the last few years. Before you died, I mean. Before you *died*." Rochelle gave her head a shake. She'd done that a lot in the past twelve hours. "I still can't believe you're back."

That makes two of us. Coco reached out to touch her sister again, just to reassure herself that she wasn't dreaming. Was it possible to feel things in your sleep? Her nightmares were frighteningly realistic, but this... It was different. Warmer. Lighter. In those nightmares, the water was always cold and the crushing pressure made it hard to breathe. She picked up a slice of toast and focused on the sensations as she bit into it—the rasp of the bread on her tongue, the slippery butter, the sweetness of the jam. There was no Marmite in the house—Rochelle hated it. Joss used to order it in bulk from the internet.

Yes, this was real.

Rhys gave her leg a gentle squeeze, reminding her without words that she was okay. That *they* were okay.

"Changed how?" Coco asked.

"We used to have fun together. Go to the movies, go

bowling, go to the diner. Sometimes you'd even come for a bike ride, but exercise wasn't exactly your thing unless there was a horse involved."

"Really? I've been learning to play tennis."

Rochelle choked on her coffee. "Tennis? Are you joking?"

"No, I swear."

"Are you good at it?"

Celine burst into laughter, and when Coco glared at her, she grinned. Her presence here was a relief. Remi was still annoyed by Coco's escape—it showed in his eyes—but Celine was so happy to be somewhere other than the château that a little of her joy rubbed off on her husband. She'd spent ages staring out the window last night, not because anything exciting was happening on the quiet street in small-town USA, but because it was different to everything she knew.

"At tennis? I'm absolutely terrible."

"Figures."

"Gee, thanks. About the horses—I read on Facebook that I used to work at a ranch?"

"You did. Every Saturday and Sunday morning, although Mr. Austin couldn't afford to pay you much. And then you started your new job and quit horse riding too. And the community theatre, and you loved the theatre. I know you said that your work was important, but Joss, it sucked all the happiness out of your world."

"It was obvious?"

"To everyone. I mean, I tried to talk to you about it, but you just insisted the ridiculous hours were part of your long-term career plan. That you didn't want to spend the rest of your life being poor."

Glancing around the house, it seemed that plan hadn't

worked out so well, had it? And perhaps being poor wasn't so bad anyway? Living with Rhys in Uxbridge, Coco had learned to appreciate the small things, the people rather than the possessions, and she'd been happy apart from the nightmares. And look at Celine and Remi—they had unimaginable riches, and yet they were still miserable half the time.

"I was an architect, wasn't I?"

"An architectural assistant. Did you know that you helped to design the new public library in town?"

"Really?"

"The old one got taken out by a freak tornado. It's on YouTube."

"Wow."

"But the new building's much nicer. When it opened, you took me for a walk around and pointed out all the little touches you'd added. The curved windows, the seating area that overlooks the shelves, the book-shaped fountain..." Rochelle's mouth twitched at the corner. "The funhouse mirrors in the bathrooms..."

"I put funhouse mirrors in the *bathrooms*?"

"Your boss thought you were crazy, but everyone loves them, especially the kids. Going to the library is fun now, and it's showing in the kids' school grades too."

Was that why she'd pushed herself so hard? Because she believed in her job and thought she could help people? Maybe. But if she'd lived to work, that left one massive question...

"If I spent all day, every day at the office, then how did I have time to date?"

"You didn't."

"But the baby..."

"I always figured you got involved with somebody from

work. Unless you had a one-night stand or a secret thing with the pizza delivery guy—I mean, all you did at home was eat and sleep."

A one-night stand? Coco didn't feel like a one-night-stand sort of girl. And as for the pizza delivery guy...ugh. She just couldn't imagine herself getting naked with a man she barely knew. Could rebirth have changed her personality that much?

"Let's focus on work for now. Did I mention anyone's name?"

"Uh, probably? I'm really bad at remembering names. At the salon, I write them all down and check the schedule before each appointment. Faces, I can do, but names? Pffft."

"Did you ever meet any of my colleagues?"

"A few. The first year, you took me to the office Christmas party as your plus-one because you didn't want to go on your own. Some creep hit on me. Slicked-back hair, dimples, thought he was God's gift because he could bench-press two hundred pounds."

"Did he have any tattoos?"

"Not that I remember. Why? Does that matter?"

A lump formed in Coco's throat as she nodded. Talking about her own death hadn't become any easier, and remembering it was worse. She closed her eyes for a second, and the man's arm was *right there*, swirling in the dark water, waiting for her to choke.

"Coco does have *some* clear memories," Rhys explained, and she sagged with relief because she didn't have to try and speak. "The man who killed her had a quote from Ralph Waldo Emerson tattooed on his arm. 'All life is an experiment.' Plus he had an outrageously expensive watch and dark hair. That's as much as we know."

"H-h-he was strong too. He held me u-u-underwater."

Rhys curled an arm around Coco's shoulders, and she leaned into him, borrowing his strength once more. She'd thought coming to America would help to bring her closure, but it had also torn open old wounds. And talking about her demise was like pouring salt water onto the jagged flesh.

Over and over and over again.

The colour drained out of Rochelle's face, and she gripped the chipped edge of the dining table until her knuckles turned white.

"I'm so sorry…"

"What's done is done," Remi said, checking his own watch. "We don't have much time here, so let's focus on the goal."

Rochelle glared at him, but she also put her hands in her lap. "The only person around here with fancy-ass quotes tattooed on his arms is Lance Drecker, and it wasn't him."

Now it was Remi's turn to look annoyed. Probably people didn't snap at him often. "And how do you know that?"

"Because Lance Drecker got both of his legs blown off in Iraq, and he's been in a wheelchair ever since. There's no way he could get over the sand to the lake."

"How about rich people?"

Rochelle barked out a laugh. "This is Lark's River."

"And we're a stone's throw from Reno."

Coco reached out for her sister's hand. "Please? There must be someone. That watch cost a hundred thousand euros."

Rochelle gasped. "What kind of lunatic spends that much money on a watch? He could put a down payment on a house instead. Or donate to the food bank. Or fund the church's youth program for *years*."

At least Remi was self-aware enough to display mild embarrassment. "Yes, well, some people would choose the watch. And we still need to find the man who wears it."

"Then try the partners at the architecture firm. I don't know how much they get paid, but Joss always said that if she made partner someday, our money worries would be over."

The wig itched like crazy, and Coco sat on her hands so she wouldn't be tempted to scratch. If she dislodged the hairpiece, the private investigator might get curious, and if one thing was clear from the meeting so far, it was that Monica was sharp.

Remi hadn't wanted Coco at the meeting at all. Too risky, he said. What if somebody recognised her? But Rochelle just scoffed and pointed out that she was a beautician, and not only that, she also did the make-up for the community theatre group in her spare time. Now Coco had long blonde hair, fatter cheeks, blue eyes rather than brown, and a thinner nose thanks to contouring. Even Remi had grudgingly admitted that she looked totally different.

So now she was sitting in the living room at the rented house while Monica gave them a rundown of everything she'd managed to dig up in the past twenty-four hours.

Remi had directed her to check out the partners at Hatcher, Marquez and Phillips, and she'd prepared a thirty-page report complete with photos. This journey back into

Jocelyn's life was…unsettling. Coco had hoped that the facts might stir a memory, a glimpse of recognition, but her mind was a blank.

It hurt.

It hurt that she'd been turned from something into nothing.

"The firm employs thirty full-time architects plus their support team," Monica started, businesslike. Everything about her said "no-nonsense," from her short-cropped hair to her sensible boots. "Although the office is between Lark's River and Reno, the staff travel to cover the whole of Nevada and California too. A number of their clients are in LA. Phillips is the oldest of the partners—he turned fifty-seven in March. Arguably, he's the most talented of the three, and also the best-known. Before he moved to Lark's River, he worked in New York and designed several famous buildings."

"Why'd he come here?" Rochelle asked. "I'd have stayed in New York."

"He came for a woman and stayed for the casinos."

"Huh?"

"He traded his wife of twenty-five years in for a mistress and a gambling habit. I think we can rule him out as a suspect. If Ron Phillips owned an expensive watch, he'd have swapped it for poker chips long ago. You still won't tell me who your witness is? The person who saw the suspect?"

Remi shook his head. "I'm afraid I can't."

Monica just shrugged. "You're paying the bill. Moving on to Marquez… Ms. Bordeaux—Jocelyn—reported directly to him, and it seems that his work ethic rubbed off on her. He got to his position by grit and determination. His father was a janitor, and his mother picked crops, but he scraped up enough money to go to college and qualified as an architect. He built them a house, and he has no debt, but I wouldn't class him as rich. Those school loans were a millstone around his neck for much of his life."

"Which leaves Carl Hatcher."

"Ah, yes. Mr. Hatcher." Monica's voice had a "saving the best for last" tone to it. "Now, he *is* rich. Not because he works hard or even because he's particularly gifted, but because he inherited a fortune from his father. I'd go so far as to say that work is a game for him. He enjoys short days, long lunches, and golf. He's worked on a number of interesting projects—the public library in Lark's River is one of note—but he's in the game for the prestige rather than the money. He's also married."

Icy prickles crawled up Coco's spine as her gaze met Rhys's. Could Hatcher be the one? Would she really have had an affair with a married man?

"Any idea what car he drives?" Remi asked.

Monica consulted her notes. "A red Porsche 911 Turbo. One year old, top of the line."

Red. Expensive. Now Rochelle stiffened too.

"What does one of those look like?" she asked.

Rhys found a picture on the internet and held up his phone. "Is this the car you saw?"

"I think so. I mean, I only saw it for a minute, but it was all curvy like that."

They were on the right track, weren't they?

Remi thought so too. "The pieces fit so far. How old is Hatcher? Young enough that a girl Jocelyn's age might contemplate an affair with him?"

"Thirty-seven. His father died young. If you scroll to page eight of the report, there's a recent photo."

Coco studied the picture. A brown-haired man in a good

suit, smiling for the camera in front of a wood-and-stainless-steel building. It appeared to be a corporate publicity shot, something that would go in a brochure or on a website. Hatcher didn't look particularly special, but he wasn't ugly either. Plus he kept in shape, and he had good teeth. Coco had decided that she liked a man with good teeth. Rhys's were perfect. In one of their chats, he'd confessed that he'd worn braces for three years when he was younger and the kids at school had nicknamed him "zipper lips."

Would Jocelyn really have dated that guy? She couldn't rule it out. Would Coco? No way. Her tastes had changed for the better, and she wouldn't go near a married man either.

"How did Hatcher Senior die?" Remi asked.

"Fell overboard on a fishing trip and drowned."

The prickles turned into stabby little needles.

"Were there any witnesses?"

"Just one—his son." Monica focused on Remi. "Mr. Klein, I suggest you tread very carefully with this."

"Oh, I intend to." Coco had seen Remi angry, and she'd seen him upset, but she'd never seen his eyes look as cold as they did at that moment, or as grimly determined. Even Celine shifted uncomfortably. "I didn't get to my position by letting my guard down. In business, there's always somebody waiting to knife you in the back."

"What's the next step? Do you want me to keep digging?"

"If you wouldn't mind. But I'm also going to pay Mr. Hatcher a visit."

"Is that a good idea?"

"I'll let you know when I come back."

CHAPTER 33
COCO

"Do you think Remi's okay?"

Celine had been standing by the front window in the rental house for the last half hour, which made a change from pacing, Coco supposed.

"Nobody's going to hurt him in an office filled with people."

"What if somebody follows him?"

"Why would they? He's got a good cover story." As a billionaire hoping to build the perfect vacation home in the town his wife had "simply fallen in love with," Remi had been granted a meeting right away. "Besides, Monica's waiting outside the building."

Just in case Hatcher went anywhere interesting afterwards. Remi planned to keep things low-key today, but Coco wouldn't put it past him to push a few of Hatcher's buttons. How would he react if they got close to finding out his secrets? Would he run? Or would he fight?

"But if— Here he is!"

Remi's rented BMW turned into the driveway and drew to a smooth halt beside the marble fountain outside. Yes, the fountain. Everything about this house was over the top. Remi probably felt right at home.

"Well?" Celine asked as soon as he stepped over the threshold. "What happened?"

"Can I close the door first?"

"If you must. Was it him?"

But she did move back and give Remi space. Rhys appeared too, drying his hands on his pants. He'd offered to make dinner because Remi didn't want to order pizza again. Coco had helped him for a while because the kitchen in the rental property was so beautiful that it *made* you want to cook, but after she'd gotten distracted and nearly chopped off a finger, Rhys had taken the knife away and told her that he'd finish.

"Hatcher was wearing a Blancpain Villeret Carrousel. It's remarkably similar to one in my collection."

Remi had a whole collection of expensive watches? Actually, that really wasn't a surprise.

"So it's him? Hatcher's the psycho who murdered me?"

"It seems a strong possibility. Not only because he was wearing the watch, but because he was an arrogant *fils de pute*. A man who likes to get his own way. While I was there, he berated his assistant for putting too much cream in his coffee, but he still kept staring at her derrière. Did you know he has a young daughter?"

"What?"

"A toddler. He keeps a picture of her on his desk."

"The man's an asshole," Rochelle muttered, and she was completely correct. Jocelyn hadn't been much better if she'd gotten involved with him.

"What about the tattoo?" Celine asked. "Does he have the tattoo?"

"He was wearing a long-sleeved shirt."

"So all we have to do is keep following him until he rolls up his sleeves. It's hot here—can't you ask to meet him outside somewhere?"

"I could."

"*Bon*. And then we'll know that he's the murderer."

"Yes, but knowing it and proving it are two different things. *We'll* know he did it, but so far, we have no evidence to present to the police. They've closed the case, remember?"

That was when it really hit Coco. The fury. The regret. The thought of never getting justice was a punch to the gut. *Closure, my ass.* Monica had used her contacts to get ahold of the police file, and Remi was right—there was no evidence. No defensive wounds, no footprints, and any trace material had been washed away by the water. The only eyewitness that day had been a woman out with her dog who'd seen Jocelyn hurrying along the sidewalk towards the lake, alone.

They'd found the man who killed her—*killed her*—and he was going to get away with it. He was going to carry on going to his fancy job and living in his fancy house with his no-doubt fancy wife. His wife... Did she even know what her husband was capable of? He'd murdered two people for sure—Jocelyn and her baby—maybe three if his father's death hadn't been an accident, and Emily Hatcher was still sharing his bed. Could ignorance be bliss? Or was it a ticking time bomb? What if she was the next to die?

For her, there would be no miraculous resurrection. No rebirth under a tree in the middle of the night. Hell, they still didn't know how Coco had even got into the damn plant food.

Carl Hatcher's next victim was a dead woman walking.

Jocelyn was gone.

And Coco... Fury warred with loss, but all that came out was tears.

CHAPTER 34
COCO

"I can't decide what's worse, not knowing who killed me or knowing who did and not being able to do a damn thing about it."

They'd confirmed it now. Hatcher had the tattoo. Monica had tailed him from the office to the gym, where he removed his wedding ring, followed her into the sauna, and invited her out for drinks. Monica assured Remi that she was fine, that she had a black belt in karate and carried a knife in her bikini top, but the thought of her getting so close to Hatcher still made Coco shudder.

What had Jocelyn ever seen in that sleaze? Had he told her his marriage was over? Sweet-talked her with false promises? Bribed her with a promotion? Monica said he didn't look like much in his Speedos, so it certainly hadn't been the dick.

"It sucks," Celine agreed. "He's getting on with his life as if nothing happened. I bet his wife has no idea that you even existed. I mean, a baby? She'd have divorced his ass for sure."

Remi raised an eyebrow. "Divorced his ass?"

"When in Rome, do as the Romans do. Or speak as the Romans speak."

"The Americans."

"Whatever."

Coco flopped backwards onto the couch, thunking her head onto the cushion. She wished she'd thunked some sense into herself last year. Or the year before. Who knew how long the affair had been going on? And hell, she wished she could apologise to his wife as well. Jocelyn had lost her damn mind even before she died—that was the only explanation.

"I was so freaking stupid! Did he tell me he loved me? Was I blinded by his money? Not knowing is gonna drive me crazy for the rest of my life. My *second* life. The better one."

Rhys, the voice of reason, squeezed her hand. "We'll probably never know the full story, but you've got to stop letting him screw with your head. If you give him that, then he's still got power over you."

"Easy for you to say—it's not your head he's screwing with. I just wish there was a way for me to do the same to him."

Remi drummed his fingers on the dining table, which wasn't irritating at all. Grrr. He'd taken up residence behind his laptop again, both to catch up on emails and to research Hatcher.

"Maybe... Hmm... Maybe there is."

Everyone turned to look at him.

"What do you mean?"

"As far as Carl Hatcher is concerned, you're nothing but a ghost. And I wonder, does he believe in the supernatural?"

What did that devious smile mean?

"I don't get it."

"Perhaps you've heard that Le Château de Villance is haunted? There are always rumours around the town."

"I might have heard it mentioned," Rhys said.

"There are no ghosts, of course, but I encourage the stories. Even though logic tells people that ghosts don't exist, the scared child deep inside wonders if they do. If spirits really walk the earth on a different plane. So, I play sounds at night from time to time—footsteps, a baby crying, a woman's scream. It helps to keep the townsfolk away from the place."

"Wish you'd bloody told me."

Remi's grin was a little too cheerful. "You fell for it?"

"No."

"You did."

"That walk from the château to the cottage gives me the heebie-jeebies, okay? You need more lights along the path."

"I'll install some if you're going to be staying there for any length of time."

Was that an option? The future was still so up in the air, Coco hadn't thought beyond the trip to America. But she'd go wherever Rhys wanted to go. Did he like living in France?

"So what are you saying?" Celine asked. "That we should play footstep sounds to scare Hatcher?"

"No, I'm saying that Coco should become the ghost. If Hatcher thinks she's come back to visit, that'll definitely mess with his mind. Fear mixed with guilt mixed with the conviction that he's always right—who knows what will happen?"

"You sure scared me when you showed up at my door," Rochelle said. "I thought I was gonna have a heart attack."

A heart attack would be acceptable. Could it truly work?

Even if there was only the slimmest chance, they had to try, didn't they?

"I like it. I really like it. I could drive him insane."

"You'd be good at that," Rhys said, but he was smiling even as Coco elbowed him in the side.

"How soon can we start?"

"As soon as we've made a plan." Remi's smile grew even wider. "And *I'm* good at making plans."

At Remi's request, Monica brought in a "local security specialist." He introduced himself as Bones, and while he might have smiled, the atmosphere turned oppressive when he walked into the room. As if he'd sucked all the air out of it. Coco sure was glad the man was on their side and not Hatcher's.

Together with Monica, Bones had spent the last three days researching Hatcher, which included following him as he went about his business.

"He's still at it," Monica reported after the first day. "He took a young blonde out for a swanky dinner while his wife was at home with their daughter. Cute kid. The daughter, not the coed he was kissing. Three years old and looks just like her mom."

A pang of pity hit Coco along with a wave of disgust. "Our actions are going to ruin his family's lives too, aren't they?"

Coco was already dead. Hatcher deserved to be. But his wife and child—they were innocent.

"He's already sleeping with girls on the side, and he

killed one of them. Maybe more—who knows? Is he really a good father?"

"I guess not, but…"

"Look, hun. I grew up with parents who stayed together even though they hated each other. When I turned eighteen and they finally divorced, it was a relief, not a hardship. I only wished they'd done it sooner. We'd all have been happier."

The Hatchers didn't come across as unhappy in the photos. That smiling girl… Why had Coco been so worried about having a baby of her own? Even if its father was a jerk, she could have raised the child and loved it enough for two.

"It's your decision," Rhys told her. "If you want to call this off, you can."

Monica gave her a weird look. Shit.

"I knew Jocelyn," Coco explained. "She was an old friend. I hadn't seen her in a while, but I wish we hadn't grown apart."

"What if he kills someone else?" Celine asked. "What if the new girl ends up dead in a lake as well?"

There was only one decision Coco could make, wasn't there?

"Then we have to carry on."

It was like a game of chess. They plotted a move, then tried to predict Hatcher's reaction. The endgame? Checkmate. They wanted Hatcher to admit what he'd done. Since they couldn't prove it to a court, a confession was the only viable way to get justice, and any recording would need to be made in person because a legal wiretap required either agreement from all parties involved in the conversation or a court order, unless it was a 911 call. In-person recording was legal in Nevada as long as one party had consented.

"How do I look?" Coco asked, giving Rhys a twirl.

"Beautiful, as always."

"No, really?"

The boot-cut jeans and hooded sweatshirt were anything but pretty, but that wasn't the effect they were going for. Coco needed to look on the creepy side of normal. Rochelle had made her face appear pale and gaunt, and today's contacts were pure white. They made her vision fuzzy, but it wasn't as if she'd need to drive. According to Rochelle, she'd had a licence, but she'd also been fond of speeding. Oops. Coco was back to her own hair today, although they'd told Monica she was wearing a wig—how fortunate that she looked similar enough to Jocelyn to play her body double, eh?

"Yes, really," Rhys said. "I still pinch myself when I wake up beside you in the mornings."

He was so damn sweet.

"You're lying, but I'll take the compliment."

Coco wrapped her arms around his neck and kissed him, but they'd barely got to tongues before Remi cleared his throat behind them.

"We don't have time for that. Are you ready to go?"

"As I'll ever be."

Hatcher was a creature of habit. Every Monday, Wednesday, and Thursday he left his office at five o'clock on the dot and headed to the gym in his shiny red Porsche.

And on the way to the gym, halfway along a busy street, there was a crosswalk. At ten past five, Coco was standing in place with an earpiece hidden under her hair. The hood was pulled low over her eyes as she waited for the signal.

"He's turning the corner," Rhys said from his spot fifty yards away.

Bones had come up with the communications system, and it felt like something out of a spy movie, minus the martini. He didn't elaborate on where it had come from. Bones seemed to be a "don't ask, don't tell" kind of guy.

Coco's heart jittered as she caught a flash of red in her blurry peripheral vision.

"Okay, I see him. I'm about to step out."

The plan called for her to walk in front of Hatcher's car, pause, take the hood down and make eye contact, then continue to the other side of the road. From there, she could dart through a service alley to the parking lot where Remi and Celine were waiting in the rental car. Once they'd picked her up, they'd circle back for Rhys. Bones and Monica were farther along the street, one in each direction, in case of any problems.

Right, here goes...

Coco stepped off the kerb, then slowed so Hatcher would have to stop or run her over. And he couldn't run her over, not with so many witnesses around.

He stopped.

She stopped.

He fiddled with the radio.

Asshole.

Then he looked up and their gazes met. He did a double take, and Coco gave him what she hoped was a slightly eerie, slightly mysterious smile, stifling a laugh when the car lurched forward and stalled.

Got under your skin, did I?

Coco made it to the alley, and the sound of a horn and then Hatcher's alloy wheels scraping the kerb as he drove off was music to her ears.

Phase one of the plan: complete. A point to Team Jocelyn.

"Oh, he was definitely rattled," Rhys said as Remi twisted the muselet off a champagne bottle—because apparently that metal cage thing that went over the top had a name—and popped the cork. There wasn't much to celebrate yet, but Coco had discovered that Remi didn't need much of an excuse to break out the good wine.

"Excellent."

"Maybe he'll have a stroke?" Celine said cheerfully. "Do you think he'll have a stroke?"

Rhys held out two champagne flutes, one for himself and one for Coco. "If he does, it couldn't happen to a nicer guy."

Coco closed her eyes for one delicious second, remembering Hatcher's face. "He went white. Whiter than me, and I was a ghost." A giggle burst out. "How much do alloy wheels cost?"

"Original equipment? Around five thousand dollars each," Remi said, because of course he knew these things.

Rhys spluttered into his champagne. "Are you serious? That's more than my whole car."

"Deadly serious. And don't even get me started on the cost of Ferrari wheels. Canapé?"

This was a whole other world, wasn't it? And where the hell had Remi managed to find foie gras in Lark's River? What had he done, sent the jet back to France to pick up groceries?

"I wish I'd been there," Celine said. "What are we doing next?"

"Hatcher's presenting at a conference in Reno on Monday. I thought it would be beneficial if Jocelyn made an appearance. If he's on stage, he won't be able to do anything without looking as if he's gone quite mad."

"What's the conference about?"

"It's called Homes of the Future. Something to do with renewable energy and sustainable living—Hatcher actually mentioned it during our meeting last week. And while Coco is occupying Mr. Hatcher, Mr. Bones has agreed to make some minor modifications to his home."

Rochelle stuck her fingers in her ears. "I'm going to pretend I didn't hear that part."

"What about his wife and kid?" Rhys asked. "Won't they be there?"

"On Mondays, Emily Hatcher goes to yoga while her daughter is at preschool. And this Monday, Emily also has a lunch date with her friend Lauren."

"How do you know all that?"

"Monica is good at her job. I don't pretend to be an expert in everything—far from it—but I do know how to hire good people."

Not for the first time, Coco sent a silent thank you to the stars for bringing Remi and Celine into her life and Rhys's. Remi might have been grouchy at times, but without them, untangling her past would have been so much harder. And she wouldn't have had Celine as a friend either.

"Thank you. Thank you for everything you've done."

"*Pas de problème.* And I should thank you as well—Celine and I were long overdue for a vacation, but I needed that push to take the leap." He held up his glass of champagne. "*Santé.*"

Everyone followed suit. "*Santé.*"

CHAPTER 35
COCO

"Do I look like a businesswoman?" Coco asked.

Today, she wore a plain black skirt suit borrowed from Rochelle, and Bones had supplied her with glasses containing a hidden earpiece. Rochelle had also painted her nails in red, blue, and gold—the colours of the Wonder Woman logo. She swore it was lucky.

Celine gave Coco a thumbs up.

"You'll knock him dead."

Here's hoping.

"What if it goes wrong? What if he doesn't see me?"

"Then we try something else," Rhys said. "This is a marathon, not a sprint."

"You'll be there the whole time?"

"Right behind you. Just remember not to turn around."

"I won't. I mean, I won't turn around, not that I won't remember."

Three of them were going into the venue—Coco, Rhys, and Remi. Only Remi seemed vaguely comfortable with the idea.

"When you've been to one conference, you've been to them all. A compère who likes the sound of their own voice wrangles speakers who may or may not want to be there, and during the breaks, delegates compete to see who can collect the most business cards. Quite frankly, they bore me to death. I only go when I have to."

"What if somebody asks me a question?"

"Make up an answer. It's unlikely they'll know whether you're lying or telling the truth, nor will they care either way."

Even so, Coco had spent a couple of hours last night reading up on sustainable building techniques, just in case. She didn't want to sound like a complete idiot if someone engaged her in conversation.

According to the schedule, Hatcher's presentation was due to start at ten o'clock and last for fifty minutes, including a Q&A session at the end. Coco planned to take her seat at five past ten. If she arrived right after he started speaking, it would be all the more difficult for him to excuse himself and come after her.

Plus it would give him more time to squirm.

At five minutes to ten, Coco waited outside the auditorium with Rhys, focusing on her breathing. In on five, out on seven. Celine swore that would help her to stay calm, but it wasn't bloody working, was it?

"You'll be okay?" Rhys asked.

"Oh, fine."

A lie, but she had to do this. The way to inner peace was

through justice, and she couldn't afford to be the weak link in the team. Rhys didn't look as if he believed her, not completely, but he leaned in to press a soft kiss to her cheek.

"Really, I'm okay, I swear."

Then Remi tapped on his microphone three times—his signal for Rhys to come inside—and it was showtime.

"Remember, give me a minute's head start. We don't want people to think we're together."

"A minute. Got it."

When Coco walked into the auditorium, she felt rather than saw Rhys standing by the back wall. She'd feel him anywhere—double entendre intended. But she ignored him and slipped into an empty seat on the end of a row halfway to the front.

Hatcher was talking about the merits of green roofs and rainwater-harvesting systems, which on another occasion might have been interesting, but not today. The butterflies flapped and flitted in Coco's belly as she waited. And waited. And waited.

The moment when Hatcher finally noticed her was beautiful. Just beautiful. He tripped over his next sentence, then gaped like a catfish. Whispers started in the audience when he tried to speak again and choked on his words.

"Is he okay?"

"Is he having a stroke?"

"Perhaps it's dehydration—it's awful hot in here."

Good. Hopefully it would give Hatcher a taste of hell. Did hell even exist? Coco sure hoped so because Hatcher deserved to spend the remainder of his miserable life dancing in the flames.

Their eyes met, and this time, she mouthed, "You'll pay," as the colour drained from Hatcher's smarmy face.

She was tempted to give him the finger as well, but somehow that seemed…unprofessional.

Then Hatcher took a shaky step towards the edge of the stage. Oh. Oh, shit. Coco froze until Rhys spoke into her ear.

"Leave, sweetheart. Leave right now."

Heart thumping, she came to her senses and hurried to the door. *Damn these pumps.* How the hell did Rochelle walk in them? How could *anybody* walk in them? The sound of feet clomping down the steps at the side of the stage sent her into a cold sweat, and she stumbled into the wall. Now people were staring.

"It's okay, sweetheart," Rhys whispered. "Just go out the emergency exit like we planned."

Would she make it that far? Hatcher was taller and probably hopped up on adrenaline by now. What if— Then she heard the sweetest sound in the world and took back every bad thought she'd ever had about Remi.

"Carl? Are you okay? You look as if you've seen a ghost."

"I… Maybe…"

"Can somebody get this man a glass of water? Now! Is there a medic here? He's gone quite pale."

The emergency exit was right there, and Coco burst out into the October sunshine, blinking in the glare. Where was Monica? Coco spotted her SUV idling thirty yards away and walked to the passenger side as fast as Rochelle's stupid shoes would allow. There was a lot to be said for sneakers. Or even ballet flats.

"That went well," Monica said as she pulled smoothly away.

Was she being sarcastic? Or did she genuinely not realise how close Coco had been to having a coronary? A quick glance suggested she was serious.

"Uh, I guess it went okay."

"You shook up the suspect and got away clean. That's a win in anyone's book."

Right. Okay.

Score two to Team Jocelyn.

Remi and Monica said it was essential to keep up the pressure, so that evening, Coco found herself dressed in Jocelyn's prom dress. Rochelle couldn't bear to throw it away, so she'd folded it between layers of tissue paper and tucked it into one of the boxes stacked in her room.

"Did I really wear this? It looks like...like someone took a wedding dress and chopped parts out of it."

What was left of the layers of chiffon was filmy rather than poufy, and the sparkles stitched to the bodice twinkled under the overhead light. The dress barely did up anymore, but as long as Coco didn't want to breathe, it was okay.

"That's exactly what you did do. You found the dress at Goodwill and customised it with scissors and a million diamantés."

"I sewed all of these on?"

"No, you glued them on. And somehow, they got stuck to everything. I was still finding them months after you died."

"Sorry."

"At first, I cried every time, but then I told myself it meant that you were still out there somewhere, trying to cheer me up. And I guess it was true."

Tears pricked at Coco's eyes, and she sniffed them back.

Now wasn't the time to ruin her make-up. But she was so damn lucky to have people who still believed in her, even after everything she'd done. After all the mistakes she'd made.

"I can take a turn at vacuuming now that I'm back?"

"I'll hold you to that. Hey, how about wetting your hair? You know, to emphasise the drowning part?"

"Why not? Every little thing helps."

Tonight, they'd be paying a visit to Hatcher's home, a postmodernist behemoth with a wind turbine in the backyard. Had Coco been there before? Did the philandering prick sneak his mistresses inside when his wife was out? The thought made her sick. Or perhaps that was the nerves? Either way, she felt nauseated. Death sure took a toll on a girl's life.

The others were waiting in the living room, nibbling from platters of snacks on the coffee table. Bones had prepared a video tour from his earlier trip to the house, and Monica had put together a map of the grounds. The mansion sat on a two-acre lot surrounded by a manicured lawn and meticulously pruned trees. Hatcher had been bitching at the homeowners' association for years to let him build a wall, according to Monica's research, but they were standing firm on the "no fences" rule.

"They called the house Emica," Bones said, rolling his eyes. That was the most emotion Coco had seen from him. "Short for Emily and Carl—get it? Tacky."

Urgh.

Jocelyn had been such an idiot.

For the next hour, Coco concentrated on learning the layout of the grounds—every terrace and tree, every bench and bush. And there were a *lot* of benches. Stone benches, wooden benches, even one made out of plastic. Hatcher made a habit of watching the news in his living room at nine p.m., usually with a glass of red, and the plan called for Coco to stand at the window, mouth her words, and then leave before he could get outside to challenge her. They'd decided to stick with "you'll pay" for the moment. Simple and to the point.

Remi had rented a second car to give them more flexibility, and when Rhys pulled over a hundred yards away from Hatcher's home, Bones left the vehicle first, melting into the darkness like a shadow. Remi and Celine were in the BMW half a mile away in case backup was needed. Naturally, Remi hadn't wanted Celine to come, but Bones said that a couple sitting in a parked car wouldn't arouse suspicions in the same way a single man did, and Monica had gone to her daughter's dance recital that evening. She'd offered to cancel, but nobody wanted her to break a promise, and Bones assured her he could handle Hatcher.

Coco had shuddered at the words, but then she thought about it and decided Hatcher deserved everything he got.

"He's sitting down," Bones said over the radio. "Whenever you're ready."

"I don't feel ready. I don't think I ever will."

"You want to abort this?" Rhys whispered.

"We can't. It's not just about me, is it?" Her chest felt tight as she sucked in a breath. "Let's get it over with."

Rhys gripped Coco's hand as she walked to Hatcher's gates, and when they got there, he took the black coat she'd borrowed from Rochelle to hide her bastardised wedding dress from curious neighbours.

"Good luck, sweetheart. I'll be waiting right here with the car when you come back."

The ornamental trees provided a little cover as Coco hurried across the yard. The living room was at the front of the house, on the right-hand side as you faced it. She headed for the lit window, which didn't have any drapes, just a wooden blind that appeared to be more decorative than functional. Certainly Hatcher never seemed to lower it.

And there he was.

Jocelyn's former boss didn't look entirely relaxed, but he had his feet up on the couch with a glass of wine in his hand. Red wine, white leather. Brave man. Coco stifled a smile as she tapped on the window, and the sight of the wine splashing all over Hatcher, the couch, and the floor when he dropped the glass was a memory to treasure. His jaw dropped when he realised who was watching him, and he clutched at his chest as she mouthed, "You'll pay." Was his heart…? No, shit, he was coming after her again. He practically sprinted out of the living room, heading for the front door, and Coco ran. Thank goodness she'd worn sneakers this time.

Where was the car? Rhys?

A branch whipped against her arm, but she couldn't afford to slow down. Security lights flashed on as Coco spotted the Honda to her left. Five seconds later, she wrenched the door open, breathing hard.

"He's coming! Go, go, go!"

Coco ducked into the footwell as Rhys pulled smoothly away, not a care in the world. By the time Hatcher appeared in the mirror, they were almost out of sight.

Bones chuckled into the radio. "He's standing on the sidewalk, confused as fuck."

"Did he get a good look at the car?"

"Doubt it. You timed that perfectly."

A fluke, but they needed that sort of luck. Score three to Team Jocelyn.

CHAPTER 36

COCO

When Hatcher left for work the next morning, Monica reported that he looked more rumpled than usual, and he hadn't shaved either. She was on surveillance duty while the rest of the team ate breakfast. Celine had made French toast—which didn't come from France, according to Rhys—and served it with whipped cream, powdered sugar, and mixed berries. But Rochelle insisted the only way to eat it was covered in maple syrup, and Coco had to concede that she was right.

"His clothes are creased like he slept in them," Monica said through the speaker.

"Maybe he did," Remi said. "He's fond of running after Coco, and sprinting onto the street in pyjamas or even naked would draw attention he doesn't want."

Rhys was on Team Whipped Cream. Coco could barely see his French toast underneath it.

"I'm worried that he keeps chasing her."

"As am I. And I'm concerned about why—surely if he believed she truly was a ghost, he'd understand that catching her was impossible? We need to convince him that although he can see her, she's not really there."

"How?" Coco asked. "I mean, I *am* there."

"Perhaps we could hire a magician?" Rhys suggested. "A conjurer? We'd only need Coco to vanish before his eyes once to shake him."

"What about using a hologram?" Celine asked.

Remi shook his head. "All of those ideas would mean involving others in our scheme, and I'd rather avoid that."

Good point. It was hard enough keeping Coco's identity secret from Monica and Bones as it was, and the plan would only work as long as Jocelyn's remarkable resurrection remained hidden from the world. No victim, no murder. Not for the first time, a shiver of fear and doubt ran through Coco. What if, after all their efforts, Hatcher got away with his crime?

Then a gleam appeared in Celine's eye. "I have an idea."

Remi groaned. "How much money will it cost me? I've seen that look many times before."

"Like, thirty bucks? All we need is a digital recorder and a notepad."

"A digital recorder?"

Celine laid out her plan, and before she even got halfway, Remi was shaking his head again. "No. No, a thousand times no."

"It's not a *terrible* suggestion," Rhys said, and Celine beamed at him. She really did have a beautiful smile.

"Hatcher's dangerous."

"We'll be in public," Celine pointed out.

"I don't care."

"*You* met with him."

"That's different."

Celine folded her arms and stared him down. "Whether

you like it or not, I'm my own person, and I can make my own decisions."

How could Remi argue with that? He might have created Celine, but the soul and backbone she'd ended up with were all hers.

"For the record, this is a terrible idea."

"Your objections are noted. Isn't that what you always say to your colleagues when they tell you one of your ideas is bad?"

"My ideas always work. I just associate with a lot of overly cautious bureaucrats."

"Well, my idea will work too." Celine hit her husband with that killer grin. "Please don't turn into an overly cautious bureaucrat. I like you exactly the way you are."

Two days later, Celine straightened her jacket as the team prepared to leave for Sun Valley.

"You've got the digital recorder?" Remi asked. He still wasn't entirely on board with the plan, but short of spiriting Celine back to France in the middle of the night, there wasn't much he could do to stop her. She was determined to play her part, and for that, Coco was thankful. Besides, if Hatcher had an eye for the ladies, Celine would be hard to resist.

"Of course I do. What reporter would forget something so important? I have a chewed pen and a notepad as well."

When Hatcher had received a call from the editor of a new sustainable-living magazine—who was actually Monica—he'd jumped at the chance to be interviewed.

Maybe he thought it would help to restore his reputation after the disastrous performance at the conference? He never had finished his talk, and the Q&A consisted of the audience asking each other what the hell just happened.

Yesterday, Celine had spent hours researching sustainability, and Remi helped her to compile a series of open-ended questions designed to get Hatcher talking, not that they cared about anything he had to say. They merely wanted him present while Coco made her appearance.

The location—Fredericks Café in Sun Valley—had been chosen in the hope that Hatcher wouldn't be familiar with the area. The prospect of a forty-minute drive hadn't fazed him. He'd told Monica it would be an excellent opportunity to take his Porsche out for a spin. Rhys and Remi had spent a day walking around the area, mapping out the streets surrounding the café and planning several getaway options in case the worst happened and Hatcher decided to give chase again. Coco was definitely wearing sneakers under her dress this time.

Another advantage of the meeting place was that Hatcher would be out of his house for at least three hours on a day when his wife took their daughter to a music-and-movement class at the Lark's River community centre. That meant Bones would have the opportunity to make a few more modifications to the place unnoticed—alterations that would come in useful for Phase B of Operation Justice.

Remi looked more nervous than Celine as their departure time loomed.

"I hate her being involved in this," Coco heard him tell Rhys.

"It's risky, but the whole of life's risky, isn't it? Look at her—she's smiling. I know you think that keeping her safe is the most important thing, but making her stay in the château all the time is like clipping a bird's wings. Sure, she's alive and out of sight, but a bird's always happiest when it's allowed to fly."

Remi glanced at his wife, and a smile tugged at the corners of his lips as well. "I understand that, but what if somebody recognises her?"

"It's a valid fear, but consider the context. If you took her out to a gala, then you'd obviously have a problem. But what if she and Coco went for lunch together in another town? Celine could wear a disguise—a wig and glasses or something. Who's going to notice? Or the two of you could go on a quiet holiday somewhere out of the way."

It was strange to hear Rhys giving advice to Remi, but Coco had come to realise that underneath the veneer of money and his standoffish personality, the Frenchman was human after all. He had the same foibles and insecurities as everybody else.

"Perhaps I *have* been stifling her."

"Give her some freedom. It would make you both stronger."

"First, let us see how I cope while she does this interview."

Holy hell, what a rush!

They'd been back at the rental house for ten minutes, but Coco was still riding high on adrenaline. A smile had replaced Remi's earlier frown, and Celine was relaxed in his arms, basking in the glory of a mission completed.

"Will someone tell me what happened?" Rochelle

asked. "It sucks having to work while the rest of you plot revenge."

Rochelle had run out of vacation days—she'd used most of them after Jocelyn's death to arrange the funeral and cry—and her boss was a bitter divorcee with the body of Dolly Parton and the personality of Satan. Asking for personal time was out of the question.

"Chill, we recorded everything," Celine told her. "You won't miss a thing. Listen, listen..."

She placed the digital recorder on the kitchen table as Remi got busy with the coffee machine, and the hairs on the back of Coco's neck prickled as she heard her ex-lover's voice. He sounded so...so egotistical. What had she ever seen in him? He talked—no, lectured—on energy-saving building materials and the benefits of solar power with the arrogance of a man who was always right, even when he was wrong. After a couple of minutes, Celine got bored and fast-forwarded through that part.

"No offence, but the man's a jerk."

"No offence taken. Jocelyn must've been brainwashed."

Rochelle squeezed her hand. "Sometimes, love does funny things to us. Or so I've heard."

Why did she glance towards Bones when she said that? Surely not...

"Love? More like a lobotomy."

"It looks as if your brain's in working order again now." Rochelle jerked her head in Rhys's direction and dropped her voice to a whisper. "He seems like a real nice guy."

The prickles turned to warmth. "He is. He really is."

"Hey, hey," Celine said. "This is the good part."

Oh, she was right about that.

"Mr. Hatcher, are you all right?" fake-reporter Celine asked on the tape. "Did something happen outside?"

Silence.

"The car? Is there a problem with that car?"

"It's... It's..."

"A Mustang? It's a Mustang, right?"

"Not the car. The girl."

"What girl?"

"Beside the car." Hatcher's voice was tight, his words clipped. "The girl standing beside the car. I'm sure I know her."

"I'm sorry, but I don't see any girl."

"She's standing next to the fender. A dark-haired girl in a white dress."

Coco had been hiding behind a pickup farther along the street, and when Remi gave the command, she'd popped up in Hatcher's line of sight. Their timing was perfect. Remi had been enjoying a latte in the café, hidden away in a corner with a hat pulled low over his eyes but on hand in case any emergencies arose. He'd wanted to stay close to Celine, and nobody could blame him for that. True, he needed to loosen up, but baby steps were better than no steps at all.

"The fender of the red car?" Celine asked on tape.

"Yes, right there."

"I still don't see her."

"She's looking at me." Hatcher's voice took on a pleading tone, but it seemed that he wasn't only trying to convince Celine, he was trying to convince himself as well. "Now she's pointing. How can you miss that?"

"Mr. Hatcher, did you happen to have a little something to drink before this interview?"

"No, I did not!"

Remi had given Coco the order to disappear at that point, and while Hatcher was looking at Celine, she'd ducked behind the car out of sight. A very shocked cat that had been preening itself in the sunshine bolted under the car while Coco pretended to look for an item she'd dropped.

"Okaaaaay," Celine said, her voice dripping with disbelief. "It's just that you seem to be seeing things that aren't there."

"She is there."

Perhaps Celine had also been an actress in her previous life, because her dramatic silence said more than words ever could.

"You think I'm crazy."

Still Celine said nothing.

"I'm not crazy. I'm not," Hatcher muttered. "*I'm not.*"

"Uh, do you want to end the interview here? I have enough for the article."

"Yes. Yes, that would be best."

They gave him one more glimpse of Jocelyn before she hopped into Rhys's Honda and headed back to Lark's River. The performance had gone perfectly—Hatcher was getting more unnerved by the day. Remi already had the customary bottle of champagne ready.

"Let's step it up a notch. How did the installations go?"

"As planned," Bones said from his seat in the corner. He didn't touch the champagne. The man seemed to live on smoothies and protein shakes. "Ready when you are, boss."

Remi smiled a devious smile. "Technology is a wonderful thing."

CHAPTER 37
COCO

Hatcher had five senses, and so far, they'd only messed with one of them. Since ignoring the other four seemed like such a waste, Bones had installed an array of tiny state-of-the-art speakers in Hatcher's home while he was out, tiny widgets hidden in the fixtures and fittings. One among the branches of a weeping fig tree in the atrium, a pair in the living room, another in the bedroom... Hatcher's ears were about to take a haunting.

"We can activate them in any combination?" Remi asked.

"Yes, but it's beneficial to activate several at once. That way, your target can't tell where the voice is coming from. The batteries will last a week, and then I'll have to pay another visit to change them."

"I hope this will be over in a week."

As well as the speakers, Bones had added a trio of scent diffusers to waft Jocelyn's favourite perfume through the house when Mrs. Hatcher was out. According to Rochelle, she'd favoured Hugo Boss Femme, and there had been an almost full bottle that Rochelle had gifted Joss last Christmas in one of the storage boxes. Coco found it hard to think of herself as Jocelyn, even though she and Rochelle had fallen back into an easy relationship. In truth, she didn't much like the person that Jocelyn had turned into, and she was starting to think that the opportunity to start over with a new identity was a blessing rather than a curse.

A true once-in-a-lifetime chance.

Remi must have been generous with the surveillance budget because Bones's additions also included fourteen cameras that transmitted to a secure viewing portal. Now they could watch Hatcher's descent into madness if all went well. Secretly, Coco thought that Remi was enjoying their vigilante espionage a little too much, but since he'd spent years holed up in a stuffy castle, she couldn't entirely blame him.

The champagne was out again when they settled in for their evening viewing. Rhys had jokingly asked Remi if he had shares in a vineyard, and he answered in all seriousness that he did. It was in Vallée de la Marne, tours ran daily, and they were welcome to visit any time. Maybe a vacation was on the cards when they returned to France? Rochelle came in with a plate of chips and dip, and Celine had made two different flavours of popcorn. Was this a revenge mission or a party?

Because at this moment, Coco didn't have much to celebrate. Just the sight of Hatcher going about his daily life made her feel sick.

"He's so two-faced. How can he tell his wife he loves her when he was flirting with Celine earlier?"

"Practice," Remi said. "He's probably been doing this for years."

"Seven years," Bones added. "That's how long they've

been married. Emily Hatcher comes from a good family."

Monica went home each evening, but Bones had started hanging around. He said that he wanted to be on hand in case the equipment malfunctioned, but he seemed to spend an awful lot of time sitting with Rochelle. Coco wasn't sure how she felt about that. Bones was kind of scary, but now that she'd spent more time around him, she'd come to understand that he was also loyal and dependable. Unflappable. Would it be terrible if he was interested in her sister? Maybe not. And nothing could be worse than dating Carl Hatcher.

"The Hatchers of this world like to hide their sordid indiscretions beneath a veneer of respectability."

And the prick also liked to get his rocks off. When he stripped off his clothes and fisted his mediocre cock, Coco rushed from the room and puked in the downstairs bathroom. Even though his wife was a willing participant in the act, the fact that they were having sex still turned Coco's stomach. Yeuch. The whole relationship was based on secrets and lies, and she'd been one of those secrets.

Gentle hands held her hair back, and she felt Rhys's presence. When he was close, he soothed her soul.

"You okay, sweetheart?"

"No."

"Sorry. That was a dumb question."

"I don't want to watch that or even listen to it."

"You don't have to."

"He's such a slimeball. I feel so, so sorry for his wife. If only I could apologise to her for what I did…"

Rhys gripped her wrist. "Oh, no. No way. Your visit to Rochelle was bad enough. I doubt that Emily Hatcher would be quite so understanding."

"I'm not going to go. I swear, I'm not."

Coco spoke the truth, but Rhys still poured the drinks for the rest of the evening and watched her carefully to make sure she took her sleeping pill. Yes, she probably deserved that.

She'd learned her lesson, though, and she wouldn't do anything else stupid. She wouldn't hurt Rhys, Rochelle, or Remi and Celine. Life might not be perfect, but she had too much to lose now.

Phase B of the project started the following day when Hatcher decided to spend the morning working from home. Or, at least, his own special version of working from home, which involved his credit card, a webcam, and a box of tissues.

"Ugh," Celine said. "That man has a problem."

Remi covered her eyes. "He does seem to spend most of the time thinking with his dick."

Hatcher was a psychopathic sex addict. "He's disgusting."

"So why don't you tell him that?"

"Really? Now?"

"I can think of no better moment."

Hatcher was on his way back from flushing the evidence when Coco whispered into the microphone.

"You make me sick."

The camera in the hallway gave them a great view as he jolted violently and dropped his phone. The video's resolution was good enough to show the colour drain out of his face as he stared wildly around, trying to work out where the voice had come from.

"I'm watching you. I'll always be watching you."

Thankfully, Remi shut off the microphone before she burst into giggles. This was actually fun. Tormenting a tormentor. Giving him a dose of his own medicine. When Jocelyn was alive, Hatcher had turned her into a wreck long before he'd killed her.

"W-w-where are you?"

"Don't answer," Remi instructed. "Make him paranoid." He turned to Bones. "Try the perfume."

Mr. Tall, Dark, and Unsmiling typed commands into his laptop, and on-screen, Hatcher sniffed the air and turned a shade whiter.

Maybe, just maybe, this would actually work.

"How are you feeling?" Rhys asked Coco later as they lay in bed.

"Okay, I think. As long as I don't start analysing things too much. Then the worries come and I start to get stressed."

Talking about her feelings was easier now, and a problem shared really was a problem halved. Or quartered. She'd made good friends. If only Jocelyn had done the same, they wouldn't be in this situation. Although that would mean she'd still have been scraping by in Lark's River, working her ass off for twelve-hour days at Hatcher, Marquez and Phillips. Perhaps the old saying was right—all things happened for a reason.

"I know this hasn't been easy," Rhys said. She loved the way he curved around her, his cock nestled against her ass. The way he stroked her arm and pressed soft kisses against her shoulder. "I wish I could turn back the clock for you."

"I don't."

"Why?"

"Because if I hadn't met Hatcher, then I wouldn't have met you. This new life... It's better than the old one. Does that sound crazy?"

"Yes, but I... Hmm. If I say that I'm glad you died, I'll sound like a right arsehole."

"Don't worry; I'll know what you mean."

"Then I'm glad we're together, right here, right now."

"Rhys?"

"Mmm?"

"Did you buy condoms yet?"

She heard his sharp intake of breath, but then his arms tightened.

"Yes."

"Then I want to feel you. All of you."

"Now? Are you sure?"

"I've never been more sure of anything in either of my lives."

When he finally slid into her, she realised that she'd come home. With Rhys, she was where she belonged. Her body remembered the basics of sex, but her memory was a blank, so she expected the frantic thrusting and grunting she'd seen from Hatcher earlier. But what she got was slow, languid kisses, filthy whispers, and a warmth that spread from her core to every inch of her body. A little sweat, a lot of flutters, and finally a supernova of pleasure that left her boneless on the mattress.

"Holy fuck."

"No, that was making love. A fuck is something totally different."

"Good different?"

"Hell yeah."

"Then I think I'm going to love that too. And you. I love you. So, so much."

"Same, sweetheart. Everything happens for a reason, and I'm damn glad I was the one to find you in the greenhouse that morning."

"I still want to know how I got there."

"And we'll find out, but let's take one step at a time. And enjoy each other. Balance the negative with the positive."

"How many condoms were in that package?"

"Uh, forty?"

"Forty? Wow."

"It worked out more economical."

Aw, Rhys was cute when he got defensive.

"I'm not complaining. But you'll need to buy another forty soon."

Balance the negative with the positive. Good thing they'd gone through three of the condoms last night because the shit hit the next afternoon.

Hatcher had been at home all day. He'd managed to shave, and until his wife left at ten to go shopping with their daughter, he'd held himself together. But after she'd kissed him on the cheek and told him they wouldn't be back until the evening, he'd poured himself a large glass of Scotch and begun pacing.

"Murderer," Coco whispered. She always whispered. They'd agreed it sounded creepier.

Hatcher's reactions were dulled by the alcohol, and his eyes wobbled in odd directions as he looked around for a ghost.

"I didn't mean to," he croaked.

They'd wanted an admission, and now they had it. But it didn't bring the relief that Coco had hoped for, only anger, and nor was it admissible in court.

"You held me under."

"You were going to ruin everything. You insisted on having a baby I didn't want."

"And you killed both of us."

"My wife would have left me if she'd found out."

And he'd have fucking deserved it. The man's whiny voice and self-pity made Coco's blood run hot.

"I thought you cared."

Rhys brushed away Coco's tears and wrapped an arm around her. Damn, this was hard, but it would have been so much harder alone.

"You thought I cared?" Hatcher said. "Then you were naive. Naive or stupid."

"Well, now I'm angry."

"What the hell do you want from me?"

"I want you to confess. Tell the world your sins."

"There you go, acting all unreasonable again. Are you crazy? I'd go to prison."

"Compared to hell, prison will be a happy place."

"You bitch," he shrieked. "Why won't you leave me alone?"

Bones clicked his mouse, and the lights in Hatcher's chandelier blinked off.

"What the fuck?" Remi mouthed.

Bones grinned, and that was actually scarier than his... What was the male equivalent of resting bitch face?

"Just a little bonus, boss."

CHAPTER 38
COCO

For three days, Coco worked around the clock to drive Hatcher crazy. Rhys became chief coffee maker as she spent half the night staring at the monitors set up in the living room of the rental house, watching the asshole toss and turn.

"It's working, isn't it?" Coco asked after whispering sweet, murderous nothings to Hatcher as he paced the hallways in the early hours.

Rhys squeezed her shoulders and passed her a chocolate chip cookie.

"Well, he's started talking to himself, so I'd say we're headed in the right direction."

That wasn't the only change in Hatcher. He began lashing out at his wife as he teetered on the edge of insanity. Coco felt awful for her, but Remi adopted a pragmatic approach.

"Short-term pain for long-term gain. She'll be better off without him."

Maybe that was true, but it didn't make watching the abuse any easier.

"Darling, you haven't showered for three days. Are you ill?"

"Shut up! Just shut up! I've been busy."

"Why don't you take a break? We could go out for dinner."

"Leave me alone."

Emily Hatcher made herself scarce for the rest of that day, but Coco did no such thing. Exhaustion took a back seat as she mainlined caffeine and whispered into the mic at every possible opportunity. By the weekend, the warring spouses could barely look at each other without bickering.

And then it happened.

"You say you're fine, but you smell like a sewer. What on earth is wrong with you? And why haven't you been to work all week?"

"For fuck's sake, Jocelyn! Stop questioning me!"

Emily Hatcher froze. "Who the hell is Jocelyn?"

"Nobody. She's nobody."

"I don't believe you!"

"Believe what you want." Hatcher threw his tumbler of Scotch at his wife, but thankfully, his aim was off. Amber liquid splattered across the white walls in the living room as the glass smashed into glittering shards. "And get the hell out of my way."

Not to be deterred, Emily hurled a golf club back at him, but her aim was no better and it lodged in the TV, sparking. Slap a price tag on it, and they could have called it modern art.

"You bitch!"

"Asshole! I'm leaving, and I'm taking my daughter with me."

"Do whatever you want."

As Mrs. Hatcher packed enough luggage for a round-the-world cruise, Team Jocelyn held a conference in the kitchen over a nice bottle of red wine with Camembert Remi had no doubt paid an extortionate amount to have couriered in from France.

"At least Emily's out of there," Coco said. "I was so worried that he'd hurt her."

Remi stroked his chin like a Bond villain. "Yes, and that means we can up our game now. Time to break him completely."

"What about something with water?" Bones suggested.

"That would have an element of poetic justice. Does he have a boat?"

"Hatcher sold his father's boat after he died and never replaced it."

"Guess it had served its purpose."

Could Carl Hatcher really have killed his father? Jocelyn and Rochelle had never known theirs and barely knew their mother by all accounts, but Coco still couldn't imagine wanting either of them dead. Had Hatcher Senior been a tyrant? An abuser? What had shaped Carl into the utter bastard he'd become? Or was it genetics that made the man tick? Coco had spent a lot of time thinking about nature versus nurture over the past few weeks, and late in the evening, she'd talked with Remi over glasses of wine. She had to admit that her rebirth made a fascinating science experiment. They knew enough from Rochelle to presume that Coco had gotten Jocelyn's soul—there were plenty of similarities between them, everything from a shared love of avocados to the way Coco flicked her hair when it got in her face. But there were also differences. Coco looked at some of the things Jocelyn had done and just couldn't understand why. Joss Bordeaux had acted horribly towards the end.

Actually, maybe she could understand why. As she sat there, surrounded by friends and with Rhys's arm around her shoulders, she realised there was one big difference between the two of them: love. Coco had known love from all sides, while Joss's only comfort came from her sister.

Which was why she'd stay as Coco. Now that she knew more about Joss, she didn't want to become her again.

"Why don't we flood his house?" Celine asked. "We could turn on all the taps."

Bones shook his head. "Too difficult. We'd have to block the plumbing, and he's spending more and more time at home."

True. They'd thought that with the ghostly goings-on, he might want to get out of the house, but he was in no fit state to work. Instead, he stayed with Jocelyn, spiralling into madness. Or perhaps he thought she'd follow him to the office? Hmm, the office...

"What about the architecture firm? Could we do anything there? The whole place is empty overnight."

Bones sipped from his glass of ice water, his face impassive. "I'll take a look."

Two nights later, the sprinkler system at Hatcher, Marquez and Phillips malfunctioned, and by the time the first member of staff arrived the next morning, Hatcher's glass-walled office was under several inches of water. Model buildings bobbed around, bumping into chairs and tables, and the electrics for the whole building had shorted. Bones hid nearby to watch the action and provided a blow-by-blow account as Hatcher showed up in his pyjamas, unkempt hair flapping in the breeze.

"The staff seem more shocked by his appearance than by the damage. He's splashing through puddles in his slippers. Someone should send him home. Wait, now he's yelling at the fire crew. Asshole's not gonna make himself any new friends there."

"Did you enjoy your swim?" Coco asked when he got back.

In response, he hurled an expensive-looking vase at the mirror in the hallway. The camera opposite caught the twinkles as both shattered into smithereens. Hatcher needed to sign up for anger management lessons. Was it fury that had led him to kill Joss? Had he snapped after an argument? Or had he planned her death and executed her and their child in cold blood?

On-screen, Hatcher headed for his dwindling liquor supply and grabbed a bottle of what looked like vodka. This time, he didn't bother with a mixer or even a glass, just poured the liquid down his throat and then coughed. If nothing else, he'd turn into an alcoholic. Or maybe he'd always had a drinking problem? There were so many things they didn't know about him, but it really didn't matter. Life behind bars would be more effective than twelve steps anyway, and that was where he should be. *Prison.*

"We need something more," Remi said. "Something big. A stunt that makes him believe his life is in danger."

Bones merely smiled his creepy smile. "Leave it with me, boss."

The next morning, Hatcher ran out into the hallway barefoot, and the air turned blue from his curses. Guess he should have swept up that broken glass. He'd been awoken by the crackle of flames, and when he hobbled to the front window, he was treated to their flickering beauty.

They hadn't set the house on fire—they weren't monsters—but his detached double garage was blazing nicely. He'd parked the Porsche inside the same way he did every time he drove it, and as Coco watched from her hiding place, a loud *pop* came from what was left of the building.

"That was a tyre," Bones said. "Show yourself now, while he's still inside."

Coco slipped out of the bushes and stood in the dancing light just long enough for Hatcher to get a good look, then ran down the driveway and along the street to Rhys's waiting car. When Hatcher made it outside, still limping and wincing, they were both long gone.

"He's searching the bushes," Bones whispered.

"Shit, will he find you?" Rhys asked.

"Nah, I'm in a tree. He walked right past."

By the time the fire trucks had departed, leaving the blackened remains of Hatcher's Porsche dripping rivulets of sooty water over the once-white garage floor, Coco was back in the living room at the rental house, sipping a mug of hot chocolate courtesy of Rhys. He'd been her rock through all of this.

"Did you enjoy the show?" Coco asked Hatcher when he walked back into his hideous home.

"I knew it was you!" he yelled. "I knew it! And I told them, I *told* them, but they just looked at me like I was crazy. They're the fools, not me."

According to Bones, the fire crew had been whispering

about having Hatcher committed, but a padded cell was too good for him.

"That was just a taster. Next time, I'll wait until you're inside."

The last vestiges of Hatcher's bluster gave out, and he sank to his knees in the hallway, a dozen distorted versions of his own terror staring back at him from the jagged remains of the mirror.

A broken man.

"Fine. Fine! You win. I give up." He snatched his phone out of his pyjama pocket—why did men always get pockets?—and began jabbing at the screen. "I knew you were a bitch from the moment I met you, but at least you were a good fuck. You stupid, nasty little whore."

"Who's he calling?" Rhys whispered, his arm tightening around Coco.

The police. He was calling the police.

"Come and pick me up. I'm a murderer. Just get me away from her."

A pause.

"No, I'm not joking. I killed a girl. Jocelyn Bordeaux. I held her and my bastard child under the fucking water until she stopped breathing, and now she's trying to kill me. For crying out loud, would you come and take me to jail?"

When he hung up, he curled into a ball on the floor, still clutching the phone, and sobbed until the police led him away in handcuffs.

Justice was finally served.

CHAPTER 39
EPILOGUE - RHYS

Rhys leaned over Coco's shoulder as she read the front page of the *Daily Lark*, careful not to spill his glass of champagne. Sure, it was only eleven in the morning, but somewhere in the world it was cocktail hour, and they needed to celebrate.

Remi, Celine, and Rochelle crowded around as well. They should have bought extra copies of the newspaper, perhaps even framed one... After all, it was a memorable occasion. The article was short and to the point, and also horrifying.

Shocking news emerged yesterday in Lark's River as local architect Carl Hatcher telephoned the police and confessed to the murder of his mistress, Jocelyn Bordeaux. Ms. Bordeaux's death had originally been ruled a suicide, but in light of this new evidence, Sheriff Lawson has confirmed that the case will be reopened. An anonymous source close to the investigation tells us that there are concerns over Mr. Hatcher's fragile mental state. Could he be planning an insanity defense?

According to our source, Mr. Hatcher hears Ms. Bordeaux speaking to him at night and spends much of his time cowering at the back of his cell. Several times, he's begged officers to keep her away from him—a spectacular fall from grace for a man once considered one of Nevada's shining stars.

Following Mr. Hatcher's arrest, a second girl has come forward to claim that he tried to drown her in a bathtub when she threatened to inform his wife of their affair. The terrified young lady told us that he promised to finish the job if she mentioned his indiscretions to anybody.

Another unexplained death—that of college girl Ann Farber, who drowned in her parents' hot tub last year—will also be investigated further after Ms. Farber's roommate informed police that she'd seen the deceased in the company of Mr. Hatcher shortly before she passed away. And finally, police in Henderson have confirmed they'll be taking another look at the death of Mr. Hatcher's father following his drowning eleven years ago. A common theme, maybe?

How many more victims might this man have had?

The families of Mr. Hatcher and Ms. Bordeaux were unavailable for comment, but this reporter will keep you updated as the investigations progress.

"I wasn't the only one," Coco whispered.

Rhys squeezed her shoulders. "Because of what you did, he won't get away with any more murders."

"What *we* did. I couldn't have done it without all of you guys."

Remi sighed. "Work will seem boring after this adventure."

"The château will seem boring," Celine said. "Now that I've tasted freedom, how can I stay there forever?"

"You don't have to, *ma chérie*. The past month has been a learning experience for everyone. I understand now that I was too harsh on you, that my fears made your life difficult, although that was never my intention. Going on vacation in France is out of the question, but the world is a big place. What do you think of the Caribbean? Perhaps I could buy a villa? A beach?"

Celine flung her arms around him. "I'd love to go to the beach."

"A flat in Swindon is definitely gonna be boring," Rhys said. "It's been one hell of a trip."

"Swindon?" Celine's expression morphed from joy to horror. "But I thought you were coming back to Villance?"

"We don't want to outstay our welcome."

"But you won't. Having more people to talk to, having friends, it's changed my life. Tell them, Remi."

"The cottage is yours for as long as you want it."

A free home? That was one hell of an offer. And the cottage was certainly a step up from whatever Rhys might stretch to on his income. Could he really leave England? He'd always assumed their time in France would be temporary, that a return home was just around the corner. *Home.* England had always felt like home, but when it came down to it, what was keeping him there? Nothing. He could still visit Uncle Albert from time to time—hell, he could even afford to fly to Wales with the money he'd save on rent.

And he needed to do what was best for Coco. She was his future.

"Are you sure?"

"We've already spoken about it."

Then the decision was easy. Looked as if Rhys would have to brush up on his language skills and probably his etiquette too. But damn, he was going to live in the grounds of a bloody castle. If somebody had told him that a year ago, he'd have laughed his arse off.

He squeezed Coco's hand. "Villance?"

But Coco was watching her sister, and Rhys realised there was one person who wasn't happy with the way this was going. Rochelle looked positively stricken.

"You're leaving again? B-b-but you only just came back."

"Coco can't stay in Lark's River," Rhys said as gently as he could. Remi had already magicked up a new passport for her to fly back to Europe. "Sooner or later, she'd be recognised, and then the Hatcher case would go up in smoke."

"What about somewhere else in the US? Sacramento? Stockton? A miracle brought my sister back, and I can't bear to lose her again."

Visions of visas and work permits swam before Rhys's eyes. Moving to the US was difficult—Jorge's sister had managed it but only because she had a job with a big bank in New York. With Remi's help, living in France would be feasible, but California...

"Then why don't you move to France?" Remi asked.

"Huh?"

"I don't want to speak ill of your living arrangements, but do you have a lot to leave behind? You don't seem to like your boss much, you can't afford your rent, and your social life seems...limited."

Tears trickled down Rochelle's cheeks. Was a propensity to cry genetic? "I'm trying my best, okay?"

Coco leapt up to hug her sister, scowling at Remi at the same time. "We know. Not everyone's a billionaire."

"Remi isn't trying to insult you," Celine explained. "What he means is that we have plenty of space at the château and we'd love to have you stay with us. Isn't that right, Remi?"

Remi looked like a cornered deer, but he nodded anyway. "Of course. And the cottage also has a spare bedroom."

"And Marguerite—one of our staff—she mentioned that the lady who did her nails in Villance moved to Paris recently, so there's a gap in the market there. You could fill it." Celine beamed. "Oh, this is perfect."

Rhys couldn't think of a better solution, but it was up to Rochelle. It would mean her leaving everything she'd ever known.

"Uh, I'll have to think on this."

Well, at least it wasn't an outright "no."

CHAPTER 40
EPILOGUE - COCO

*T*hree months later...

Coco gazed out the window at the beautiful gardens and then stood back to admire the living room of her new home. No, *their* new home. Small but perfect, it had everything she and Rhys needed. And what Rochelle needed too, of course. Now that she'd found her sister again, they couldn't bear to be parted by an ocean, and after several late-night heart-to-hearts, Rochelle had decided to give France a try.

Their French was still clunky, but with Remi and Celine living next door, they were getting plenty of practice at speaking the language. Some days, Celine refused to speak English for an added challenge.

Coco was still getting used to the new, happier Celine. Now that she sported a choppier hairstyle and Rochelle's clever make-up, Remi had agreed to her going out as long as they took a car to Limoges or Clermont-Ferrand, or borrowed his helicopter to go to Paris. Last weekend, they'd stayed in Nice for four days of sun and shopping. A five-star hotel and a billionaire's borrowed credit card sure had a way of putting a smile on a girl's face.

Yes, they'd had to put up with constant phone calls from their men while they were away, but it was a small price to pay for freedom. Even Rochelle hadn't escaped the stalking, not now that her little dalliance with Bones had come to light. Yes, Bones. Whose name was actually Bryn. Remi had been impressed with his performance in Lark's River, both his technical abilities and his discretion, and had offered him a position on his security team. Coco had been wary at first, but as he'd thawed, she realised that his surliness hid a dry sense of humour and an unflinching loyalty towards her sister. She had a feeling Rochelle wouldn't be needing the spare bedroom in the cottage for much longer.

Which was something of a relief since they'd be needing it soon themselves. They'd tried to be careful, but it seemed that Coco had more in common with Jocelyn than she'd first thought. Thankfully, Rhys had nothing in common with Carl Hatcher. Yes, he'd been shocked when the pregnancy test came back positive, but now he was listing baby names and ordering tiny T-shirts on the internet. This time, her baby's father would be everything she could hope for—kind, dependable, and calm.

Calm... Not like Remi. When he'd found out a month ago that Celine was expecting too, he'd freaked. Even though she was still in the first trimester, he'd hired a Polish midwife and a nanny, and the stream of builders trooping in and out of the château gave Celine a constant headache.

"All the baby needs is a crib," she'd told Coco yesterday.

"It doesn't need its own version of the Sistine Chapel on the ceiling, or a bed shaped like a perfect replica of the 1969 winner at Le Mans, or an actual freaking zoo."

"He's just excited."

"I know this. But sometimes I wish he'd sit in front of the TV and drink beer like a normal man."

Not that Rhys did a lot of beer-drinking. Fit4Life had taken off, and he was already working on a sequel, for relaxation this time. Even Rhys seemed stunned at the success. Not only was the fitness coach a marketing demon, but the make-up vlogger had also told her friends about it, they told their friends, and it jumped to number one in its category in the app store. Hundreds of thousands of users subscribing at four pounds per month meant the baby was going to have a very lovely crib indeed. And when the baby was a little older, they could take the holiday of a lifetime— Australia, Asia, the Americas, they'd visit them all. Together.

The back door burst open. Celine. During the daytime, she rarely knocked, but Coco didn't mind. It was just nice to have the company.

"Hey, hey! Remi wants to talk to everyone. Ooh, are those cakes from Chanté?"

A groan escaped Coco's lips. "If this is about paint swatches again..."

"Oh, I found an article that said pregnant women shouldn't go near wet paint, so now he's picking out wallpaper. Can I steal a cake? Remi's still on his crazy health kick, so we only have banana muffins."

"Sure." Rhys picked up fresh cakes most days. Since Remi had hired Chanté to cater the VIP tent at Villance's harvest festival, business at the café had improved, which was a relief because Coco craved fresh cream and nobody made better éclairs. And the cream, although fattening, was definitely an improvement on Jocelyn's gummy bears and Marmite. "But what does Remi want to talk about? Wallpaper?"

"No, no, not that. He said Joe Ellis emailed this morning."

Joe Ellis? The investigator in Las Vegas? With Hatcher in prison, the only mystery still to be resolved concerned Coco's origins. The plant food. According to Bryn, who Remi had tasked with overseeing the process, Ellis had been working undercover for weeks.

They'd had to let Bryn in on the secret. Since he was dating Rochelle, there wasn't an easy way to keep him in the dark. Was he shocked? Yes. Entirely surprised? No. He and Monica had assumed something weird was going on, and with Remi's background in biotech, they'd bet on illegal cloning.

"Truth is sometimes stranger than fiction," he'd muttered. "Magic trees? I believe you, but anyone else would think you were as crazy as Hatcher."

Remi had chuckled at that. "True. And I've learned my lesson—you can mess with a person's body, but not their soul."

So what had Ellis found? Coco prised Rhys away from his computer, and they all headed across to the château. In honour of the growing babies, Remi had switched out champagne for smoothies, and half a dozen glasses of green liquid were waiting for them on a tray in the living room.

"Try this. It's made from spinach, kale, apple, blueberry, almond milk, banana, and chia seeds."

Urgh. It was sweet that he'd gone teetotal in solidarity with Celine, but kale was meant for the compost heap, not for drinking.

"Thanks, but I just ate breakfast."

"I'll have yours," Bryn offered.

Rhys tentatively took a glass and sipped. "Not bad. You can hardly taste the kale."

Coco really didn't care about the smoothies. "What happened in Las Vegas?"

"We're waiting for Rochelle. I don't want to repeat myself."

A minute later, she showed up, and they all waited expectantly. This last loose thread had been bugging Coco for months, but she didn't feel the same simmering anger at whoever had turned her into plant food that she'd felt towards Hatcher. After all, they'd helped to achieve justice in a roundabout way. But it was still wrong. The dead deserved to be treated with respect.

"So, we know that Jocelyn's body was prepared for burial by Peaceful Spirit Funeral Services, and yet her DNA ended up in plant food manufactured by Eastlake Horticultural. Eastlake is based in Las Vegas, while Peaceful Spirit is a chain headquartered in Reno. It took some digging, but Ellis found the link between the two."

"Which is?" Coco asked, impatient.

"Two brothers. Rhett and David Englebert. Rhett founded Eastlake, and David is the CEO of Peaceful Spirit."

"That still doesn't explain how I got made into plant food."

"I'm getting to that. Ellis found that both companies have suffered from operational issues in the last year. Eastlake has been struggling with its supply chain since a number of slaughterhouses it partners with have been closed—either temporarily or permanently—due to action by animal rights campaigners. The company hasn't been able to obtain the by-products needed for several of its fertiliser lines, namely blood meal and bonemeal. Meanwhile, Peaceful Spirit managed to get into trouble with the environmental inspector. The company is... How should I put it...? It operates in the high-volume, low-margin sector. Cheap, no-frills services. The Costco of funeral care providers. They have several mortuaries, and each processes hundreds of bodies each month."

Rochelle wiped a tear away. "I wish I'd been able to afford better."

It wasn't her fault. None of this was her fault. "You did the best you could under awful circumstances."

"If you'd held a fancy funeral, Coco wouldn't be here today," Remi reminded her. "Anyhow, the volume of waste products they were washing down their drains, specifically blood, caused a substantial load to the BOD at both the Chalk Bluff and Clark County sewage plants, and management was told to fix the problem."

"What's BOD?"

"Biological Oxygen Demand. According to Ellis, that's the amount of oxygen required to break down the organic matter in the sewage. If sewage with a high BOD is discharged into a watercourse, it kills the fish because they can't get enough oxygen to breathe." Remi cocked his head. "We all learn new things every day."

"So let me guess," Rhys said. "They decided to kill two birds with one stone and send the waste products from the funeral homes to the fertiliser factory?"

"Exactly. A year ago, management issued a directive to collect the blood for 'recycling.' So that's exactly what the staff have been doing. They drain the blood into twenty-five-litre jerrycans, and every other day, they load it into a truck. Ellis has been working as a mortuary assistant at the

Las Vegas mortuary for the past month, and he has photos and documentation to prove this."

Coco felt nauseated, and she was fairly sure it wasn't from morning sickness. She'd been fortunate with that so far. Celine, on the other hand, had been puking all over the place.

"Is that illegal? It must be illegal."

"Yes, it is. If the blood goes through a sewage treatment plant, it's properly degraded and disinfected. If it's simply packaged into pots and sold in a garden centre, then it could contain any number of unknown pathogens."

"And any number of people's DNA," Rhys said. "Why did the trees bring Coco back and not somebody else?"

Remi shrugged one shoulder. "One of life's mysteries. I doubt the trees are sentient, so I expect they just latched onto the first fragment of DNA that reached their roots."

"You're saying that Coco's only here through pure dumb luck?"

"That seems a reasonable assumption. But good luck, certainly."

A shudder ran through Coco. If Albert had stirred the pot before he mixed the fertiliser, or poured it differently, perhaps she wouldn't be here at all. Joss would probably have agonised over that fact, but in Coco's view, her time on this earth was too short. However she'd been gifted this new life, she intended to make the most of it.

But she still wanted the people who'd stolen her blood and sold it for profit to pay.

"So what can we do about Eastlake Horticultural and Peaceful Spirit?"

"I need to fly to Las Vegas. Ellis has set up a meeting with an officer from the LVMPD in three days. With a…" Remi checked his notes. "A Detective Jack Callahan. Which means you need to look after Celine. She's not to go near the horses alone, or sit for too long, or stand for too long, or use the hot tub... And I bought her more vitamins. You should take those too."

Coco rolled her eyes. "Yes, Mom."

"You should take the vitamins, sweetheart," Rhys said.

Remi put his hands on his hips. "I only do these things because I care."

Yes, he did. And Coco wasn't really complaining. Better for Remi and Rhys to worry too much than not enough. And thanks to them and now Joe Ellis, she had closure on her past.

The future stretched out in front of her like a sunrise over the ocean, and she intended to embrace it.

Now she could start to live again.

WHAT'S NEXT?

And if you'd like to find out a little more about the origins of the Coco du Ciel trees, you can read that story in *A Vampire in Vegas*.

When nightclub hostess Vee Pelletier stumbles across singer Serenity Strange's body in a storeroom at Club Dead, the search begins to find her killer...but it won't be easy. The list of suspects is longer than the line of beautiful people waiting to get in.

Detective Jack Callahan has earned a reputation for solving the unsolvable, but this case may be beyond even his formidable skills. The deeper he digs, the darker the trail gets. And Serenity's killer isn't the only person with secrets. Vee's keeping a devilish one of her own...

For more details: www.elise-noble.com/vampire

If you enjoyed *Coco du Ciel*, please consider leaving a review.

For an author, every review is incredibly important. Not only do they make us feel warm and fuzzy inside, readers consider them when making their decision whether or not to buy a book. Even a line saying you enjoyed the book or what your favourite part was helps a lot.

WANT TO STALK ME?

For updates on my new releases, giveaways, and other
random stuff, you can sign up for my newsletter on my
website:
www.elise-noble.com

If you're on Facebook, you might also like to join Team
Blackwood for exclusive giveaways, sneak previews, and
book-related chat. Be the first to find out about new stories,
and you might even see your name or one of your
suggestions make it into print!

And if you'd like to read my books for FREE, you can also
find details of how to join my advance review team.

Would you like to join Team Blackwood?

www.elise-noble.com/team-blackwood

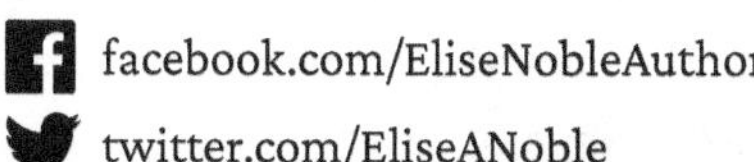

facebook.com/EliseNobleAuthor

twitter.com/EliseANoble

instagram.com/elise_noble

END-OF-BOOK STUFF

Coco du Ciel started out life as a short story written for a contest—the prompt required some kind of mutant plant—and since I'd enjoyed writing it, I decided to expand it as a challenge to myself. Why a challenge? Because I wrote it all in third-person POV, something I find difficult and don't particularly enjoy. The original draft was also written entirely from Rhys's POV (who was then called Daniel—I'm forever changing names *rolls eyes*), although I decided to add Coco's POV in a later draft because I thought we needed to hear from her. I also felt like writing a regular guy for a change, not a billionaire or a Navy SEAL, and for those reasons, *Coco du Ciel* ended up being a little different to my other books. But I need to vary the way I write every so often to keep from getting bored.

My next book will be back to the non-magical world with a new series. When I thought of the idea late in 2020, the voices in my head were so insistent that I had to clear the rest of my planned writing schedule to tackle Baldwin's Shore instead. The first three books are standalone stories with an overarching plot running through them as well, and the fourth book will follow on from both Baldwin's Shore Book 3 and Blackwood Security Book 15 (Hallie's Story). A fun-for-me-to-write crossover that involved a lot of jigsaw pieces!

And if you want to get a little hint of where the coco du

ciel trees came from, you can find that story in *A Vampire in Vegas*.

Speaking of mutant plants, I've finally started to tackle my jungle of a garden. I'm no Albert, lol. Since I started publishing books, gardening fell by the wayside, and ivy took over. But after spending so much time at home over the past year, I got sick of the sight of it, so now the whole thing's been razed to the ground and I'm starting again from scratch. A blank canvas. So far, I've built raised veggie beds and planted them with seeds. Which the dogs then dug up, so I guess we'll be having potluck salad at some point this summer. Next job: regrouting the patio. My life is just one big adventure...

Thanks so much to my awesome team as always—to Nikki for editing, to John, Lizbeth, and Debi for the final proofread, and to Jeff, Renata, Terri, Musi, David, Stacia, Jessica, Nikita, Quenby, and Jody for initial beta reading.

And thanks to you, the reader!

Elise

P.S. If, like Rhys, you ever need the emergency number in France, it's 112. Or 191 if you want air rescue. Which also happens to be the number for Vodafone customer services in England. The guys at French air rescue speak perfect English. Don't ask me how I know that.

Also by Elise Noble

Blackwood Security

For the Love of Animals (Nate & Carmen - Prequel)

Black is My Heart (Diamond & Snow - Prequel)

Pitch Black

Into the Black

Forever Black

Gold Rush

Gray is My Heart

Neon (novella)

Out of the Blue

Ultraviolet

Glitter (novella)

Red Alert

White Hot

Sphere (novella)

The Scarlet Affair

Spirit (novella)

Quicksilver

The Girl with the Emerald Ring

Red After Dark

When the Shadows Fall

Phantom (novella) (2023)

Pretties in Pink

Chimera

Secret Weapon (Crossover with Baldwin's Shore)

The Devil and the Deep Blue Sea (2023)

Blackwood Elements

Oxygen

Lithium

Carbon

Rhodium

Platinum

Lead

Copper

Bronze

Nickel

Hydrogen

Blackwood UK

Joker in the Pack

Cherry on Top

Roses are Dead

Shallow Graves

Indigo Rain

Pass the Parcel (TBA)

Blackwood Casefiles

Stolen Hearts

Burning Love (TBA)

Baldwin's Shore

Dirty Little Secrets

Secrets, Lies, and Family Ties

Buried Secrets

Secret Weapon (Crossover with Blackwood Security)

A Secret to Die For (TBA)

Blackstone House

Hard Lines

Blurred Lines (2023)

Hard Tide

Hard Limits (2023)

Hard Luck (TBA)

The Electi

Cursed

Spooked

Possessed

Demented

Judged

The Planes

A Vampire in Vegas

A Devil in the Dark (TBA)

The Trouble Series

Trouble in Paradise

Nothing but Trouble

24 Hours of Trouble

Standalone

Life

Coco du Ciel

A Very Happy Christmas (novella)

Twisted (short stories)

Books with clean versions available (no swearing and no on-the-page sex)

Pitch Black

Into the Black

Forever Black

Gold Rush

Gray is My Heart

Audiobooks

Black is My Heart (Diamond & Snow - Prequel)

Pitch Black

Into the Black

Forever Black

Gold Rush

Gray is My Heart

Neon (novella)

9 781912 888429